ALSO BY JESSICA BRODY

The Karma Club

MY LIFE
UNDECIDED

MY LIFE UNDECIDED

Jessica Brody

FARRAR STRAUS GIROUX
NEW YORK

TJ

Copyright © 2011 by Jessica Brody

All rights reserved

Distributed in Canada by D&M Publishers, Inc.

Printed in May 2011 in the United States of America
by RR Donnelley & Sons Company, Harrisonburg, Virginia

First edition, 2011

10 9 8 7 6 5 4 3 2 1

macteenbooks.com

Library of Congress Cataloging-in-Publication Data

Brody, Jessica.

 My life undecided / Jessica Brody.— 1st ed.

  p. cm.

 Summary: Fifteen-year-old Brooklyn has been making bad decisions since, at age two, she became famous for falling down a mine shaft, and so she starts a blog to let others make every decision for her, while her community-service hours are devoted to a woman who insists Brooklyn read her "Choose the Story" books.

 ISBN: 978-0-374-39905-4

 [1. Decision-making—Fiction. 2. Conduct of life—Fiction. 3. Blogs—Fiction. 4. Books and reading—Fiction. 5. Family problems—Fiction. 6. High schools— Fiction. 7. Schools—Fiction.] I. Title.

PZ7.B786157My 2011

[Fic]—dc22

                          2009051277

To my little sister, Terra,
for making hard choices and doing it with style

Life is like a game of cards.
The hand you are dealt is determinism;
the way you play it is free will.

—Jawaharlal Nehru
(First Prime Minister of India)

CONTENTS

MY LIFE
UNDECIDED

PROLOGUE

The sirens are louder than I anticipated.

Not that I ever in a million years anticipated sirens at the beginning of all this. Otherwise, obviously, I never would have agreed to it.

Hindsight.

It's a bitch.

But even when my unnervingly calm best friend, Shayne, informed me that they were coming, I never expected them to be this loud. Or this . . . I don't know . . . *conspicuous.* They're like beacons blasting through the dark night, waking the neighbors, calling out to anyone within a five-mile radius, "Hey! You! Look over here! Brooklyn Pierce has screwed up . . . *again!*"

Why don't they just send out a freaking press release or something?

Although, I have no doubt this will make the front page of tomorrow's paper. Or at least the top-clicked story on a few local blogs. Because really, what else is there to talk about in this boring little nothing-exciting-ever-happens town? The fact that the First Church of Who the Heck Cares got a new pastor last week?

No, this will definitely be *the* news.

And I will definitely be at the very center of the scandal . . . yet *again.*

I guess you could say I'm some sort of a magnet for unfavorable attention. Prone to these types of "media-frenzy" disasters.

When I was two years old I fell down an abandoned mine shaft and was stuck down there for fifty-two hours while rescuers worked around the clock to save me. They had to drill through twenty feet of solid rock because apparently the hole in the ground was big enough to fit a 25-pound toddler but not exactly big enough to fit a 210-pound firefighter in full rescue gear.

The story was all over the news. According to Wikipedia, the entire nation "stood by" and watched on live TV as they pulled me to safety. It made the front cover of twenty different national newspapers and magazines, my parents got a phone call from the president himself, and there was even talk of turning the story into a TV miniseries event.

From that point on, I was known across the country as "Baby Brooklyn, the little girl who fell down the mine shaft." One wobbly, toddler-size step in the wrong direction and my life was forever tainted by disaster. I was permanently marked as a screwup. I have no recollection of the event whatsoever, but the memory continues to follow me wherever I go. Famous for something I'll never be able to remember. Immortalized for one very unfortunate lapse in judgment.

My parents have been telling me for years that I make "bad decisions." But I never believed them. Because, you know, they're parents. And since when are parents *ever* right about anything?

But I'm slowly starting to wonder if maybe I was just *born* that way. Like poor judgment is in my DNA or something. Genetically predisposed to make crappy choices. Although my mom has always blamed herself for the incident, it was *me* who decided—in the seven lousy seconds it took her to zip up my sister's jacket—that it would be a good idea to chase the little green lizard right off the hiking trail and down an abandoned mine shaft.

And what have I learned since then? Thirteen years later? Well, judging from the slew of various emergency vehicles lining the street . . . not a whole lot.

So it isn't until right now, at this very second—with the sirens blaring, the crowd of people gathering to try to steal a gossipworthy peek, and the overall chaos of a good idea turned very bad—that I start to think my parents might just be onto something.

Because when you're being handcuffed and lowered into the backseat of a squad car, you kind of have to start reconsidering the way you live your life.

CHARRED TO A CRISP

The police station smells like burnt toast. As if someone popped a piece of sourdough in the toaster oven and forgot about it. Or maybe the flecks of smoky odor are just lingering in my nostrils from the fire. Rebellious stowaways clinging to the inside of my respiratory system like an annoying guest who refuses to leave long after the party is over.

And trust me, the party is *way* over.

I don't know how much the firefighters were able to salvage of the house. When I was taken away in the police car, the flames were still relentlessly devouring the place.

It feels like I've been in this stuffy little room forever. I think it's the break room because there's a table in the corner with a pot of coffee resting on a rusty electric warmer and every five minutes some cop comes in, pours himself a Styrofoam cupful, and gives me one of those "Boy, did you screw up" raises of his eyebrows.

There's absolutely nothing to do in here. Nothing to read and nothing to watch except the clock on the wall. And trust me, that thing has *got* to be broken. I swear it only ticks every five seconds.

There's a fat, balding man who keeps popping his head in to tell me that he's "working everything out," and that I "shouldn't be worried." He's supposedly a social worker who's been assigned to my case. And all I can think is Great, now I'm a *case*.

I keep waiting for them to bring Shayne in. At least then I'd have someone to talk to. She was right next to me when the cops showed up . . . and the fire trucks, and the ambulances, *and* the news vans. Her last words to me before I was handcuffed and taken away were "Don't worry, Brooks, we're in this together."

But for the last six hours, there doesn't seem to be anyone in this but me. Oh, and Phil, the way-too-happy-to-be-here-so-early-in-the-morning "social worker." I figure they're probably holding Shayne in another room. They always do that in the movies. Separate the criminals to see which one will talk first. Well, if they think I'm going to rat out my best friend, they've got another think coming.

I mean, the whole thing *was* initially her idea. But I'm the one who said yes. I'm the one who got us into the house. I'm the one who turned on the stove . . .

Fortunately, it wasn't *my* house. It wasn't anyone's house, in fact. That was the brilliance of it all. Or at least, that was *supposed* to be the brilliance of it all. It's funny how the word "brilliance" can take on a whole new meaning when you're sitting in a police station at seven in the morning.

Perspective.

Also a bitch.

Because according to Phil, the fact that it wasn't my house may not necessarily be a good thing. It's all so confusing and overwhelming. Everyone's been throwing around words like "trespassing," "arson," "jail time," and "underage drinking," and I

have no idea what any of it means. Well, apart from the underage drinking. That one, unfortunately, I'm pretty familiar with.
Especially now that the spiked punch is starting to wear off and
the hangover is settling in. Believe me, it's not making this situation any better. I really wish I liked the taste of coffee right about
now. Even that stale pot on the table over there is starting to look
better than this tornado of a headache that's brewing above my
temples. I try to sleep by resting my head down on the table, but
the hard surface of the wood only exacerbates the throbbing.
Would it kill them to bring me a Tylenol? Or a tranquilizer?

The door squeaks open again a little after ten a.m. and just
when I think I'm about to get another disappointing glare from
one of Colorado's finest, the uniformed officer with the name
"Banks" engraved into his badge looks down at the clipboard in
his hands, then up at me, and says, "Brooklyn Pierce?"

I nod, my pounding head still cradled in my hands. "Yes?"

I pray he's going to tell me that I'm going home. Or that
Shayne is in the other room waiting to see me. Or that the get-
out-of-jail-free fairy has come to wave her magic wand and spring
me from this place.

But he doesn't say any of these things. Instead his forehead
crumples and he studies my face with this confounded expression, as if he's trying to remember the capital of some obscure
Central American country. "There's no chance that you're *Baby*
Brooklyn, is there? That little girl who fell down the mine shaft
all those years ago?"

Fantastic, I think with a groan. Just what I need right now. A
reputation for making headlines.

"Yes, that was me."

Officer Banks raises his eyebrows, seemingly impressed at

my celebrity status. "Wow. No kidding? So what was it like down there? Were you scared?"

"I don't remember," I reply through gritted teeth. "I was *two*."

He seems to be oblivious to my displeased tone because he just keeps on talking. "How did you end up down there again? Chased a rabbit or something?"

"Lizard," I mumble.

"I bet you regret that decision, huh?" Banks remarks with a chuckle that grates on my nerves. "Not the smartest thing in the world, was it?"

"Is there something you wanted to tell me?" I nod hopefully toward his clipboard.

"Oh, right," he replies, snapping himself back into the moment. "Good news. Looks like you're going home."

Thank GOD!

I jump up from my chair and rush toward him, feeling like I want to wrap my arms around his portly middle and squeeze him. Obviously, I restrain myself.

"Thank you, thank you, thank you!" I exclaim. It's about freaking time they let me out of this hellhole.

I think about my soft, comfy bed, my fluffy white pillow, my clean, cotton pajamas. Fresh underwear. Toothpaste and mouthwash. All the things you take for granted until you're stuck in a place like this for six hours straight.

But my relief is short-lived. Because the next words out of his mouth are the scariest ones I've heard all night. Scarier than "arson," scarier than "trespassing," even scarier than "jail time."

Officer Banks drops his clipboard down against his thigh and offers me a sympathetic wink. "Your parents are here."

FRIENDS DON'T LET
FRIENDS MAKE FAJITAS

It's not like I didn't consider the parental factor in this equation. I've just purposely been choosing *not* to think about it. Preferring to live in a world (if only imaginary) where parents simply don't exist.

They have a word for that, you know? It's called "denial."

"They were able to get on an early flight out of Boston," the officer tells me as he opens the door and leads me through a series of hallways.

Boston. It all started with Boston, Massachusetts. Or as my perfect, prudent, would-never-burn-a-house-down older sister would be quick to correct, *Cambridge*, Massachusetts. Home of Harvard University. A school for people who make *good* decisions in their lives. Decisions that don't end in police stations that smell like overcooked Pop-Tarts.

In other words, a school for people like Isabelle Pierce.

And at the beginning of every October there's a weekend especially dedicated to the proud parents of these outstanding, would-never-burn-a-house-down kinds of people. It's called

"Family Weekend." But it may just as well have been called *"Parents'* Weekend," because as an official member of the "family," I don't remember receiving an invitation. Not that I would have gone. Not that I would have even *thought* about going. Especially when I learned that "Family Weekend" is also called "Brooklyn Gets the Entire House to Herself Weekend." Although, I imagine that over time, both titles will be thrown out completely and replaced with just "The Weekend Brooklyn Burned Down a Model Home."

A day we can all eventually look back on and share a good laugh about.

Riiiiight.

I blame Izzy. If she hadn't gotten into such a prestigious, stuck-up school to begin with, my parents never would have left for the weekend and I never would have even been given the opportunity to say yes to Shayne's (at one time) genius idea. If my sister had just been a huge screwup like me, she'd probably be living at home, attending some lame-ass community college in downtown Denver, and none of this would have happened. I'd be asleep in my bed right now, soaking up the last few blessed hours of the weekend, instead of here, walking the last few steps to my execution.

"YOU BURNED DOWN MY MODEL HOME?!"

My mother clearly sees me before I see her and she doesn't waste any time.

"How could you *do* something like that?" she roars before I have even stepped both feet into the lobby.

"Camille." My father places a tender hand on her shoulder. "We promised we'd handle this rationally."

"That was at 35,000 feet," my mom growls back. "This is

the lobby of the Parker Police Department. Rationality is completely out of the question right now."

"It was an accident, I swear," I try, but my dad shushes me with a look that says "If you want to live, you'll be quiet."

"An accident?" my mom thunders. "An accident! And I suppose sneaking into my office, stealing my keys, and throwing a raver in the model home of my biggest development project to date was an accident, too?!"

I'm pretty sure my mom means "rager," but I'm smart enough to refrain from correcting her. Probably the first *wise* decision I've made in a while.

Officer Banks clears his throat and we turn to look at him. Surprisingly, he doesn't appear to be all that uncomfortable standing in the middle of our family spat. I suppose he sees this kind of thing constantly. After all, it's not like the police in this town have anything better to do than break up teenage "ravers." Parker, Colorado, isn't exactly crime-infested. Last year they caught a college student selling weed out of the back of his mom's SUV and people are still talking about what a scandal it was. Unfortunately that doesn't bode well for my plan to forget this whole thing ever happened.

"Why don't we discuss this when we get home," my dad suggests, giving the officer an apologetic nod.

Without another word, my mom wheels around and storms out the door. I can almost see the smoke trailing behind her.

"We'll have to call Bob," my dad says as he steers the car onto Highway 83. The bright mid-morning sun blinds me after I've been cooped up in that police station all night. My mom is staring vacantly out the passenger-side window. Actually, her expression only *looks* vacant. I know her well enough to know that emptiness is the last thing on her mind. It's that look she gets when she feels like someone has betrayed her. A disconcerting mix of anger, sadness, and "what did I do to deserve this?" It's enough to make you vomit up guilt.

"Who's Bob?" I have the courage to ask. It's the first thing I've said since we left the station. My mom, surprisingly enough, still hasn't uttered a word.

"Our family lawyer," my dad responds.

"Oh," I mumble feebly, feeling dejected and emotionally drained. But what I really want to ask is *"We have a family lawyer?"* Funny how I never knew that before today. I guess it's because we never really needed him until now. Or I suppose I should say . . . until *me*.

"Hopefully he can fight the arson charge," my dad thinks aloud. "The trespassing is going to be a tough one to deny, though. You were the only one with access to the key to the model. And the underage drinking charge is a wash. Your blood alcohol level was off the chart when they brought you in. We're lucky no one got hurt at this thing. We could have been slapped with a serious lawsuit on top of everything else."

Lucky.

There are a million emotions I'm feeling right now, but "lucky" certainly isn't one of them.

My dad navigates the labyrinth of streets in our subdivision until we're parked in our garage. Before the engine is even turned off, my mom unbuckles her seat belt, opens the door, and stomps into the house. Sometimes I think her silence is worse than her yelling. And right about now, I almost wish she'd go back to screaming at me. At least then I'd know what she's thinking.

My dad, on the other hand, is composed. Collected. His usual balanced self. I can count on one hand the number of times I've seen him lose his cool in my lifetime. People are always saying that my mom and dad complement each other perfectly. Like a balloon tied to a rock. I never really understood what they meant until now.

"What does arson mean?" I ask my dad, clicking off my seat belt but staying firmly planted in the seat. Despite my previous impatience to get home, right now I'm in no rush to go inside.

My dad takes a deep breath. "It means they think you set the fire on purpose."

I can feel the panic rise up in my throat. "But I didn't!" I screech. "I swear I didn't!"

My dad glances at me in the rearview mirror. Despite the disappointment that's evident on his face, there are small traces of compassion there, too. "I know, Brooks," he says, an unsettling edge to his usually warm tone. "And that's why we need a lawyer."

Technically, it *was* me who started the fire. But I'm not lying when I say it was an accident. I may be decisionally challenged but I'm no pyro. I just thought the party would be that much better if we had fajitas. Granted, I wasn't exactly in my right mind when I came to this conclusion. And I think I've proved once and for all that drinking spiked punch and cooking fajitas simply don't mix. Especially when the "fresh vegetables" you use to cook them turn out to be made of plastic, like so many things found in a model home. Needless to say, the "green peppers" and "tomatoes" started to burn pretty quickly and the elegant fabric napkins that I used to remove the charred props from the pan turned out to be more flammable than I'd anticipated. The next thing I knew, a hundred drunk teenagers were running around the house screaming "Fire!" and then I ended up in handcuffs.

It wasn't supposed to be like that, though.

It was supposed to be the party of the century . . . of the *millennium*. An event that would guarantee me a place on the map. A spot in the Parker High School hall of fame. At least that's what Shayne had promised me.

Oh God, Shayne. I hope she's not still at the police station. I'm sure her parents would have come to get her hours ago. Wouldn't they?

I trudge into the house, snatch the phone from the cradle in the kitchen, and carry it upstairs with me. I haven't yet informed my parents that I'll be needing a new cell phone because mine is buried under a pile of charred rubble in the middle of an uninhabited multimillion-dollar subdivision. Somehow, it didn't seem like the right moment to start making demands.

I close my bedroom door and dial Shayne's number. It rings twice and then goes to voice mail so I leave a hurried and rather frantic message.

"Shayne," I breathe into the phone, "I didn't see you at the police station. I hope you're okay. I just wanted to let you know that I'm fine. Well, for the most part. I'm home now. But it looks like I have to go to court on Monday morning. Lame, right? I'm so sorry. This whole thing totally sucks. I just hope you're not in too much trouble. Anyway, call me and we can talk about everything. Oh, and I lost my cell phone in the fire so you'll have to call me at home. Okay. Bye."

I hang up and toss the phone onto my desk.

Please let her be okay.

I feel wretched. About everything. About Shayne. About my looming court date tomorrow morning. About the model home—or what *used* to be a model home. Landing this new subdivision project was supposed to be my mother's big break as a real estate developer. It was supposed to be her company's "golden ticket" to glory.

I guess I'm not the only person who fell off the map tonight.

When I finally collapse onto my bed, I'm tormented by the thoughts and images swirling around in my head. Fire and regret. Sirens and remorse. Uniformed police officers and their disapproving stares. As exhausted as I am, sleep is virtually impossible. And as heavy as my eyelids feel, they stay open for the rest of the morning.

My guilt keeps me awake.

No Offense

Shayne says ponytails are lazy. You can wear them to the gym and you can wear them when you're lounging around your house, but if you show up at school with your hair stuffed in a rubber band all it says to the world is "I was too tired to try this morning."

She's big on appearances. Perceptions are key. Your representation to society dictates what people think of you. And given that everyone thinks the *world* of Shayne, it's hard not to take notes when she dishes out her valuable nuggets of advice. I mean, if there were ever a representation of perfection and poise, it would be Shayne.

I don't want to get out of bed on Monday morning and face the music, but I can hear Shayne's voice in my head, reminding me that there are no days off in the world of perception. No sick days. No allotted vacation. Keeping up appearances is a full-time job. Because when you're fortunate enough to be welcomed into Shayne's exclusive company, people look at you differently. Or I guess I should say they look at you *constantly*. For as long as we've been friends, I can't remember ever *not* having an audience.

Shayne is like a local celebrity. People take notice of everything she does. And when you're standing right next to her, they take notice of you, too.

As on many lethargic days, this is the thought that finally pulls me out of bed and gets me into the shower. Consequently, this is also the thought that drives me through my ninety-minute daily beauty regimen. Wardrobe selection is just the beginning. And even that can be a daunting task because it requires finding a combination of clothing articles that are body-flattering, expensive-looking, in season, adequately provocative while still school appropriate, have not appeared in any photos bearing the caption "fashion police" or similar, *and* do not consist of something you've been publicly seen in for two to three months. Then comes makeup application, hair-styling, buffing, polishing, lotioning, spritzing, bronzing, tweezing, moisturizing—all the while keeping one encompassing question in your head: "Is this good enough?" If the answer can't be followed by an exclamation point, it's time to start over and try again.

"Presentable" is never sufficient. "Spectacular!" is the only option.

And today I have to tack on the additional question of: "Can I wear this in court?"

Lawyer Bob claims to know me from when I was little. He says my sister and I used to come over and swim in his pool in the summertime. I don't recall any of this. And I certainly don't think it entitles him to put his hand on my knee when he's talking to me. I'm fifteen now, not five. At one time it may have been endearing. Now it's just creepy.

But I don't complain because he seems to be doing a pretty effective job convincing the judge at the courthouse that I'm not a danger to society and should be let off easy for my "criminal acts."

I really hate that term, by the way. I wish they'd stop using it in the same sentence with my name. But what am I going to do? Turns out swiping the key to a model home (regardless of whether or not your mother is the developer of the property) is actually *illegal*. It's called "trespassing," and judging by the perma-scowl on the judge's face, I'm assuming it's highly frowned upon as well.

Bob seems to be wrapping up his little speech now. Talking about reports from the fire department and lack of malicious intent. It's all Greek to me, but it sounds impressive and I suppose that's what matters. He finishes with an unceremonious nod of his head and then slides back into the seat next to me.

"I think we got this." Bob leans in and huffs into my ear. "The fire marshal has already confirmed the fire wasn't set on purpose and this judge is very sympathetic to first-time offenders."

There's another word I've come to strongly dislike in the last thirty-six hours. "Offenders." Where does that term even come from? It's not like I've personally offended anyone. No one even lived in the house. It was full of plastic props and photo frames filled with pictures of catalog models. No one should feel "offended."

Well, except maybe my mom. She's sitting in the front row of the courtroom. That look has yet to make it off her face. She's barely said two words to me since yesterday morning. I can't tell if she's mad or depressed or just constipated from eating too much clam chowder in Boston.

But believe me, I didn't do this to offend her. Honestly. I

didn't even think about her when I was saying yes to Shayne's request to use the model house for our weekend bash. And maybe that was the problem. Maybe I *should* have considered my mother.

Maybe I should have considered a lot of things.

Like whether or not I'm going to spend the remainder of my sophomore year behind bars.

My mom is tightly clutching my dad's arm. For the life of me, I can't tell whose side she's on. Does she *want* me to go to jail? Or does she want me to get off with a warning? Could she really be mad enough to want to see me locked up? I mean, I know I screwed up but I'm still her daughter. At least as far as *I'm* concerned.

"Brooklyn Pierce." The judge's rough, scratchy voice startles me and I turn back around and face front. I can tell that she's addressing me directly because she's looking right at me. Not at my lawyer. Not at my parents. But straight at me.

I swallow hard and try to drown out the pounding in my ears as I await my fate.

"I've seen a lot of cases involving underage drinking," the judge begins, a thick, jagged line appearing across her forehead, "but I have never, in my twenty-five years in this courthouse, witnessed such a disappointing, disgraceful, blatant lack of judgment on the part of a teenage girl."

Okay, that can't be good.

I can hear a whimper from somewhere behind me. I'm pretty sure it's my mom. My dad's soothing whispers do little to calm her.

Bob reaches down and rests his hand back on my knee. I think this is supposed to be reassuring, but it only makes me more restless.

The judge is still talking. "If you don't change your behavior, young lady, and find some common sense, I have no doubt that you will end up right back in this courtroom. And believe me, next time, I will *not* be as lenient."

Lenient? Did she say *lenient*? Lenient is good, right? Lenient is what Bob keeps saying we're hoping for. Lenient means I don't spend the next year in an orange jumpsuit.

"You only get one warning, Ms. Pierce," the judge states sternly. "And this is it."

Woo-hoo! She's letting me off on a warning!

My insides are boiling with excitement. I nearly jump out of my chair with joyous laughter.

"Two hundred hours of community service and I never want to see you in my courtroom again."

Wait, WHAT?

The gavel slams down, and before I can say anything, Bob is out of his seat and patting me awkwardly on the head with a huge grin. "We did it, Brooks! Congratulations!"

Congratulations?

"But what was that last part she said?"

"Community service!" exclaims Bob as if he's pitching a trip to Disney World to his five-year-old daughter. "Isn't it fantastic?"

"Two *hundred* hours of community service?" I can barely get the words out. "But that's like . . . my entire life!"

Bob waves away my concern with a flick of his hand. "Oh, it'll be over before you know it. Just you wait and see. Trust me, Brooks. This is *good* news."

"It is?"

His head falls into a resolute nod as he closes up his file folder and drops it into his briefcase. "You should be jumping for joy right now. You could have been looking at a far worse sentencing than community service."

I suppose he's right. I should be grateful. Even my mom appears to be happy about the news. I actually got half a smile out of her before she turned up the aisle and exited the courtroom. I guess she wasn't rooting against me after all.

Two hundred hours is a freakishly long time, though. I don't even think I'd want to watch TV for that many hours. Let alone service the community.

As my dad is shaking Bob's hand and offering up all kinds of enthusiastic gratitude, I can't help but glance around the courtroom in hopes of seeing Shayne. I still haven't heard back from her. I can only *hope* that she's at school with everyone else.

But what if she's not?

What if she's sitting in a dirty jail cell somewhere because *her* judge wasn't quite as lenient? I just don't know if I could live with myself if that were true.

My mom, my dad, and I file out of the courthouse and walk through the parking lot in silence. As soon as I get into the car, I check the clock on the dash. It's just after ten in the morning. I've already missed two hours of school.

It's somewhat ironic. Of all the times I've tried to come up with clever ways to ditch class, *this* particular scenario never came to mind.

But as much as I'm absolutely dreading stepping foot in that building and facing the gossip and stares and ridicule, I'm anxious to see if Shayne is there. To see if she's all right. But as we drive down the freeway, closer and closer to the promise of a possible resolution, I'm struck by an unnerving thought. If she *is* there—if she *is* okay—then why haven't I heard from her?

SHAYNE'S WORLD

Shayne Kingsley is the center of the universe. The bright, shiny object around which everything else orbits. If anything bad were to happen to her, the galaxy would simply collapse onto itself. Everything would be completely out of whack and we'd all just spin off into space to be consumed by a giant black hole.

Shayne and I have been friends since the fifth grade. And the last five years have been, by far, the best of my life. Because when Shayne Kingsley lets you in, everything just gets better. People treat you like royalty. Guys ask you out. Evites to parties from people you've never even met start appearing in your inbox. It's the most amazing feeling in the world.

You could say Shayne has a Midas touch. Everything she comes into contact with turns to gold. If you're a girl and she befriends you, you're almost guaranteed a spot on the home-coming court. If you're a guy and she makes out with you, you'll never have trouble finding a date for the rest of your life.

It's been that way for as long as I can remember. Since grade school even. Some doubted her popularity would transfer once we entered high school, but she quickly proved them all wrong. Even as a freshman last year, Shayne managed to become one of the most popular girls at Parker High, hooking up with a senior football player right out of the gate, only to break his heart a few weeks later when she discarded him like a used tissue. But that's just part of her MO. Always keep them at an arm's length. That way you'll always give off the impression of being pursued.

Now she's dating a sophomore at CU Boulder. He's in one of the most popular fraternities on campus and he's constantly inviting her to all their fabulous parties and formal dances.

But regardless of who she's dating, Shayne is just magnetic. People are simply drawn to her.

It must run in the family because Shayne's father is ridiculously successful. He's by far the richest man in our town. And one of the wealthiest in the state. I'm not quite sure what he does exactly—and honestly, I don't think Shayne knows either—but whatever it is, he does it well. He's always in the middle of some "big deal" that he can't talk about. And Shayne just sits back and reaps the benefits. She's never had to ask twice for anything she's wanted.

I arrive at school right as third period is ending. The hallways are filling up fast as I head for my pre-algebra classroom, thankful that it's one of the classes Shayne and I have together. I can feel people staring as I hurry past. They know. They *all* know. I don't know how they couldn't. It doesn't take long for news of something like this to spread.

I burst into the room just as the bell rings but my face falls when I see that Shayne's usual seat is empty. I slink to the back of the class and slide behind my desk. A dreadful feeling is settling into the pit of my stomach. Something is not right. Something has gone terribly wrong.

The weirdest part is, when Mr. Simpson conducts his daily roll call, he skips right over Shayne's name. He goes straight from Jason Kim to Heidi Larson. As if she's simply been erased.

I feel like I'm in some sort of alternate reality. A parallel universe where Shayne Kingsley is no longer the center of everything. In fact, she doesn't even exist.

After taking attendance, Mr. Simpson quickly starts in on his lesson plan, blathering excitedly about equations and how there are two sides to every one and they always have to balance out. No matter what.

But I'm hardly paying any attention. My mind is reeling. I make a swift decision and launch my hand in the air, stopping Mr. Simpson mid-sentence.

"Yes, Brooklyn?" he prompts. "Do you have a question?"

"Um, yeah," I begin hesitantly. "Why didn't you call Shayne's name during attendance?"

He appears disappointed that my question isn't on topic but answers it anyway. "She transferred to my sixth-period class."

This information nearly knocks me out of my seat. "What? When?"

Mr. Simpson lets out a jovial laugh, as if he finds this whole exchange incredibly absurd. "She came in to talk to me about it this morning. Some kind of scheduling conflict with her electives."

The dreadful feeling spreads to my limbs now and I struggle to stay upright in my chair.

"Now can we continue talking about equations?" he asks with an amused grin.

I nod numbly as I sink further and further into my seat. Inside, my mind is screaming.

She's here.

She's okay.

She's not in jail.

And I know that can only mean one thing . . . she's been *purposely* ignoring me.

The Queen of Charades

Okay, there's got to be another explanation. Maybe her cell phone was destroyed in the fire, too. Maybe her mom grounded her when she found out about the party and she's been unable to talk to anyone. I mean, there can be a *lot* of other conclusions to draw here. It seems silly and irrational for me to automatically jump to the worst one.

I have to talk to her. I can't just sit around here and wildly speculate. I have to give her the benefit of the doubt and allow her a chance to explain herself.

And fortunately I know *exactly* where she'll be after fourth period.

You know those famous restaurants in L.A. and New York where celebrities purposefully go to be photographed by the paparazzi? Well, that pretty much describes our high school cafeteria. On a much smaller scale, of course.

It's the place to see and be seen. If you're dating the captain of the football team, this is where you would publicly make out with him to let everyone know. If you've just broken up with your boyfriend, this is where you would make a point of sitting next to the hottest guy in school and flirting shamelessly to prove that you're so completely over it. And at the heart of it all . . . is Shayne's table, smack-dab in the center. I'm not sure if its location originated from Shayne's desire to be the center of the attention or because of the student body's desire to keep close tabs on her and her friends. It's kind of a chicken-or-the-egg thing. But regardless, there it is. In the middle of the cafeteria. A metaphorical spotlight pointed right down on it at all times.

I didn't have time to make a lunch today because of the whole, you know, criminal situation, but I'm not really that hungry anyway. So I bypass the food line and just head straight for the center table. I can see that Shayne is already seated before I arrive.

As usual, she's surrounded by a group of people and talking animatedly about something or other.

I take a deep breath and start a slow approach to the table. As I get closer I notice that my usual spot on Shayne's right-hand side is occupied by some girl I've never seen before. And across from her is another stranger. In fact, as I slowly glance around from face to face, I notice that the whole table is practically *filled* with newcomers, most of whom I don't even recognize. Sure, there are still a few of the regular crew, like Bailey Reynolds, Krysta Garrett, and Brittany Harlow (who I like to call the conjoined triplets, because they're *always* together and they have *exactly* the same haircut), but everyone else is brand-new. People who *never* would have had the slightest chance of sitting at Shayne's table a week ago.

It doesn't make any sense.

I decide it's time for some answers. She can't just not return my phone calls, transfer out of my math class, and invite a bunch of nobodies to sit at our table without having to explain herself. I don't care who she is. So I march up behind her and brusquely tap her on the shoulder.

She turns, and upon seeing my face, brandishes one of her perfectly rehearsed beauty-pageant smiles. I must have seen that smile a million times. And my heart lurches in my chest.

Because I know, all too well, that this is the smile she puts on for appearances. It's an insincere, diplomatic mask that she only wears when she's being especially fake. Behind it . . . there is nothing.

"Hey, Brooks," she says breezily, the practiced smile never faltering.

"Hi, Shayne," I reply, taking a glance around our now unfamiliar table. "I missed you in pre-algebra last period."

"Oh, yeah!" she says, giving the side of her head a light smack with her palm. "I totally forgot to tell you. I had to change my whole schedule around so I could do this independent study thing."

A total lie.

Shayne would never be caught dead taking independent study.

But I play along with a nod and say, "Oh, I see," even though I don't. What I *do* see, quite clearly, is that Shayne is throwing every trick in her book at me. All the phony, face-saving tactics she has stored up in her arsenal.

A lot of people might admire Shayne from afar. But what they don't know—what *I* know—is that being the most popular girl in our school is a full-time job. One that Shayne has an uncanny knack for making look easy.

"So how have you been?" she asks, running two fingers down a strand of her silky blond hair.

Her question makes me want to scream. *How have I been? HOW have I been? I've been to the police station, the courthouse, and nearly to jail! That's how I've been!*

But I don't. I restrain myself. I remember my five-year training course in "The World According to Shayne Kingsley" and flash my most unaffected smile. "I've been okay."

She clucks her tongue against the roof of her mouth and with a slight frown goes, "I heard about your little stint with the police. How are you holding up?"

My grin widens. The corners of my mouth feel like they're being yanked toward my ears with invisible strings and my cheeks are starting to cramp. "Oh, no biggie," I chirp, dismissing her bogus concern with a wave of my hand. "I never found out what happened to you, though."

Shayne raises her eyebrows inquisitively, like she doesn't have the faintest clue what I'm talking about. "What do you mean?"

"On Saturday night. After the party. What happened to *you?*"

She laughs as if the answer to this question is obvious and the only plausible explanation for me asking it is to make a joke. "That was an insane party. I have to admit, I was pretty hungover the next day. I was supposed to meet Jesse for brunch at his dorm and I just couldn't pull myself out of bed!"

I can't believe this. She's *totally* dodging the question. And making me look like a complete idiot in the process.

Or on second thought, maybe I *can*.

After all, I've spent the past five years of my life watching her do the same thing to so many other poor fools while I stood by, knowing exactly what she was up to and ready to share a conspiratorial giggle once she was finished. And yet I never once, in a million years, even *considered* the possibility that she might one day do it to me.

"Whatever happened to 'I'm right behind you' and 'we're in this together'?" I ask, cringing at the desperation that's seeping into my voice. Definitely not the impression I wanted to put out today but that doesn't stop me from continuing. "Did you forget that the party was *your* idea?"

Shayne cocks her head to the side, looking like a lost puppy as she says, "I'm not sure what you're referring to." And then before I can even think of what to *possibly* say next, she motions to the packed table and with a flawless look of phony disappointment goes, "I'd totally ask you to sit down, but as you can see, it's kind of full today."

I nod as if I understand, but really, I'm just trying to fight back the tears that are springing to my eyes. I refuse to give her the satisfaction of seeing me cry. Or better yet, I refuse to give her the *ammunition*.

I turn to the conjoined triplets, hoping to find just the slightest trace of sympathy on their faces, but they refuse to even look at me, keeping their eyes glued to their matching plastic salad containers.

"So I guess I'll see you around," Shayne says, all chipper and bubbly, like she's an assistant on some cheesy game show offering me the crappy consolation prize of a lifelong supply of denture cleaner.

And before I can even mutter a response, she turns back to her waiting "audience" and continues telling her story, right where she left off.

Without even missing a beat.

Meanwhile, I'm left standing in the middle of the cafeteria, the imaginary spotlight beaming blindingly down on my face, illuminating my pain and humiliation for everyone to see. For everyone to talk about.

Mr. Simpson was absolutely right. There *are* two sides to every equation. Even this one.

Because just as Shayne has been known to turn nothing into something—water into wine, straw into gold, Kmart into Dolce and Gabbana—the opposite is also true. And with just a flick of her magic wand, what she giveth, she can taketh away.

SOUTHERN COMFORT

I burst out the back door of the school feeling breathless and weak. Like someone's been chasing me for miles. Except in reality, there's no one behind me. There's no one anywhere near me. I am alone. Freakishly alone.

I collapse onto a small patch of grass and pull my knees to my chest, burying my head between my kneecaps as I rock slowly back and forth. The tears are flowing freely now, spilling out and dripping down the sides of my legs.

How can Shayne do this to me? How can she use me like that and then just throw me away? I'm not some random guy she met at a party. I'm her best friend. Or at least I'm *supposed* to be.

One wrong move, one pair of handcuffs, one community service sentencing and I'm tossed aside. Shunned. No longer deemed an asset but rather marked—*branded*—as a liability. A screwup. Just like I've always been. Except now the whole school knows about it. Now the queen of all of them has cast me out of the kingdom.

And as I sit here alone on the grass, staring up at the red-brick building that used to welcome me, I feel completely and utterly rejected. Like a failure. The weight of my crappy choices crashing upon my shoulders.

Why did I have to say yes to that party? Why couldn't we have just gone to the movies? A basketball game in her dad's reserved clubhouse-level box? Stayed home and baked cookies? Then none of this would have happened. Everything would be back to the way it was. The way it *should* be.

"You know you're not supposed to be out here," a voice says, startling me back into the present moment.

I whip my head around, realizing that I'm not alone after all. Evidently, I have company. And he's cute.

Really cute.

Tall and dressed well in a pair of dark wash jeans and a button-up white shirt. He's leaning casually against the side of a nearby tree trunk, one hand in his pocket, the other holding on to the end of a half-smoked cigarette. His longish dark blond hair sweeps dramatically across his forehead, just tickling the tops of his lashes. And he has these piercing crystal blue eyes that look like two sapphires.

Who the hell is that?

I quickly attempt to wipe the embarrassing tears from my face, absolutely certain that I'm leaving behind unsightly smudges of black mascara, identical to the ones smeared across my kneecaps.

"Oh, hi," I mumble, wanting to crawl under a bush somewhere. "I didn't see anyone there."

If he notices that I've just been sobbing like a baby (and I'm not sure how he can't), then he certainly doesn't let on because instead of bringing up the topic of my tearstained face (and knees), he simply steers the cigarette to his mouth, takes a long drag, and says in a smooth, totally heart-melting Southern accent, "You could get in serious trouble for being out here."

I have to laugh at this. It feels good after all the crying. "And you couldn't?"

He blows out the smoke and smiles. Actually, it's more like a knowing smirk, followed shortly after by a blasé shrug. "I suppose I could. But Martin and I have an understanding."

"Who's Martin?"

He takes another drag. "The school security guard."

"Oh, *him*," I say, the disdain evident in my tone. I remember him all too well. He's the one that busted Shayne and me last year for sneaking off campus during lunch. "I didn't realize he had a name."

"Everyone has a name," he replies with another smirk.

"Well, yeah," I fumble. "I mean, I just . . . didn't . . . you know . . ." Finally I give up, sighing exasperatedly. "Who are you?"

He chuckles and tosses his cigarette to the ground, smashing it underneath the heel of his dark brown work boot. "Hunter Wallace Hamilton . . . the third," he says, like he's introducing himself to royalty.

I snicker. "*That's* your name?"

"My full name, anyway. Most people just call me Hunter."

"I've never seen you before," I blurt out, instantly wishing I hadn't. Because it's an incredibly lame thing to say. Especially to someone who looks like Hunter. But it's true. I think I would have noticed someone this hot before. Or, at the very least, Shayne would have and pointed him out to me. And then started dating him two seconds later.

"That's probably because I'm new," he's quick to inform me, his Southern drawl sweetening the air like the smell of spun sugar. "Just moved here from Atlanta. Today's my first day."

"And you're already on a first-name basis with the security guard?"

"Hey," he says, raising one hand in the air. "I have my priorities straight. Those are the kinds of people you have to befriend if you want to get away with certain things." Hunter pushes himself off the tree, takes a few steps toward me, and pulls a pack of Marlboros from his front pocket. He holds them out to me. "Want one?"

When I hesitate, he nods to my puffy eyes and drawls, "It'll help."

I figure I'll take any ounce of help I can get these days, so I pull a cigarette from the pack and secure it between my lips. Hunter removes a lighter from the other pocket, squats down next to me, and flicks the wheel. A flame sparks.

My heart flutters in my chest as his hand hovers inches away from my face. He's even more spectacular up close—with this small shadow of facial hair around his cheeks and chin. It's so sexy I nearly drop the cigarette from my mouth.

He has to be a senior. No doubt about it. How many underclassmen can grow facial hair like that?

As the flame comes in contact with the end of the cigarette, I attempt to emulate the smokers I've seen and suck in hard. Hot smoke immediately drenches my lungs, singeing my throat and devouring all the oxygen in my body. I break out in violent coughs, hacking up spouts of gray clouds. It feels like a three-hundred-pound wrestler is standing on my chest.

Hunter plops down on the grass next to me and slaps me on the back. "Aww, kiddo. You should have told me it was your first time."

I'm unable to respond with anything but more coughs as I feel further humiliation sink in. *Kiddo?* How's that for a low blow?

"You still haven't told me *your* name."

It takes me a minute to respond. Mostly because I'm still hacking up my lung. But also because this guy is so freaking hot, I'm having trouble forming words.

"Uh, Brooklyn?" I manage to get out.

"Are you asking me or telling me?"

I try to squeeze out a smile. "Sorry. No, it's Brooklyn. Brooklyn Pierce. But most people just call me Brooks."

"Nice to meet you, Brooks," he says politely as he reaches out his hand to me.

Like an idiot, I just stare at it in confusion.

"Maybe it's a Southern thing, but where I come from, we shake hands when we meet someone we like."

I instantly blush at his comment and then shove my hand into his. "Sorry," I say again.

"Brooklyn Pierce," he echoes thoughtfully. "That sounds familiar. Are you famous for something?"

I exhale another rugged cough and attempt a second skillful (looking) drag on the cigarette, this time being careful not to inhale. "Yes. Being a screwup."

He seems to find humor in that as he leans back on his hands. "I highly doubt that. Seriously, why do I know that name?"

"Well," I begin tentatively. "It's either because you just saw my best friend reject me in front of the entire school a few minutes ago or you saw me being pulled out of an abandoned mine shaft by twenty rescue workers on national TV thirteen years ago. Take your pick."

Hunter nods and I watch the familiar realization dance across his face. "Oh, right! Baby Brooklyn! I saw that *Dateline* special they did on you a few years ago. 'Baby Brooklyn, Ten Years After the Rescue.'"

I sigh. "Right. That."

"That was quite a story."

I take another fake drag off my cigarette. "Yeah."

He seems to sense my unwillingness to take this particular walk down memory lane and wipes the grass from his hands and pushes himself to his feet. "Well, it looks like you could use some alone time. So I'll leave you be for a while. It was nice to meet you."

I shield my eyes from the sun and squint up at him. With the bright midday sun creating a halo effect around his head, he almost looks like some kind of angel. A very *hot* angel. "Uh . . . nice to meet you, too," I manage.

Without another word, he gives me a quick salute and slips through the back entrance of the school. The space around me falls silent, and without the distraction of my cute new Southern friend, I instantly remember why I came out here to begin with. My eyes tear up again and I slowly start to slip back into that dark, wallowing place.

I try another drag on the cigarette, coughing significantly less, and just when I think I really *am* alone this time, I hear another voice come from behind me. This one, however, isn't smooth and sexy with a hint of a twang. In fact, it's more like a frightening, vicious roar. And I quickly realize that my nightmare of a day isn't over yet.

"What do you think you're doing?!"

Measuring Down

"**Detention?**" my mom bellows as soon as I get into the car later that afternoon. I guess this answers the question of whether or not she's speaking to me again. "You got detention on top of everything else that's happened?"

I stay quiet, knowing silence is probably my safest bet at this point. Especially when anything I say can and *will* be used against me.

"For *smoking*!" she seethes in a disgusted tone. "My fifteen-year-old daughter! A degenerate *and* a smoker!"

I break my vow of silence to come to my own rescue. "I'm *not* a smoker. I swear to God it was my first time and I didn't even like it."

My mom grunts. "First time smoking. First time throwing a party. First time burning a house down. Wow, Brooks, you're on a real roll here. What is going *on* with you?"

I wish I knew. I really wish I did. Because maybe then I could fix it. It's not like I *enjoy* being in all this trouble. It's not like I get some kind of demented kick out of being caught by men in uniform. It wasn't exactly a thrill to have to deal with Martin the security guard again or stay an extra *three* hours after school today, staring at the back of some guy's shaved head. Trust me. I'm not looking forward to going back to *that* for the next five days.

"I don't know what we're going to do with you, Brooklyn," my mom continues ranting. "I'm going to have a long talk with your father tonight. We're going to have to figure out what the heck we're supposed to do about all this. You have got some serious judgment issues, and honestly, I don't know where it comes from. Your sister has always been so . . ."

And there she goes. Talking about the ever perfect, ever wise, ever brilliant Isabelle Pierce. I immediately tune her out, focusing my mind on better things, like my brief but dreamy five minutes with Hunter Wallace Hamilton III this afternoon, and those heart-stopping blue eyes of his, until my mom's voice is just a distant drone. It's not like I need to listen. I already know what she's saying. *Why can't you be more like Izzie? If she can manage to graduate at the top of her class, serve as captain of the girls' tennis team,* and *get into Harvard all at the same time, it shouldn't be that hard for* you.

But what my parents don't understand is that, actually, it's harder.

I read this article once that said that younger siblings statistically perform worse in school (and in life) than first-borns. Because firstborn children start out with a clean slate. A benchmark-free existence. Whatever they do—whether it's achieve excellence or barely manage to scrape by—is the measuring stick against which the other siblings are compared. And when you have a measuring stick like Izzie, you might as well just throw in the towel and get used to mediocrity. Which is exactly what

I've learned how to do. Because really, what's the point of try-ing when, according to the scientists, I'm destined to come up short anyway?

My mom's diatribe lasts the entire car ride home. Thank-fully, once we get there, she tells me she's too angry to speak to me anymore, and I slink into my room and close the door. I swear she's *this* close to disowning me. I wonder if that's even possible. Can you legally disown your *own* children? I would ask Google but the moment my dad gets home and my parents have finished their little private *chat* in the kitchen, my computer is confis-cated and moved into the den and my Internet privileges are indefinitely revoked. Along with my phone privileges, my TV privileges, my leaving-the-house privileges, and my basic right-to-having-a-life privileges.

I'm pretty much grounded until I'm forty. And I say "until I'm forty" instead of "for life" because I assume by the time I reach forty my parents will finally be old and senile enough to forget why they grounded me in the first place.

The house is like a prison. No cell phone. No text messag-ing. No *instant* messaging. No Facebook. No Twitter. No tele-vision. No movies. No dates. And instead of driving me, like they usually do, my parents are making me take the *bus* to school every day.

So I guess Bob was right. There *are* worse punishments than community service.

And here I thought I wasn't going to have to serve jail time.

Then, as if that isn't bad enough, to top it all off my parents decide that once the contractor starts rebuilding the fire-damaged model home, I'm going to work at the construction site twice a week. Some kind of punishment-fits-the-crime idea that they're both especially proud of. So as soon as the inspectors give my mom the go-ahead, I'll be doing hard-ass, clothes-ripping, nail-hammering, large-object-lifting manual labor . . . for free. Which I'm pretty sure is illegal but what am I supposed to do? Sue them?

Things get progressively worse as the week goes on. School is basically a living nightmare. I've become invisible overnight. *Insignificant.* From royalty to nothing. People barely even notice me in the hallway, let alone recognize me. They bump into me like I'm not even there. Like they didn't even see me standing right in front of them. Because as it turns out, without Shayne standing next to me, I'm nobody. All this time, I thought I was important. I thought I was *somebody* at this school, when really I only existed as an extension of her. An appendage. Like an arm or a leg or a strand of hair. Not as my own person. In the context of Shayne, I was a goddess. In the context of just myself, I am blank space.

I guess the one positive thing about being cast out of Shayne's high-heeled posse is that I actually get to sleep in during the week. No more waking up at the crack of dawn to beautify myself to Shayne's ridiculously high standards. I mean, why should I continue to care about what I wear or if my lips are glossed or if my eye shadow complements my skin tone when I'm no longer the center of any attention? When no one gives a crap about me anymore? In fact, just to show my rebellion, I actively *choose* to wear my hair in a ponytail and don my most comfy (and therefore *least* trendy) pair of jeans *every single day* this week. And you know what? It feels freaking awesome.

My classes are particularly boring now that Shayne has

conveniently transferred herself out of the three we had together. In English, Mrs. Levy asks us to choose between reading *The Old Man and the Sea* by Ernest Hemingway and *The Grapes of Wrath* by John Steinbeck, and honestly, they both sound like total downers. Especially since Shayne and I used to pick our assigned reading together and then download synopses off the Internet. Now it looks like I'll be cheating alone.

I've been trying to keep a low profile at school. Which is probably why I haven't been able to spot Hunter Wallace Hamilton III again, much to my disappointment. Because don't think for a second that I haven't looked. I have. Pretty much every time I skulk down the hallway. Chances are, he spends most of his time in the senior hall with the rest of the cool people (e.g., *not* me). And you're really not allowed in the senior hallway without a pass. Not a real, physical pass, like a hall pass or something, but a metaphorical pass. Like a boyfriend who's a senior or a recognized kinship with someone who's been granted lifetime, unlimited access. Someone like Shayne Kingsley.

And I think we've already established what happened to *that* particular "kinship."

On the plus side, my homework load has lightened significantly. Because when you live in Shayne's World, there are actually two different kinds of homework. The kind you do for school and the kind you do for her. Or rather, for her continued acceptance. Because not only do you have to look dazzling at all times, you also have to be up-to-date on every reality show, celebrity blog, fashion magazine, album release, movie opening, awards show, and anything else Shayne deems "important." It's a very time-consuming endeavor.

DishnDiss.com is the bible, the ultimate source for every

gossip-worthy tidbit released to the public (and a few things that weren't *meant* for public knowledge). Shayne reads it religiously. She lives by it. And therefore, if you want to be in her inner circle, so must you.

But now, there's no reason to keep up-to-date on these things. Shayne doesn't even speak to me anymore, let alone quiz me on my retention skills. So I haven't visited the blog once since Sunday night. Not that I have much access to the Internet these days. Mostly just during my daily hibernations in the library during lunch.

I've staked out a permanent hiding place there so I don't have to sit by myself in the cafeteria. The problem is there's no food allowed in the library, so by the time sixth period rolls around, my stomach is starting to growl and my blood sugar is dangerously low. And when you tack on the extra bonus that I now have to go to detention every day after school this week, I'm basically famished by the time I get home.

Not to mention the total humiliation of having to actually *sit* in that detention room.

So by the time the week draws to a close and my mom picks me up after school on Friday evening, believe it or not, I'm actually looking forward to the first day of my court-ordered community service tomorrow. Because I figure anything has got to be better than *this*.

Servicing the Community

I was wrong.

When I step foot in the lobby of Centennial Nursing Home on Saturday morning and witness firsthand where I'm going to be spending two hundred precious hours of my life, seven words flash through my mind: *They have* got *to be kidding me.*

Lawyer Bob assured me this was *the* "primo" community service gig. A walk in the park. All I had to do was play some bingo, maybe a few games of checkers, and it would be over before I knew it.

But he didn't mention anything about the smell.

This place absolutely *reeks* of old people. And that's probably because they're *everywhere.* Hunched over in wheelchairs blocking off entire hallways, sitting on the couch in the lobby mumbling to themselves, inching their way down the corridors with walkers at two feet an hour. And to be honest, it's kind of freaking me out. I mean, it's not like I've never been around old people before. I *do* have grandparents. It's just that I've never been around this *many* of them at one time. And a lot of these people look like they're on their last leg . . . literally. That guy sitting in the corner who looks like he hasn't moved in weeks is missing his leg from the knee down. I wonder if he lost it in some freak boating accident or maybe a shark attack.

I take a deep, long breath—*all right, let's get this over with*—and start to weave my way through the obstacle course of parked wheelchairs and walkers standing between me and the front desk. Then, out of nowhere, a crusty, chapped hand reaches out and grabs my arm. I let out a shriek and whip around to see an old man with a bandage taped over one eye clutching on to me like he's drowning and I'm the life preserver.

"Dih yoo brih ma si-gah?" he asks, his one eye all intent and determined.

I stare back at him in horror. "W-w-what?"

"Dih yoo brih ma si-gah?" he repeats, this time a little louder. As if volume was the initial problem.

"I'm sorry," I say, glancing uneasily down at the iron death grip he's got on my arm. You wouldn't think that a man this frail would be capable of hanging on for dear life like that. "I don't understand what you're saying."

"He asked if you brought his cigar," a helpful nurse translates as she approaches and carefully pries the man's hand open. I immediately feel the blood rush back to my fingers. "Every week there's a young volunteer who goes to the tobacco shop and brings him back a cigar," she explains. "She kind of looks like you." Then she turns to the man and speaks loudly and slowly. "That's not Betsy, Mr. Jacobson."

"Wah?"

"That's. Not. Betsy!"

As she continues to try to explain the difference between me

and some girl named Betsy, I approach the front desk and introduce myself to the young Asian woman sitting behind it. Her
name tag reads "Carol Yang."

She flashes me a warm smile. "Good morning! How can I
help you?"

"Um, yeah, hi," I say. "I'm Brooklyn Pierce. I'm here for my
first day of court-ordered community service."

And just as quickly as it came, her smile vanishes, and now
she's looking at me like I'm some kind of violent criminal who
should be locked away and never released.

"Oh, right," she sneers dismissively. "Well, do you have your
paperwork?"

I produce the documents that Bob received from the courthouse and set them on the desk.

But Carol sighs and pushes them back toward me with the
tip of her finger, as if the criminal acts the paperwork represents
were somehow contagious. "Volunteers report to Gail. I'll page
her."

She picks up a nearby telephone and practically yells into
the receiver. "Paging Gail Goldstein. Gail Goldstein, please come
to the front office." I cringe at the high-pitched squeal that blasts
through the overhead speakers, echoing her exact words with an
underwater, gargled effect. It's as soothing on the ears as metal
scraping against glass, but apparently I'm the only one who
heard it because everyone else in the room doesn't bat an eye.

No surprise there.

A few moments later, a short, tubby woman with dark, silver-
streaked hair and black horn-rimmed glasses waddles into the
room and proceeds to look me up and down, as if she's assessing
a horse that she's thinking about purchasing. I assume this is

Gail although she doesn't introduce herself. She just starts talk-ing. Incredibly fast and with a very thick East Coast accent. I can understand her only slightly better than that one-eyed guy who is still waiting for his cigar to manifest.

"You'll need to sign in with me as soon as you get here and check out before you go. I have to report your hours to the courthouse so I need to know exactly when you arrive and when you leave." These fifty or so words escape her mouth in a total blur, but I manage to catch the gist of it and nod my under-standing.

She pulls my paperwork off Carol's desk, secures it to a clip-board in her hand, and scribbles something on the top sheet. Then she motions for me to follow her and starts off down the hall, rattling off rules like an auctioneer on Red Bull. "Always wash your hands after you've interacted with a resident. Don't try to help a resident into or out of a wheelchair. Never give our residents anything to eat or drink. No matter how nicely they ask. And try to avoid using generic questions like 'How are you?' when interacting with the residents. Unless you really want to know how they're doing. Which I assure you, you do not."

"Why not?"

Gail stops at a door marked "Activity Room" and turns to face me. She shoots me a stern, almost warning look. "This is a nursing home. People don't come here to get better. They come here to die. So you can imagine most of them are not exactly in the best shape. As the activity director of this facility, it's my job to make their last days—weeks, months, whatever—as en-tertaining as possible."

I swallow hard and fight back a wince, praying that nobody actually kicks the bucket while I'm in the vicinity.

Gail ignores my reaction and pushes open the door. "C'mon," she orders. "Let's find something for you to do."

That task is easier said than done, however, because it quickly becomes evident that I pretty much *suck* at community service. Over the next few hours, I manage to get booed off the bingo stage for calling out the numbers too fast (apparently one bingo ball an hour is the going rate around here), I nearly kill a diabetic man by giving him a glass of lemonade, and I unintentionally cause a riot in the activity room by proposing we play Monopoly instead of Rummikub. Because according to today's activity schedule, eleven o'clock is Rummikub hour and suggesting any modification to that schedule is the equivalent of suggesting anarchy.

No matter what I do, I can't seem to avoid screwing up. It's like I destroy everything I touch. Gail is starting to go hoarse from all the reprimanding she's doing, the nurses are giving me dirty looks everywhere I go, and to top it off, some really sick-looking guy just sneezed on me.

"Well, Brooklyn," Gail says with a frustrated sigh after she's successfully pacified what will now go down in history as the Great Rummikub Riot of Centennial Nursing Home, "I'm just not sure what I'm going to do with you."

As I listen to the soft clanking of Rummikub tiles being maneuvered across the tabletops behind us, I'm kind of hoping she'll just give up and sign the court document saying I've successfully completed my two hundred hours so I can be on my way. But judging by the determined look on her face right now, I kind of doubt that's going to happen.

The intercom squawks to life, interrupting her thoughts as that same high-pitched squealing voice announces, "Gail Goldstein, please report to room 4A. Gail Goldstein, please report to room 4A."

I'm not exactly sure what's going on in room 4A, but from the way Gail's shoulders are slouching and her face is bitterly grimacing, I'm willing to guess that it's not good. Or at least not something she wants to deal with right now.

But then suddenly her entire demeanor shifts. Her eyes brighten, her lips curve into a scheming smile, and I can almost make out the lightbulb flickering over her head. "Actually," she begins, seeming pretty darn proud of herself, "I think I might have *just* the job for you."

"What?" I ask warily, sensing that my future is looking dim.

"I'm going to have you read to the resident in 4A."

"Read?" I verify, feeling somewhat relieved by her response. I can think of much worse things for me to do in a place like this. "As in just read aloud . . . from books?"

Gail bobbles her head from side to side in a gesture of ambiguity. "Well . . . yeah. For the most part."

She motions for me to accompany her as she heads back into the hallway. "Come on," she says cheerfully—almost *too* cheerfully—"I'll introduce you to Mrs. Moody."

With a skeptical frown and a reluctant step, I follow her out the door and down the long corridor of rooms, scanning the plaques on the wall for the one marked "4A," the whole time wondering if the name "Mrs. *Moody*" is actually a real name, or some kind of indicative nickname.

Mood Swings

"**Mrs. Moody**," Gail coos softly as she raps on the door three times.

"Whaddya want?" comes a rough, crabby voice from the other side, proving in an instant that "Moody" is both a name *and* a state of mind.

"I hear you've been giving the nurses some trouble again." Gail's tone, on the other hand, is exactly the opposite. Soft and peaceful like a lullaby. Not in any way resembling the way she's been addressing *me*.

"They're trying to poison me!" the old woman howls in response.

Gail steps inside but I opt to remain in the hallway. For some reason, it just feels safer.

"Oh, Mrs. Moody," I hear Gail say soothingly as I watch her pick up random items lying on the floor and place them on a dresser that's visible from the doorway. "No one is trying to poison you."

"I can see it in their eyes," the raspy voice insists. "You can tell *everything* from the eyes, you know? And there's evil there. Evil, I tell ya!"

"Well," Gail promptly changes the subject, "I brought someone who wants to visit with you."

Gail's hand emerges from behind the door and she beckons me forward. I step timidly into the room, half expecting to find a snarling, wart-covered monster on the other side. But instead I see a small, extremely frail-looking white-haired woman lying in her bed, the covers pulled protectively up to her bony, sagging chin.

"Who are you?" The woman's eyes narrow in on me. "I didn't order you. Go away."

"Now, now, Mrs. Moody," Gail coaxes. "Don't be like that. This nice young woman has come to spend time with you."

Excuse me?

She wants me to spend time with *this* crazy old bag? No. Absolutely not. I did NOT sign up for this.

Mrs. Moody squints her beady little eyes at me and vigilantly scrutinizes my face before finally declaring, "I don't trust her. Keep her away from my stuff."

I take that as a clear sign for me to exit and I start back for the door. But Gail is too fast, and before I've moved an inch her hand is firmly wrapped around my elbow, holding me in place.

"She clearly doesn't want company," I hiss under my breath.

"Just give her a minute," Gail reassures me.

But when I look back at Mrs. Moody, whose death stare still hasn't softened, I'm not feeling that reassured.

"Mrs. Moody," Gail says, approaching the bed and adjusting the sheets around the old woman's petite frame, "this is Brooklyn Pierce. She's one of our volunteers today and she specifically told me that she wants to read to you."

No. No, I didn't. I don't remember saying that AT ALL.

"Brooklyn Pierce?" The edge in Mrs. Moody's voice has now been replaced with a cold curiosity.

"That's right," Gail confirms.

"The little girl who fell down the mine shaft?"

I roll my eyes. *Great.* Even *this* old looney knows about my prickly past.

Gail looks at me as if to ask "Is that true?"

I nod reluctantly and grumble, "Yep, that was me."

Mrs. Moody squints again, her mouth twisting as she carefully looks me up and down. "That's impossible," she finally asserts with a glower. "That girl was only two years old."

Gail lets out a condescending laugh and I immediately wonder if mockery is the best course of action right now. I mean, this woman doesn't exactly appear to be stable. "Well, Mrs. Moody," Gail replies, sounding like she's speaking to a small child. "That was over ten years ago. The little girl would be all grown up by now, wouldn't she? She would be . . ." She looks to me to finish the sentence.

"Fifteen," I reply.

"Fifteen years old," Gail echoes.

Mrs. Moody gives another hard stare in my direction, her eyes penetrating. After a few excruciating seconds, I have to look away.

"Ah yes," she says with a slow nod. "I see the resemblance in the eyes. You can tell everything from the eyes, you know? I remember watching on TV when they pulled you out of that hole. There was fear in those eyes of yours."

Probably the same fear I feel from being in here with you.

Gail gives me a thumbs-up sign but I don't really see how this situation could possibly warrant such a gesture. This woman is obviously insane . . . not to mention a total grouch. I'm not exactly thrilled about the idea of spending time alone with her.

"So what do you say, Mrs. Moody?" Gail asks, that same patronizing tone in her voice. "Will you let Brooklyn read to you for a little while?"

The old woman clucks her tongue against her mouth as she considers this opportunity. Then finally she shrugs and says, "I suppose if it makes her happy . . ."

Gail beams. "Fantastic!" Although I feel considerably less enthusiastic about the decision. And I'm just about to express my less-than-enthusiastic sentiment when it becomes apparent that I'm not going to be given a choice in the matter. Gail has already grabbed a plastic chair from the corner and is sliding it up to the bed. Then she retrieves a stack of small, weathered paperbacks from a nearby shelf and pushes the books into my hand. She guides me toward the seat, applying pressure against my shoulders until I finally relent and plop my butt down into it.

"Okay, you two. Have fun!" she says, before scurrying out of the room.

I really don't think she could have gotten out of here any faster.

I glance uneasily down at the stack of books in my lap. The covers are so mangled and gnarled, they look like they could be well over a hundred years old. And from the dog-ear creases on several of the pages, it's clear that these books have been read—no, more like *devoured*—many times over. I casually glance through the titles in the stack (four in total) and notice that they all look relatively alike. The same white cover, the same blue banner across the top, the same author. The only differences between them are the titles and the colorful illustrations below them. It's obvious these are books in a series. But it's not a series I've ever heard of.

"You Choose the Story?" I ask skeptically, reading the label that appears across the top of each book.

She confirms with a grunt.

"*This* is what you want me to read to you?"

Anger suddenly fills her eyes and she turns away, staring at the wall. "I don't care what you do. You're the one who wanted to come in here."

"Well, yeah," I say, treading carefully. "But wouldn't you rather read something, I don't know, more age appropriate? These look like kids' books."

She lets out another primal grunt and commands, "Just read already!"

"Okay," I concede, opening the first one in the pile. "Whatever."

Halfheartedly I begin reading aloud. "'You are a famed treasure hunter on a mission to explore an uninhabited island in the middle of the Caribbean Sea. Since the island's discovery, many have attempted the journey, but few have returned. The island is rumored to be a refuge for vampires. A secret hideaway for the undead. But you have reason to believe there are long-lost treasures buried there. Gold and diamonds stashed away centuries ago by Spanish explorers . . .'"

Mrs. Moody soon turns back around to face me. She appears to be listening intently. And I'm just glad that we don't have to try to make any kind of conversation because clearly she stinks at it. By page three, it becomes obvious why these books are called *You Choose the Story*. At the bottom of the page, the narrative suddenly halts and we're presented with two choices, each leading the story in a different direction.

"'If you choose to ignore the ominous black smoke and go ashore, turn to page 4. If you want to wait in the boat and observe the island from afar, turn to page 7.'" I look up from the book. "Hey, that's pretty cool," I marvel as I fight the urge to peek ahead.

Mrs. Moody promptly vetoes option two and so we jump aboard the small rowboat and head toward the island, navigating our way through the dense black smoke that surrounds us.

For the next ten minutes, we continue on much like this. I read, and Mrs. Moody chooses the story, calling the shots with impressive confidence and zeal. "Steal the healing stone!" "Destroy the statue with the laser gun!" "Jump the ravine!" And the further we progress in the story, the more Mrs. Moody's *mood* seems to brighten. I can't say I blame her, though. As much as I hate to admit it, after a while I'm kind of starting to enjoy myself. I mean, sure I'd rather be watching TV or at the mall or something, but as far as community service goes, this isn't half-bad. Much better than getting booed off the bingo stage or trying to decipher the mumblings of a one-eyed man.

"Okay," I say, arriving at a brand-new set of choices. "Do you want to stop to eat the mysterious berries that may or may not give you magical powers or do you want to go directly to explore the cave?"

As usual, Mrs. Moody doesn't even pause to contemplate. "Eat the berries," she commands, like an evil dictator.

"Are you sure?" I ask, doubtful. "Because that old yogi man we met back at the beach warned us not to touch any of the local fruit."

She grunts my comment away. "Nonsense. He doesn't know what he's talking about. He's working for the vampires! The berries will allow us to see in the dark. We need that before we can explore the cave. I have a hunch on this one."

I'm not too convinced but I've already learned that it's not worth arguing with Mrs. Moody, so I turn to page seventy-nine and continue reading. " 'You carefully pick up a berry and pop it into your mouth. At first the red juice that flows from the fruit is sweet and refreshing, filling you with an uplifting, almost floating sensation. But soon after, you start to feel a numbness in your legs. It rapidly spreads to the rest of your body and then you collapse to the ground. You are completely paralyzed, destined to remain in a conscious coma for the rest of your life . . . or at least until the vampires find you. The End.' "

"Again," she dictates, as soon as the words leave my mouth.

"Okay." I flip back a few pages. "Do you want to eat the berries or go directly to the cave?"

"No!" she barks. "From the beginning!"

"Really? Wouldn't you rather try a different one?" I pick up another book from the stack and brandish it toward her. "This one's about time travel."

But she shakes her head. "We have to find the buried treasure."

With a surrendering sigh, I put down the time travel book

and flip back to page one, reading the same opening for a second time. "'You are a famed treasure hunter on a mission to explore an uninhabited island in the middle of the Caribbean Sea . . .'"

Over the course of the next hour, I'm seriously starting to question Mrs. Moody's judgment. Old age has really tainted her logic. So far her so-called hunches have led us to fall into a coma, become slaves to the mighty vampire king, Iblier, and be eaten by a pack of hungry werewolves.

And I thought *I* made bad choices.

But every time we meet our bitter end, Mrs. Moody insists we start over from the beginning and try again, absolutely dead set on finding this hidden treasure we've been hearing so much about.

And every time we do turn back to page one and begin the story again, this time determined to make completely different choices, I can only marvel at how convenient it would be if life were more like that. If we could simply go back to the beginning and start over after every bad decision we make.

I guess it's safe to say that if my life were a *You Choose the Story* novel, I would be just as decisionally challenged as Mrs. Moody. Cluelessly stumbling through my adolescence, hoping to locate some sort of metaphorical hidden treasure but always finding myself at disappointing dead ends.

I mean, look where my choices have gotten me so far. My best friend—or the girl I *thought* was my best friend—has deserted me, the entire school has forgotten that I even exist, I'm grounded until midlife, about to be forced into manual labor at my mother's construction site, and I'm spending my Saturday afternoons reading children's books to a senile old woman who doesn't even have enough common sense to know that you shouldn't eat mysterious berries on an island inhabited by vampires!

And that's not even taking into account the whole chasing-the-lizard-down-the-mine-shaft incident. We all know how stupid *that* was.

Mrs. Moody eventually falls asleep in the middle of one of her doomed adventures, giving me the opportunity to check my watch and see that I still have two hours left before I'm released for the day. I suppose I *could* go back out there and find Gail so that she can give me something else to do, but I really wouldn't want to bother her. I'm sure she's super busy. So instead, I prop my feet up on the edge of the bed, lean back, and close my eyes, determined to catch up on my sleep until it's time to go home.

BREAKING POINT

But it doesn't exactly happen that way.

When Gail catches me nodding off in Mrs. Moody's room she gets really pissed off and I have to spend the last hour and a half of the day scrubbing bedpans. Yeah, you heard me. *Bedpans.* As in for patients who can't get themselves to the bathroom.

So. Not. Cool.

And it's not like I can refuse. Because Gail has that whole "I could always call the court and tell them you're not cooperating" thing hanging over my head. Needless to say, I won't be taking any more catnaps at Centennial Nursing Home.

I can't keep going like this. This is pure torture. Spending my weekends in a home full of one-hundred-year-old people who might keel over at any second is no way to live.

And the worst part about it is . . . I have to go back *tomorrow*!

I did the calculations, by the way. It's pretty freaking depressing. At eight hours a day, every Saturday and Sunday, without any breaks, I'll be finished with my sentencing in, wait for it . . . THREE months! Three friggin' months! Can you believe that? That's an entire *quarter* of a year of hanging out with people who are six times my age.

That can't be good for me.

I'll tell you one thing, though. Something's gotta give here. Something's gotta change. I can't keep making stupid mistakes like this. The consequences are just far too traumatizing. If I keep going the way I have been, I'll never have a real life ever again.

But the problem is, I don't know how I can possibly fix it. I'm doing the best I can. Living my life the only way I know how. But it seems like no matter what I do, no matter what crossroads I end up at, I always pick the wrong direction. I always choose the *wrong* story.

Why does life seem to be so hard for me and yet so easy for everyone else?

I read an article in *Contempo Girl* magazine the other day about a girl only two years older than me who started some huge, successful online community dedicated to improving people's Karma.

Who are these people? And how are they managing to do such amazing things while I can't even keep myself out of detention? Why are there nearly four hundred students in my class— not to mention all the millions of people around the world—who can manage to get through the day without finding themselves in the backseat of a squad car? Why am I the only one who seems to have a problem making the right decisions?

If only there was a way to take the decision-making power out of my own hands and place it in theirs. The ones who are getting it right every day. The ones who don't have a suspected arson charge on their record.

If only there was a way to let all of *them* make my decisions for me . . .

The thought nearly knocks me off my seat at the dinner table on Saturday night. My fork falls from my hand and clatters to the floor. My parents both shoot me a questioning look but I'm far too distracted to even care.

My mind is buzzing with excitement. My heart is pumping hard with adrenaline. An idea is forming. An idea that could quite possibly be the best idea I've ever had in my entire life. And yes, I know that's not saying a whole lot.

"Mom!" I burst out suddenly, pushing my chair back and rising to my feet.

She narrows her eyes at me, most likely mentally preparing herself for my next big flop. "What? What now?"

"I need to use the Internet tonight."

She shakes her head definitively and focuses back on her salad. "No, Brooks. We've already talked about this. No Facebook. No Twitter. No—"

"No," I'm quick to interrupt. "It's for a . . . school project."

My dad looks up with genuine curiosity. "What kind of school project?"

I rack my brain for a believable lie. "Um, research," I reply hastily, "for a history paper. On the Revolution."

I know lying is probably not the best course of action right now since I'm already treading on *extremely* thin ice, but I don't have a choice. I can't tell them what I'm really up to because I'm not quite sure I fully understand it myself yet. All I know is that it might just be the one thing that saves me. The one thing that can change my life for the better.

"Okay," my mom finally agrees. "You have one hour."

And before either one of them can ask any more questions, I'm out of the room. I run my dirty plate to the sink, splash some water on it, and bound up the stairs to the den where my dad has relocated my laptop until the still-yet-to-be-determined end of my grounding.

I power it on, bouncing my legs restlessly as I wait for it to boot up. Once I get to an Internet browser, I simply cannot enter the Web address fast enough.

I arrive at the home page of a popular blogging site and click the button to start a new blog. I've never had a blog before. I guess I've never felt the need for one.

Until now.

Because that judge was right. I need to change my behavior. I need to find some common sense. Otherwise I'll keep ending up right back where I am now . . . at the bottom.

I think I've proven to everyone by now, even myself, that I'm incapable of making good decisions. That my judgment is epically flawed. And that I'm practically destined to fail in whatever I do.

So I say it's time to stop. Time to stop making decisions altogether.

From now on, the world is my guide. The people are my leaders. And I will do whatever they tell me to do. No questions asked.

I put my life in their hands.

From this point forward, *they* will choose my story.

MY LIFE UNDECIDED

SAVE ME!

Posted on: *Saturday, October 16th at 9:09 pm by* BB4Life

ATTENTION ALL BLOG READERS!
I DESPERATELY NEED YOUR HELP!!!!
THIS IS FOR REAL!!!!

Basically, my life's a mess. No, more like a disaster. And I know, most high schoolers will tell you that their lives suck. But before you click off and dismiss this as just another self-pity party for an overindulged, clueless teenager, let me assure you that I'm not writing this to pass blame. I'm not going to sit here and whine about my parents, my teachers, or my loser ex-boyfriend (not that I have one). I know that everything that's happened to me is my fault and my fault alone. A direct result of my own choices. In other words, I'm the only one to blame. (A shocking statement coming from a fifteen-year-old girl, I realize.)

But I'm getting ahead of myself. Let me try to catch you up without boring you with too many details. There was a very blatant lapse in judgment, resulting in a pair of handcuffs, a trip to the police station, a court hearing, and a life sentence of community service. And let's just say, well, this isn't the first time I've found myself suffering the consequences of a bad decision. As it turns out, I'm kind of bad decision–*prone*.

But see, that's where you come in. Yes, all of you out there (hopefully) reading this. I think I've proven that I clearly can't be trusted to make my own choices. And that's why I need YOU to make them for me. That's right. Every single one of them. I'm done with it. I'm done with all of it. From now on, every decision I'm presented with will be posted here. On this blog. Followed by a simple multiple-choice poll. Then you vote on what you think I should do and I do it. Whatever the poll outcome is, I will follow it.

No questions asked. No hesitations.

People tell me I need to find some common sense and so this is me doing exactly that. This is me fixing the problem. YOU are my source of common sense. YOU are my voice of reason. Please don't steer me wrong. I entrust my life to your (hopefully) capable hands.

So without further ado, my first set of choices.

1) In English class, we are being asked to choose between reading *The Grapes of Wrath* or *The Old Man and the Sea*. If you think I should read *The Grapes of Wrath*, please vote 1. If you think I should read *The Old Man and the Sea*, please vote 2.

2) Lunchtime. No one will sit with me in the cafeteria (due to aforementioned judgment lapse), so I've been skipping the meal altogether and hiding out in the library until 5th period starts. But I think the lack of daily nutrients is starting to take its toll. What do you think I should do on Monday? If you think I should hide out again to save my reputation, please vote 1. If you think I should suck it up and accept my fate as the cafeteria lone ranger, please vote 2.

So there you have it. This poll will close on Monday morning. PLEASE VOTE!!! I know they're not earth-shattering or life-changing decisions, but they're all I've got so far. Like I told you, my life sucks. Please continue to check back for more exciting stuff as it (hopefully) develops . . .

Thanks for stopping by!

Your ever-helpless but ever-hopeful new cyberspace friend,
BB

VIVE LA DEMOCRACY!

As soon as I finish typing and press "Publish," I feel exhilarated. Free. Knowing that the good people of the World Wide Web are going to be taking care of me from now on. It's like a weight's been lifted off my shoulders. No more decision-making. No more choices. No more opportunities for me to screw up my life (even more than I already have). I've officially thrown my hands in the air and said, "World! Take the wheel! I'm tired of driving!" Of course this would be a much better metaphor if I were actually old enough to drive, but whatever.

I mean, if the producers of reality shows can trust the public to pick the next great singing sensation or the most talented person in the country, then why shouldn't I trust them, too? After all, we *are* a democracy. We vote on everything from presidents to idols to all-star sports teams, so why not take that model and apply it to my own life?

Obviously the blog has to be anonymous, though. It's not like I can advertise who I am. Besides, that's not the point. It shouldn't matter who I *am*, but rather, what I *do*. Plus, I can't run the risk of someone from school stumbling on it and knowing that it was me who wrote it. I figure the nickname "BB" (for Baby Brooklyn) is appropriate for this occasion given the fact that it pretty much sums up everything that's wrong with me.

For the next twenty minutes I obsessively hit "Refresh" on my blog to see if anyone has voted, but the polls remain at 0 percent and the visitor counter ticks up to only 23 (the exact number of times I've hit "Refresh"). Eventually, though, my mother comes into the den with a loud throat-clear and tells me that my Internet time is up. So I reluctantly shut down and trudge back to my room.

I know I need to rest before my long day tomorrow at the nursing home (gag!), but there's just no possible way I can sleep tonight. I'm way too excited about my new idea. So instead I lie awake, staring at the ceiling, fantasizing about all the magical ways my life is bound to change from here on out, until I finally drift off around two a.m.

My alarm goes off at seven, and seeing that my parents are still asleep, I tiptoe into the den and turn on the laptop again. I wait impatiently for it to boot up and then quietly tap my fingers against the keys until I'm back at my new blog site.

Without wasting a second, I scroll down to the bottom of the posting. My eyes immediately light up when I see that there are already two votes on my poll. Two whole votes in less than twelve hours! That's gotta be a good sign, right?

The only problem is, one vote is for *The Old Man and the Sea* and the other is for *The Grapes of Wrath*. And for the other question, one person thinks I should hide out in the library at lunch on Monday and one person thinks I should suck it up and face the cafeteria crowd.

Not super helpful.

But the important thing is that people are voting. And it's only been a few hours. There are sure to be more opinions by the end of the day.

Before my parents are able to catch me using the Internet and ground me until age forty-*one*, I switch off the laptop and scamper back into my room to get dressed.

An hour later I walk back through the front doors of Centennial Nursing Home (barely) ready to face another day of odorous hallways and grumpy old people. Gail looks about as happy to see me as I am to see her.

Hey, at least the feeling is mutual.

I think she kind of hoped that after the bedpan incident, I might have opted not to come back. And trust me, the thought *did* cross my mind. But then I considered all the other horrifying community service gigs that I might be assigned in place of this and so here I am.

Despite the fact that she caught me snoozing in Mrs. Moody's room yesterday afternoon, Gail still assigns me to read to her again. Because apparently Mrs. Moody's disposition was noticeably more cheery this morning and the nurses seem to think that I might have had something to do with that. In spite of how much everyone around here wants to (and does) hate me.

I have to admit, I'm a bit relieved when Gail gives me the order and I head down to room 4A. I mean, even though Mrs. Moody is . . . well, *moody*, reading to her sure beats scrubbing smelly bedpans.

"Good morning, Mrs. Moody!" I announce, trying to sound pleasant as I push open the door and step into her room. The window shades are still drawn and the room feels dank and depressing.

Mrs. Moody, still tucked tightly under the covers, looks up at me from the bed and gives me one of her patented glares. "Who are you?"

So much for making a good impression.

"I'm Brooklyn, remember? I came in here to read to you yesterday?"

"No, I *don't* remember," she growls back. "And I don't want you to touch any of my stuff."

"*Baby* Brooklyn." I try to jog her memory and suddenly feel a new and unfamiliar sense of ownership and acceptance about the nickname. "The little girl who fell down the mine shaft."

I can tell that her memory is properly jogged because her scowl shifts ever so slightly and although she's still far from *happy* to see me, she seems to grudgingly accept my presence. "What do you want?"

"I thought maybe I could read to you again."

She lets out one of her infamous grunts and directs her gaze to the ceiling. I take that as a yes and head to the bookshelf in the corner, scanning the collection of *You Choose the Story* titles. "So what's it going to be today, Mrs. Moody? Time travel? A deep-sea adventure? Mission to Mars?"

"I don't care," she grumbles. So I pull a random title from the shelf and bring it back to the bed, dragging the chair along behind me.

"Okay," I say, getting comfortable and flipping open the book with an illustration of the Serengeti on the front. "Let's go on a safari."

I'm about to turn past the title page when I notice an old, mangled sticker on the inside of the front cover. I hadn't noticed one like it on the book we read yesterday, but then again, I wasn't really paying much attention. I was too busy trying not to take Mrs. Moody's death stares personally.

The sticker is circular in shape and in the middle are big block letters spelling out the words "This book is the property of" and then a space underneath where someone has handwritten their name.

"Who's Nicholas Townley?" I ask, barely managing to read the fading, childlike scribbles.

"No one!" Mrs. Moody snaps suddenly, much louder than usual. "I don't know anyone by that name."

"Well, then why do you have his book?"

"He's no one!" she yells again.

The cutting edge to her voice frightens me. And for someone whose emotional arsenal consists of grouchy and grouchier, that's saying a lot. I look up to see Mrs. Moody's face turning a bright, alarming shade of red as her fingers tightly clasp the edge of the blanket that's covering her. And when I peer closer, I can actually see that her delicate, bony hands are shaking.

I'm not quite sure what to do at this point. Is she having some sort of breakdown? Or a heart attack? I'm thinking that maybe I should call the nurse.

But then, as if able to hear my thought process, Mrs. Moody commands, "Just read!"

And so I do. I hastily turn the page and start reading the text much faster than the average pace. "'You are an ambitious young zoologist on a safari in the great African Serengeti, hoping to study an endangered pack of exotic tigers ... .'"

It seems to be working because out of the corner of my eye, I can see the clutch of her fingers loosening, the white splotches around her knuckles fading, and the color of her face slowly returning to normal. So I keep reading, arriving at our first choice on the bottom of page two.

"Do you want to ask the guide for help or do you want to continue out into the wild on our own?"

"Alone!" she instructs without taking a moment to think about it.

Feeling my panic slowly dissipate, I turn to the corresponding page and continue reading, laughing quietly to myself. I see her sense of judgment hasn't improved since yesterday.

But I guess I'm not really one to criticize.

After several failed attempts, we finally manage to spot one of the endangered exotic tigers we've been seeking, but Mrs. Moody proceeds to scare it away by choosing to take a flash photograph, even though I warned her that would happen. She finally drifts to sleep around failed attempt number fourteen and I close the book and slip it back onto the shelf. I pause for a moment and take the time to run my fingers across the spines of all the other *You Choose the Story* novels lining the bookcase. I simply can't believe how many she has. I quietly count them and am shocked to find over *forty* in total. I mean, don't get me wrong, the concept is fun and all, but it just seems such an odd obsession for a woman her age.

I know I should probably just let it go and chalk it up to the bizarre antics of a senile old woman, but my curiosity gets the better of me and with a quick peek over my shoulder to make sure Mrs. Moody is still out like a light—and she is—I pull one of the titles from the shelf and open it. The same mysterious sticker appears on the inside cover. Property of Nicholas Townley. I check a few additional titles, including the one we read yesterday, and they all contain the same matching label.

Whoever the heck this Nicholas Townley is, Mrs. Moody is now apparently in possession of his entire *You Choose the Story* collection. I suppose Nicholas's mother could have sold the entire lot on eBay after her son grew up and moved out of the house and Mrs. Moody could have been the winning bidder. I mean, the books *do* look pretty old. And loads of people sell their old childhood stuff on the Internet. But that doesn't really explain why she reacted the way she did when I brought up the name. Plus, Mrs. Moody doesn't exactly strike me as the kind of woman who spends a lot of time on eBay . . . or any Web site for that matter.

I glance back at the bed, sensing there's something more to this story, but not quite sure what it is I'm looking for. Or if I'm ever going to find it by watching her sleep. Her eyelids are closed, her mouth is slightly agape, and the hardened lines on her forehead and around her jaw are strained and tense, like she's dreaming about something particularly unpleasant.

Jeez, she's even moody in her sleep!

I shrug the whole thing off and slide the book I'm holding back onto the shelf. I eye Mrs. Moody's empty water glass on the nightstand, pick up the cup, and refill it from the bathroom sink. Then I tiptoe out of the room to find Gail, making a point to walk especially *slooooow* down the corridor toward the activity room, one millimeter step at a time. Since I'm definitely not in any rush to discover what thrilling task she has in store for me next.

Plus, it's not like anyone moves any faster around this place. So really, I'm just keeping pace with the rest of the hallway traffic.

DAILY POLL RESULTS SUMMARY

Date: Monday, October 18
Username: BB4Life
Blog URL: www. MyLifeUndecided.com

Which book should I choose to read for English?
(11 total votes)

The Grapes of Wrath by John Steinbeck   (8 votes)

73%

The Old Man and the Sea by Ernest Hemingway   (3 votes)

27%

What should I do at lunchtime on Monday?
(11 total votes)

Hide out in the library without food   (5 votes)

45%

Eat lunch in the cafeteria despite the dirty looks and isolation   (6 votes)

55%

TO MAKE MATTERS WORSE

The Grapes of Wrath it is!

Oh my God. I actually got *eleven* votes in one day! Eleven people read my blog.

I almost don't believe it. I have to double-check the results e-mail in my inbox just to make certain I'm reading it right. And then, just to be triple sure, I check the blog itself and look at the results posted there.

It's totally legit. Eleven people are out there showing their support for the lost and chronically undecided teenagers of the world. And eight out of those eleven people think I should read *The Grapes of Wrath* by John Steinbeck. Granted, it's not the book I would have chosen since it's pretty much twenty times longer than the other one. But that's the whole point! I'm not choosing anymore. They are. And they have chosen!

The people have spoken!

Of course, I had to wake up at the crack of dawn before my parents got up to sneak back into the den and find out what the people had to say about the future of my literary education, but so what? Pretty soon my entire life will be turned around and my parents won't have any more reason to keep me grounded. And who knows, maybe I'll end up liking *The Grapes of Wrath*. I mean, I like grapes. And wine is made out of grapes. So how bad could it be?

I'm slightly *less* excited about the second poll result, however. Fifty-five percent of the people who voted think I need to swallow my pride and get my butt back into that cafeteria today. I haven't been inside that place since Queen Shayne relieved me of my number one Lady in Waiting duties, and to be honest, I'm not too thrilled about the thought of showing my face in there . . . ever again. The vote was pretty close, too. I mean, six to five? Maybe I'll drop by the library before lunch and take a look at the results one more time . . . just in case.

After checking out the last available copy of *The Grapes of Wrath* from the library, I sit down at one of the computer terminals and direct the Internet browser to www.MyLifeUndecided.com (my blog's Web address). My shoulders droop and I puff out a defeated sigh when I find that the poll result is the same. Actually it's worse. Two more votes came in and both are in favor of the cafeteria outcast option. So I guess that's my answer then.

Grudgingly, I push back my chair and rise to my feet, mentally preparing myself for what is sure to be a torturous forty-five-minute lunch period. But I know that I made a promise to my blog readers (all thirteen of them now!), and more important, I made a promise to myself. And both of those promises have to be fulfilled.

I stare longingly at the table in the back of the library that was once my safe haven from the sheer horror and humiliation that I'm about to encounter and make my way toward the door, nearly smashing into some guy I don't know who's on his way in.

We both sashay back and forth as we try to find our way around each other. "Oh, sorry," I mumble, still completely distracted by the daunting task that lies ahead of me.

"That's all right." He offers a friendly chuckle as he finally manages to step past me and I start down the hallway toward the cafeteria. I know it's just my imagination but my feet are feeling convincingly heavier the closer I get. Like they're attempting a last-ditch effort to save me from what I'm about to do. Which is basically the equivalent of social suicide.

Remember when I told you about the cafeteria? That it's the place to see and be seen? The source of all tabloid-worthy gossip? Well, I'm about to enter it and announce to the entire world (or the world according to this school anyway) that I'm a loser. That I have no friends. That I'm no longer welcome at Shayne Kinglsey's coveted center stage table. And that I basically suck.

I make my way through the food line, choosing something light and easily digestible in case the stress of my looming brush with death becomes too much to handle and I end up having to throw it up later. The lunch lady swipes my meal card and I grab my tray and take a deep breath before stepping into the main dining area. I want to keep my eyes glued to the floor, but they act on their own accord and instantly redirect to the center table. Shayne is already seated, looking amazing in some new designer jeans that I've never seen before and surrounded by the same group of random people that I never once gave a second thought to.

Before anyone at the table takes notice of me, I move quickly toward the back. Past the band geeks, past the art freaks, past the Goths, the chess club, the honor society, the debate team, all the way into social oblivion. There's an empty table in the far corner and I drop my tray down and slide onto the bench.

Okay, I tell myself. *The poll just said I had to eat in here. It didn't say anything about lingering around afterward.*

So I quickly start to shovel large forkfuls of food into my mouth, washing them down with ferocious gulps from my water bottle. Every once in a while I steal a quick glance around, fully expecting to see hundreds of eyes on me. To hear the whispers echoing around me like digital surround sound.

But in reality, every time I look up, there's nothing.

No murmurs. No stares. No one has even batted an eye in my direction.

I might as well be right back in the library, because no one even seems to notice that I'm here.

And honestly, I'm not sure which is worse. To be ridiculed, pointed and laughed at . . . or just completely forgotten. And now that I'm sitting here, blending into the table like a chameleon, I almost feel myself longing for the ridicule. At least then I'd know that people still realize I exist.

Because the silence is actually louder than the whispers.

I pick up the pace, gobbling down food at an alarming rate, until my plate is nearly clear. I jab my fork into the last cube of faded orange cantaloupe, pop it into my mouth, and swallow.

Done!

I wipe my face and toss my napkin onto my tray. I start to stand, but am suddenly thrust back into my seat. I can't seem to catch my breath. My throat feels tight. Blocked.

I bang my fist against my chest, trying to loosen it up, but the tightness only gets worse. Now, I'm gagging. And I have a sneaking suspicion that those horrific retching sounds are coming from me.

Holy crap, I'm choking!

On a piece of melon!

Water and panic fill my eyes at the same time and I glance around desperately for help but no one is even looking over here. Everyone is still all engaged in their stupid little conversations. Not one single person in this entire cafeteria seems to notice that I'm freaking *choking* over here. As in my airway is obstructed and if I don't *un*obstruct it very soon, I'm going to die!

I try to scream or shout but no sound comes out. I wrap my fingers desperately around my throat as the soft din of the cafeteria seems to fade into the background. Am I losing consciousness? Will anyone even notice if I collapse?

I can't die in here! My obituary headline can't be "Cafeteria Loner Chokes on Melon."

Suddenly a pair of arms is around my waist, yanking me out of my seat. I can't think. I can barely see. My vision is clouding over. I hear a voice from somewhere far away tell me not to panic.

But that's about all I can do right now. PANIC!

Violent, sharp thrusts jab against my abdomen. Once, twice, again. My body jerks around like a lifeless rag doll. It feels like someone is stabbing me in the gut. But I still can't talk. I still can't breathe.

Three more brutal heaves, only this time harder, packed with more intensity.

And then . . . oxygen.

The warm, beautiful air floods into my lungs. I gasp and suck it in hungrily. I simply can't get enough. My vision starts to return to normal and I see the culprit lying on the bench in front of me—a jagged lump of barely chewed cantaloupe, looking like it's been through hell. Not very dissimilar from the way I probably look right now.

The pair of arms wrapped tightly around my waist slowly unclasp and release. I turn around to get a first look at my savior.

Although his dark curly hair and hazel eyes look vaguely familiar, I don't recognize him. But then again, if he was sitting way back here, close enough to save me, then he definitely isn't someone I would have normally conversed with. Or even acknowledged.

Then, as my vision starts to clear and I can see him better, I realize he's the same guy I just bumped into coming out of the library.

His face is lined with worry, his eyes are wide with distress behind a pair of wire-rimmed glasses, and his chest is rising and falling rapidly underneath his plain white T-shirt. "Are you okay?"

"Yeah," I reply breathlessly, still devouring the air. "Thank you."

He smiles and wipes his forehead. "You're welcome."

People are starting to take notice now. Curious eyes are starting to glance in this direction. It's about freaking time!

Although now that I've been spotted—now that I'm no longer invisible—all I want to do is get the heck out of here.

"You're Brooklyn, right?" the guy asks me, seemingly oblivious to the flutter of new attention.

"Yeah," I answer distractedly, first eyeing the front entrance that leads into the main hallway of the school, and then refocusing on the back door which leads out into the teachers' parking lot. The back is decidedly closer.

"I'm Brian Harris. I sit behind you in English class."

My head whips back to center. "You do?"

I immediately regret saying this because he looks a little hurt by it. So I try to cover and say, "I mean, you do. That's right."

"Are you sure you're okay?"

There's some kind of new commotion brewing near the front of the cafeteria and I know that someone has called in reinforcements. Teachers are congregating and making their way over here. I really need to do some damage control. And fast.

"Um, yeah. Totally," I say, trying to brush it off as if this sort of thing happens every day. And I guess, in a freakish, abnormal way . . . it kind of does. At least to me. "I'll see you in English, 'kay?"

And before he can respond, I bolt for the back exit, pushing the door open with my shoulder and ducking into the parking lot.

Apparently, I'm learning. Getting wiser. Because this time, I'm smart enough to escape *before* the authorities arrive.

After-School Matinee

As it turns out, that guy Brian—my cafeteria Heimlich-maneuvering savior—really *is* in my English class. And he really *does* sit behind me. How come I never noticed that before? Maybe it's because Shayne used to sit *next* to me (before she conveniently rearranged her whole schedule just to avoid me), and once you've been lured into Shayne's irresistible bubble, everything else not included and/or welcome in that bubble (i.e. dorky brainiac debate team members like Brian) might as well not even exist. Apparently, only when that bubble has been adequately burst are you able to realize what is really going on around you. Or in this case, right behind you.

Well, anyway, Brian apparently chose to read *The Grapes of Wrath*, too. And as soon as Mrs. Levy asked us to pair up with a discussion partner, he tapped me on the shoulder and asked if I'd like to be his.

Now, at the risk of sounding like a total bitch, I'm going to be perfectly honest here. Normally (meaning when Shayne Kingsley was dictating my every move) this is something I would *choose* to roll my eyes at and pretend not even to hear. Believe me, the very thought of this makes my stomach lurch with guilt because this guy *did* just save my life. But I think it's safe to say that "normal" went out the window about a week ago and so obviously this was not my chosen reaction to the question because a) Shayne Kingsley is (thankfully) no longer the boss of me, and more important, b) I am no longer making my own choices. So I simply smiled, thanked him for the offer, and told him I'd think about it and get back to him tomorrow. When what I really meant was "I'll put it on my blog, poll my thirteen readers, and let you know the outcome."

He looked a little put off by my response, but smiled back anyway and said, "Okay, sounds good."

And that's not the only choice I was presented with today. In seventh period, Mrs. Montgomery, the health teacher, asked us if we wanted to sign up for an extra credit field trip to see some new science exhibit that's in town. *Normally*, I would have been the first person in the room to laugh (out loud) at this ridiculous notion. *Extra* credit field trip? As in *not* required? Yeah, right! But again, no longer my decision. So I have to put it to a vote.

And finally, in the hallway, I passed by a girl handing out flyers asking people to try out for the girls' rugby team (which, if memory serves, I think is kind of like soccer). Who even knew this school *had* a girl's rugby team? I mean, seriously, where have I been the past two years?

Nevertheless, I had to ignore my initial instinct to toss the flyer into the nearest trash can and snicker about just how lame people can really be, and instead, tuck it into my bag to be decided upon later.

Thankfully my parents are going to some charity fund-raiser for my dad's work tonight and I'll have the house to myself. Which means . . . full, unlimited access to the computer! And the ability to present all of these new decisions to my panel of judges.

Of course, first I have to get through my last day of detention.

And I know from a week's worth of experience now that it royally sucks. There's absolutely nothing to do but study. And after thirty agonizingly tedious pages, I've discovered that *The Grapes of Wrath* doesn't appear to have anything to do with grapes. In fact, I don't know why John Stein-what's-his-face decided to name it *The Grapes of Wrath* in the first place. Seriously, what does that even mean?

I take out my notebook and start to sketch out a rough draft of my next blog posting but I stop writing mid-sentence when I hear the sound of flirtatious girly laughter coming from the hallway right outside the detention classroom.

My whole body freezes in fear and the pen nearly drops from my hand. I'd recognize that unmistakable laugh anywhere. It comes directly from page two of Shayne Kingsley's seduction script. The performance she puts on for whatever member of the opposite sex she's selected as the next lucky recipient of her affections.

And when I strain my neck to look through the crack in the half-ajar door, I see exactly who she's chosen.

It's Hunter Wallace Hamilton III. My new Southern friend.

The voices are kind of garbled from this far away, but I see the handshake. I see the way she lets her fingers linger around his knuckles as she pulls away. And then Hunter's own words float through my mind.

"Maybe it's a Southern thing, but where I come from, we shake hands when we meet someone we like."

Oh God. It's an introduction. He's finally met Her Royal Highness of Parker High. I knew it had to happen eventually. I knew I couldn't keep him to myself forever. Not that he was ever mine to keep or anything, but a meeting with Shayne Kingsley was pretty much inevitable. She has some kind of radar for hot men. As soon as a new one enters the area, she homes in on him and launches a strike.

And that's exactly what's going on right now. The Shayne-bot is in full-on attack mode. I know the whole routine by heart. Motion for motion. Every eye bat. Every demure glance under lowered lashes. Every playful shoulder slap and provocative slide down the arm. Because after five years of friendship and idolization, this routine has been forever burned into my memory. It's a fully rehearsed, impeccably executed, flawless production often accompanied by the use of props, costumes, and blocking. And it never fails.

I can feel the anger boiling up inside me. A fire burning deep within, ready to explode.

What on earth is she doing? She already has *a boyfriend!*

A really hot one, too. Who goes to CU Boulder and invites her to fraternity parties. But apparently that's not enough for her. Apparently she has to have everyone. She's like a dog with two tennis balls. Never satisfied with just the one, always trying to figure out how to stuff that second one into her mouth.

"Well, *Hunter.*" She pronounces his name with the trained sex appeal of a lingerie model. "It was really great meeting you. Maybe I'll see you around."

Okay, this is it. She's gearing up for the big finale, the grand exit. I call it "The Walk Away." But it's not just any old departure. It's slow and purposeful and practically requires a double-jointed hip. But the most important part—the ultimate clincher—is the one (and only one) glance back over the shoulder.

Obviously, from my viewpoint, I can only see Hunter now. Shayne's already begun her victory swagger down the hall. But I don't need to physically observe it. I can see it just fine in my head. What I *don't* want to watch, however—what I don't think my heart can take—is Hunter's reaction. So I look away. I bury my face in my notebook and try to distract myself with doodles. Furious, paper-ripping doodles.

In fact, I do such a good job with my diversion, I don't even notice when Hunter walks through the door.

WILLINGLY DETAINED

"Well, hello, Miss Brooklyn," Hunter says in that sexy Southern drawl of his as he plops down into the seat next to me.

And I'm so totally dumbfounded that he actually remembers my name (not to mention the fact that he's sitting less than
two feet away from me), all I can say is "Huhia."

Yes, I realize it's not a real word.

He takes a curious look around, as if he's genuinely interested in the decor of the room. "So this is detention, huh?"

My face instantly flushes red as I struggle to stop staring at
him like a socially inept stalker. He really *is* amazing-looking.
"Uh, yeah, I guess."

"Nicer than the detention at my old school." He finishes taking mental inventory of the room, then turns back to me with a
stricken frown. "I feel really bad about putting you in here."

Wait, what?

Although I'm still relatively speechless, he responds to the
stupefaction that's evident on my face. "I heard that you'd gotten

detention for smoking on campus and I feel completely responsible. I'm sorry."

I can't believe he came all the way in here just to apologize. Although, really, I'm still trying to get over the part about him remembering my name. I mean, sure, I've been thinking about him pretty much nonstop since we first met, but I hardly believed that *I* would have ever crossed *his* mind.

"Oh," I say, feeling stupid. "It's not your fault. I'm the one who said yes to the cigarette."

He shrugs. "Either way, I wanted to make it up to you. Do you think that would be all right?"

The way he says "all right" is positively mouthwatering. Like someone pulling apart a long ribbon of fresh-made taffy. *All riiiiiiight.* The sound lingers in the air, leaving behind a heartmelting sensation.

All I can do is nod.

"I was thinking—" he begins but is quickly cut off as Mrs. Henry, the evil teacher in charge of detention, pads over and glares at Hunter with those beady little black eyes of hers. "Excuse me, young man. What is your name?"

Hunter gives her an unimpressed once-over. "Hunter Wallace Hamilton."

The third, I add in my head, fighting back a grin.

Mrs. Henry scowls down at him. "I don't have you on my list. And that means you don't belong in here. Detention kids only. You're going to have to leave."

No! I want to scream aloud. *He was just about to tell me how he was going to make it up to me!*

Hunter reluctantly rises to his feet. I want to reach up, grab onto his perfect-fitting crewneck sweater, and yank him back into the chair. He gives me an apologetic look and then, without saying anything, turns and heads toward the door, taking with him my last ounce of hope that anything remotely exciting will happen in this room today.

Mrs. Henry watches him go, her hands cocked on her ample hips, almost as if she's making sure he doesn't come back. I wonder if she had to apply for the position of Detention Director. Because really, she fits the role to a tee. I can't imagine any other teacher in this school better suited for the part.

But Hunter doesn't get all the way to the door. He slows just short of it and turns back around. "So you have to be in detention to hang out in here?" he clarifies.

"That's right." Mrs. Henry nods authoritatively.

"And to get detention you have to be in some kind of trouble?" he asks.

I observe the exchange with measured uncertainty. Doesn't he *know* what detention is? I mean, it's not that hard of a concept.

"Yes," Mrs. Henry answers, growing impatient.

Hunter purses his lips as though he's trying to wrap his mind around the idea. As if the notion is truly difficult for him to grasp. And then his head falls into a pensive nod and he reaches into his pocket and pulls out a black Sharpie.

"Okay," he says with a surrendering shrug. "I guess that leaves me no choice then."

I watch in a strange mix of horror and disbelief as he proceeds to scribble *right* on the wall of the classroom with the black marker. Mrs. Henry gasps. The rest of the classroom breaks out in fits of laughter and respectful applause. When he's done, Hunter steps back to reveal the word "Anarchy" written on the wall.

"A little cliché," he admits, admiring his work. "But I suppose it'll do."

He pops the cap back on the Sharpie with a loud click, returns it to his pocket, and then strolls back over to the desk next to mine and slides in.

Mrs. Henry can hardly move, let alone speak. She just stares, wide-eyed, at the graffiti on her precious detention room wall.

But Hunter doesn't appear to be paying any attention to her. He simply adjusts the pant legs of his jeans and leans back in his seat, making himself comfortable. Then he turns to me with a wink and a knowing smile and says, "There. Now we can talk."

MY LIFE UNDECIDED

SOUTHERN HOSPITALITY

Posted on: *Monday, October 18th at 9:43 pm by* BB4Life

Oh my God. So much to report. So many decisions to make. I definitely need your help now more than ever!

Okay, let's get the boring stuff out of the way. First, thanks to everyone who voted on my last posting, I'm now signed up to read *The Grapes of Wrath* for English. A guy in my class (who also happened to save me from choking in the cafeteria today, but that's a whole other post) asked me to be his discussion partner for the book. Please vote yes or no below. For the sake of anonymity, from now on this guy will be referred to as "Heimlich."

Second, I've been presented with the opportunity to go on some kind of extra credit field trip (not mandatory) to see some science exhibit that's in town and to try out for my school's rugby team. I've never played rugby, never watched it on TV, and am actually quite fuzzy on the details of the game itself. So please decide for me.

And last, here comes the good stuff! There's this really cute senior who just moved here from one of the Southern states. For the sake of this blog, we'll call him "Red

Butler" because *Gone With the Wind* is my mom's all-time favorite movie and I can't really think of any other good Southern references right now. Anyway, his dad happens to be an investor in some hot new club that's opening up downtown and he's invited *me* to go to the opening next weekend! (Red Butler, not his dad.) Isn't that incredible?! There's like a whole guest list situation and everything and *I'm* going to be on it!

This is a big deal for two reasons. 1) Red is SO gorgeous and I can't think of one girl in this entire state (or any other state for that matter) who wouldn't jump at the chance to go out with him, and 2) this is my first social engagement opportunity since my über-popular yet über-backstabbing, ex–best friend / Queen Bee heartlessly ditched me last week after I took the rap for a party that was *her* idea. By the way, henceforth, she will be referred to as "Her Royal Heinous" in honor of all her completely heinous acts.

As promised, I defer to your decision-making power, but I'm absolutely dying to go to this club opening. Lots of cool people will be there (including Red, who—if I haven't already established—is so incredibly hot!). The only problem is, of course, the parental factor. I'm still grounded and forbidden to leave the house until I'm forty. But, should you all so graciously allow, I *could* devise a plan to sneak out after said parental factor has gone to sleep. What do you say? Please vote!!!

Thank you to everyone reading this. Please continue to spread the word about my blog. I need all the help I can get!

XOXO,
BB

MISPLACED

How cute is Hunter Wallace Hamilton III? I'm sorry, but I just can't stop thinking about him. Or repeating his name over and over again. I really like the way it sounds. Hunter Wallace Hamilton . . . the *third*. It's so distinguished. I feel like putting on a ball gown and waltzing around my living room every time I say it. (Not that I own a ball gown . . . or know how to waltz, for that matter.)

Because I wake up late the next morning, I don't have time to check the poll results before I catch the bus to school. So it looks like I'm going to have to check them on one of the library computers at lunch.

The morning totally drags on. Pre-algebra is the worst. Mr. Simpson continues to show his undying adoration for systems equations and I continue my attempts to tune him out. But it's a difficult thing to do all by myself. I used to have Shayne around to help me. We would play this game where we'd take turns drawing funny pictures in an effort to make the other person laugh. The first one to laugh aloud lost the game. Now that I'm sitting back here alone, it's not nearly as much fun. I manage to sketch a really impressive stick figure likeness of Mr. Simpson making out with his graphing calculator, but without anyone there to praise my efforts with a stifled giggle it's not really the same.

Don't get me wrong. Mr. Simpson's not *terrible*. He's a nice enough person, I guess. Plus, I think it's kind of endearing the way his face gets all red when he gets excited about boring math stuff. It almost gets red enough to match his hair. But as the bell rings and he says, "Brooklyn, would you mind staying behind for a few minutes?" my feelings about him suddenly take a turn for the worse.

I sigh as I gather up my stuff and reluctantly trudge to the front of the classroom. I wait for him to speak because it's not like I'm going to talk first. He's the one who asked me to stay after class, painfully delaying my trip to the library computer bank.

After a few moments of awkward silence, he opens with, "You know I had your sister in my class a few years back."

Oh, so it's going to be one of *those* conversations.

I don't quite know what to do with you, Brooklyn. As hard as I try, I can't figure out why you're struggling. Your sister was such a terrific student and you're . . . well . . .

They rarely finish the thought. They just kind of trail off and leave it hanging like that, hoping I'll get the point. Of course I get the point. I've been *living* with that point since birth. Isabelle Pierce was the dream student. The dream daughter. The dream tennis star. So what happened to you?

Mr. Simpson is clearly waiting for me to respond to his comment so I just mumble something like, "Yeah, I know."

"How's she doing at Harvard?"

I shrug and glance at the clock on the wall. Did he really keep me after class to talk about my sister's escapades at her prestigious Ivy League school? "Fine, I guess."

"I'm worried about you, Brooklyn," he says abruptly.

And here we go. Let the benchmarking begin.

I don't respond. I just shift my weight and hug my books tighter to my chest. Because it's not like I'm going to play into his poorly disguised agenda.

"For the life of me, I couldn't seem to understand why you were struggling so much in my class."

I fight back an eye roll and mutter, "Uh-huh."

"You've aced all the tests so far, and yet you're still barely pulling a C average. Which was baffling me."

I look down at my fingernails and attempt to excavate a stray piece of black lint that has appeared to lodge itself under my chipped manicure. Then I smile to myself when I think about Shayne's face if she were ever to witness my blatant lack of proper nail maintenance.

"So I did a little research," Mr. Simpson continues. "And I discovered that the only reason you're not getting an A in my class is because you hardly complete any of the problem sets. And you still manage to do extremely well on the tests."

So far, my sister has yet to make her way back into the conversation, but I know it's only a matter of time.

"And then I looked up your high school placement exam."

Uh-oh.

"You did what?" I ask, suddenly completely disinterested in the upkeep of my manicure. Or lack thereof. Why is this guy digging through my school files? Is he even *allowed* to do that?

He doesn't actually answer the question. I think he knows he doesn't have to. It's not as though I didn't hear him.

"And according to the placement exam you took at the end of middle school, you should be in advanced algebra II by now."

Oh, this is definitely not *good.*

"Um, I'm not sure what you're getting at," I say as politely as possible, raking my front teeth along my bottom lip.

"I'm just wondering why you signed up for math basics last year, when according to your placement exam, you *should* have signed up for algebra I."

"Uh . . ." I stammer. "I guess I just didn't think I was ready for algebra I. I thought, you know, better get the 'basics' down first, right?"

Mr. Simpson looks confused by my answer and I don't blame him. It's not like I'm making much sense. The truth is I purposely ignored the results of my placement exam so that I could be in the same math class as Shayne. But right now, I'm not really interested in discussing yet another one of my blatant errors in judgment with my middle-aged math teacher. All I really care about is getting the heck out of this classroom and checking my blog to see if my readers have granted me permission to go out with Hunter next weekend.

"Judging from your test scores in this class," Mr. Simpson goes on, clearly oblivious to my dwindling patience, "it appears the subject matter is simply too easy for you. And I'm starting to think the reason you're not completing the problem sets is because this class just isn't challenging you enough. I'd like to ask you to consider moving up to my algebra I class."

Great. I was kind of looking forward to snoozing through the rest of this semester but it appears that might not be an option anymore.

"So what do you think?" he asks. "I have a spot in my second-period section. I can talk to your other teachers about re-arranging your schedule to accommodate."

My shoulders droop and I release a heavy sigh. "I guess I'll have to put it to a vote," I grumble reluctantly.

"Excuse me?"

"I mean, I guess I'll have to think about it."

Mr. Simpson seems surprised by my unexpected willingness to entertain his offer. I think he probably assumed I would put up some kind of fight. And under any other circumstances I would have. Actually, it wouldn't have been a "fight" per se, but more like an all-out refusal followed by a mad dash for the door.

"Terrific!" he says, his face brightening. "Let me know what you decide."

"Oh, I will," I say as I shuffle out of the classroom and head toward the library. I have a sinking feeling that my days of doo-dling through math class are officially over.

DAILY POLL RESULTS SUMMARY ⚡

Date: Tuesday, October 19
Username: BB4Life
Blog URL: www.MyLifeUndecided.com

Should I be Heimlich's discussion partner in English class?
(27 total votes)

Yes   (24 votes)

89%

No   (3 votes)

11%

Should I try out for the girls' rugby team?
(27 total votes)

Yes   (17 votes)

63%

No   (10 votes)

37%

Should I sign up for the extra credit field trip for health class?
(27 total votes)

Yes   (22 votes)

81%

No   (5 votes)

19%

Should I go to Red Butler's dad's club opening next weekend?

(27 total votes)

Yes   (1 vote)

4%

No   (26 votes)

96%

Scout's Honor

Okay, who are these people? And why are they seriously trying to ruin my life?

Only ONE person out of twenty-seven thinks that I should go to the club opening with Hunter? ONE???? Do they not get how gorgeous he is? Do they not understand how sexy his accent is? Maybe I should have posted a photo. Except that would kind of defeat the whole anonymous thing. Well then, maybe I should have recorded his voice and posted it as a sound clip. Then they could have at least *heard* what they were voting against.

And 81 percent of these people think that I should go on that extra credit field trip for health class. How did this happen? How did my blog end up in the hands of goody-two-shoes science buffs? That's not really the audience I intended. I mean, seriously, people! Get a life. Maybe if you weren't so busy watching rugby and going to random science exhibits, you'd have a cute guy with a roman numeral after his name inviting *you* to hot new downtown clubs.

As I sit in the library seething at the screen, I'm so frustrated I can barely even get excited about the fact that my blog reader-ship has more than doubled in size. Twenty-seven voters. That's a lot. Word must be spreading quickly.

Too bad all twenty-seven of them are complete morons who are probably alone and bitter and have nothing better to do with their time than read teenage blogs and vote on other people's lives, but whatever.

I scroll through my latest entry, rereading everything I wrote, searching for something I might have left out—something that might have swayed the vote the wrong way—when I notice an unusual notation at the bottom of the posting that says "5 comments."

Comments? People are commenting? I totally forgot you could even do that!

I click on the link and am immediately brought to the com-ment page. Excitedly I scan the remarks, searching for a clue as to why these people would vote against me having any fun in this fun-forsaken life of mine.

Comment 1:
Sorry, BB, but I don't think your parents would approve. I'm proud of you for establishing a life of your own, but I think you should stay home this time.

Comment 2:
Red sounds cute. But he also sounds like a bit of a "bad boy." Probably not the best choice for you at this point in your life. Good luck!

Comment 3:

Thanks for the blog! It's super entertaining. I've forwarded it to all my friends and they're voting now too. I hope everything works out for you, BB!

Comment 4:

What's Heimlich's story? Is he cute?

Comment 5:

FYI . . . the name is *"Rhett* Butler," not "Red Butler."

I lean back in my chair and scowl at the screen. "Bad boy"? What the heck does *that* person know? And yes, it's true. My parents probably *would* disapprove of me going to a club opening downtown, but that's only because my last nocturnal activity didn't turn out so well. But still, I *really* want to go! And it's not like I'd be stupid enough to burn down *another* building.

Well, at least there's still over a week and a half before the club opening. I'm bound to get some more supporters by then.

With a sigh, I close the browser and push myself out of my seat. When I peer down at the clock on the screen, I'm very pleased to see that there's only five minutes left of lunch.

In English class, I'm so distracted by my disappointing poll outcome that I'm hardly able to focus on the *Grapes of Wrath* discussion.

"Hello?" Brian asks for the second time, waving his hand in front of my face to get my attention. "Are you there?"

I blink away my trance and try to concentrate. "Sorry. What did you ask?"

Brian smiles and repeats the question from the study guide

in front of him. "How does John Steinbeck use the dust bowl as a metaphor?"

But I don't answer that question. Instead, I ask a different one. "Where did you learn to do the Heimlich maneuver?"

Brian laughs and drops his pen against his desk, seemingly giving up on the book for the moment. "Boy Scouts, why?"

I have to stifle a laugh at the thought of Brian in a Boy Scout uniform. The mental image is just too funny. Don't get me wrong, he's not ugly or anything. But he's not exactly cute either. At least not in the conventional, Hunter-Wallace-Hamilton-III type way.

Okay, he's *charming* at most. Like that dorky, debate-team, straight-A's-since-birth kind of charming. But really that's it. Sure, there's something about his expressive hazel eyes that I can't quite pinpoint, but it's not like you can even see them very well when they're hidden behind his glasses. Plus, all that is totally counteracted by his head of dark, unruly curls.

"You were in the Boy Scouts?"

He nods. "Since I was six. My dad signed me up for Cub Scouts the minute I was old enough. Now's he's been trying to get me to complete my Eagle Scouts project. He's *all* about the Boy Scouts. It was his *'thing'* when he was my age."

I detect small traces of resentment in his statement. "And you? Are you not *all* about the Boy Scouts?"

He shakes his head. "I'm much more of an indoor person as opposed to one of those outdoorsy, build-a-bridge-with-a-Swiss-army-knife-and-a-pack-of-matches types. Just one of the many ways I've managed to disappoint my father."

I'm not sure how to respond to this, so I just stay quiet and stare down at my book.

"I never thought I'd ever use anything I learned in Boy Scouts," Brian continues, his voice noticeably lighter in tone. "Well, until you came along, anyway." He flashes me a playful wink.

I roll my eyes. "Glad I could help."

"I'm just happy it worked," he says with a smirk. "Before you, the only one I'd ever tried it on was Dudley."

"Who's Dudley?"

"Our golden doodle."

"Your *what*?"

Brian laughs. "Our dog. A golden doodle is a cross between a golden retriever and a poodle. He tried to swallow a pinecone once. Didn't work out too well."

I scrunch my nose in disgust. "You did the Heimlich maneuver on your *dog*?"

"It's not like I gave him mouth-to-mouth," Brian defends. "He was choking and I came to his rescue. Just like you."

"Great," I mumble, not really appreciating being lumped into the same category as a dog.

He picks up his pen again and starts expertly flipping it around his fingers. "So what about you? Were you ever a *Girl* Scout? Did you go door-to-door selling Thin Mints?"

"Actually, I never made it to the cookie sales."

He raises one eyebrow to inquire further.

"I went for one meeting when I was eight but was so bored by all the talk of community service and stuff that I quit the same day." I laugh aloud at the irony of this because here I am, seven years later, spending my weekends at an old-age home.

"Must be nice," he says, somewhat absentmindedly.

"What?"

"Being able to quit when you don't like something."

Mesmerized, I watch his pen twirl effortlessly around his knuckles, like a slight of hand magic trick. "That's cool," I say, nodding downward. "Did you learn that in Boy Scouts, too?"

He laughs. "This? No, this is a debate thing. All debaters do it." He catches the pen between his index and middle fingers and then sets it down. "Anyway, I'm sorry it didn't work out with you and the Girl Scouts."

I snort out a laugh. *"Why?"*

"Because I totally would have bought cookies from you."

His response kind of catches me off guard. Not the context of it, but the way he says it. With a kind of flirtatious look in his eyes. As though John Steinbeck isn't the only person to make use of metaphors. But before I can give it a second thought, Brian has already launched into the next discussion question, eagerly expressing his opinion on character development.

MY LIFE UNDECIDED

MY UNDYING DEVOTION
TO THIS BLOG

Posted on: *Monday, October 25th at 7:02 pm by* BB4Life

Okay, as it turns out, rugby is *nothing* like soccer. Except for the fact that there's a ball, a grassy field, and a goal, they're actually two *very* different games.

Just to give you a quick update on the choices you've made for me thus far, I went to the tryouts today, just like I said I would, and when I first got there, I could have sworn I was in the wrong place because the field was full of boys. It wasn't until closer inspection that I realized it really *was* the girls' rugby team, just none of them happened to *look* like girls. They all had crew cuts, strapping muscular frames, and a seeming collective disregard for any kind of traditional beauty-enhancing products. They were also, on average, all about a foot taller than me, which really wouldn't have bothered me if rugby didn't happen to be a contact sport. No, wait. "Contact" is too soft a word. "Tackle" sport is more accurate.

Yes, tackling. As in full-on, football-style dog piles in the middle of wet grass. The difference between rugby and football, however, is the existence of padding and protective gear. In rugby there isn't any. And now I've got a black eye, two toes that may or may not be sprained (since according to the school nurse, it's nearly impossible to diagnose a sprained toe), bruises in places I didn't even think were capable of bruising, and an ego that is shattered beyond repair.

I'm not complaining, mind you. I'm just, you know . . . *disclosing* the facts. The good, the bad, *and* the ugly. Because I want you to know just how far I'm willing to go to keep my promise to all of you and follow the choices you have made on my behalf.

Speaking of which, Rhett Butler's big club opening is coming up this weekend. I know a lot of you have already voted but I think I'll leave the poll open *just* a bit longer so I can be sure to gather *everyone's* opinion before I do anything. So if you're new to the blog, don't forget to vote! And although I know it's not technically *my* choice, let me just say that I really, REALLY want to go. So badly, in fact, I'd be willing to endure *another* round of rugby tryouts. Just an FYI . . .

Well, I'm off to find some Neosporin and a lot of concealer. Thanks for tuning in.

Your bruised and battered friend,
BB

DECIDEDLY SO

I've learned over the past week and a half that allowing perfect strangers to control your life is not always pleasant . . . and on some rare occasions, can be hazardous to your health.

Needless to say, I didn't make the rugby team.

And even more needless to say, I didn't mind in the slightest.

The extra credit field trip for health class was on Tuesday and allow me to sum it up for you in one word: BORING! And totally gross. The exhibit we visited was called "Bodies" and it wasn't anything like I expected. Basically it consisted entirely of dissected human corpses. No, I'm serious! Dead. Bodies. Cut. Open. On. Display.

I nearly lost my lunch three times.

At least I got to skip the last three periods of school and Brian Harris was also on the trip, so I (sort of) knew *one* person in the group. Because let's face it, the crowd I used to hang out with isn't really in the habit of signing up for extra credit field trips, particularly ones involving dead bodies. But I guess just in case I *did* lose my lunch and ended up choking on it on its way back up, at least Brian would have been able to Heimlich me again.

But having him on the trip with me did prove to have its downside. On the way back, he told me the debate team was minus one person because someone had to transfer schools and then he asked me if I had any interest in joining. And I'm sure you can guess what the consensus on *that* decision was.

"Definitely!" "Sign up!" "Sounds like fun!" "Good change of pace!" "Go for it!" To name a few of the comments left on the blog—which currently has a record fifty-two voters, by the way.

So it would seem that I'm now formally a member of the Parker High School debate team. Go ahead and carve out my tombstone because my reputation—or what was left of it—is officially dead and ready to be buried.

Not that I would have any time to do anything remotely fun anyway. Besides the fact that I'm still knocking out sixteen hours of community service every weekend, my homework load has practically doubled since it was decided that I *should*, in fact, switch to Mr. Simpson's algebra I class and I've had to catch up on the two months of work that I missed. (Thanks, blog readers / math enthusiasts!)

My parents, on the other hand, are *thrilled* with all the new choices I've been making lately. So much so that they actually moved my laptop back into my room, reinstated my Internet privileges, *and* agreed to replace my lost/fire-damaged cell phone. Yippee! I've rejoined the twenty-first century.

Not that it rings or anything. Because you kind of have to have *friends* in order to receive phone calls. But it still feels good to hold it in my hand, regardless.

And to top it all off, thanks to my fifty-two faithful and

(questionably) wise blog readers, I'm now fully versed in the Students Against Animal Cruelty movement, enduring a five-day 100 percent macrobiotic diet (don't ask) with my mother, and watching a TV show about ice truck drivers on the Discovery channel that my Tivo suggested for me. Because once the Tivo asked if I wanted to *Watch It* or *Delete It*, the decision was no longer up to me.

There is still, of course, the matter of the opening tomorrow night at the club Hunter's dad invested in. And obviously, I'm still *dying* to go. My blog readers, however, have yet to show a concurring opinion.

Although the vote has swayed *somewhat* since my last posting / guilt trip—i.e., now only 89 percent of them are set on permanently destroying my happiness, as opposed to the former 96 percent—it's still not looking good. Even if you factor in a very favorable margin of error, you still don't get anywhere near the outcome that I was hoping for.

And although I know I vowed not to second-guess my blog readers, I'm having a really hard time upholding that promise. Because honestly, what are they trying to do to me? Is it so much to ask that I get to have just a small ounce of fun? A *smidgen* of a life?

Apparently so.

It's now Friday afternoon. School has just let out and I'm on my way to my first debate team meeting when who should I bump into right outside the door to room 203 (also known as Debate Central to the insiders) but Rhett Butler himself.

"Hey, Baby Brooklyn. What's shaking?"

I'm so surprised to see him that once again I just stand there like an idiot and gawk for a good ten seconds before sputtering out anything resembling a greeting.

"Are you going in there?" He nods to the door behind me and I spin around to see the giant poster taped to the outside that says "Eat. Sleep. Debate."

My faces flushes in horror. "Uh. To the debate team meeting? No. Of course not." I try to laugh but it comes out more like a snort.

But then again, if I wasn't going, how would I even know there was a debate team meeting going on right now?

Crap.

"So, how are things?" I ask hurriedly, trying to slyly divert his attention away from my slipup.

He smiles and shifts his backpack farther up his shoulder. "Can't complain. You know that club my dad partnered in is opening tomorrow night."

How could I forget?

"I'd still love for you to come out."

Oh God. I think my heart just stopped.

"Right," I say, pursing my lips and bobbing my head in an attempt to sound (and look) casual. "Yeah, I think I'm gonna make it. I just have to . . . um . . . you know, sort out my schedule."

I figure that sounded good. Like I'm busy and in high demand. Which is actually quite humorous when you think about the fact that my life is *exactly* the opposite.

"Cool," he replies with a shrug. "Well, the club is called Raven, it's on the corner of Larimer and Fifteenth. Your name will be on the list so you won't have any trouble getting in. I hope you decide to come."

And all I can think as I watch him walk away is "I hope I decide to come, too."

FILED AWAY

The meeting is already in full swing when I shuffle through the door. Some snooty brownnoser named Katy Huffington gives me a dirty look from the front. Honestly, I don't know why she needs the "ngton" at the end of her name. Katy "Huffy" would suffice just fine.

I find an empty desk next to Brian toward the back and squeeze in. Ms. Rich, the speech and debate coach, is speaking at a podium at the front of the classroom. Her eyes seem to follow me to my seat and just when I think I'm going to get reamed for being late, they crinkle into a kind smile and she says, "Welcome, Brooklyn," as she extends her hand in my direction. "Our newest member. In case you haven't already heard, she's going to be debating with Brian, replacing Cassie Krites who recently transferred to Cherry Creek. Although we'll miss Cassie, as she was an integral member of this team, Brian has assured me that Brooklyn will have no problem getting up to speed quickly."

I smile to myself, feeling somewhat smug, and try to ignore Katy's blatant eye rolling. If Brian thinks I'm cut out for this, maybe I really am. Maybe debate is actually my true life's calling and I've been so blinded by labels and unjust social discriminations that I never even gave it a second thought. After all, how hard can it really be? I mean, I like arguing. And I'm pretty good at it. Before my sister shipped off to Harvard I practiced the fine art of argument on a daily basis. And I often won. So maybe I'm just a natural. It'd be nice to find *something* I'm a natural at.

"Brian," Ms. Rich continues, "see if you can get Brooklyn ready to compete in the upcoming Arvada meet. Catch her up on your new resolution and see if she has any ideas for fixing the inherency issues you've been having. I think your solvency arguments are passable but not impervious. They could still benefit from some revisions. And remember, you won't be able to win on topicality alone this year. The judges are going to be much savvier about the rules than last year. Okay?"

Brian nods. "No problem. Brooklyn and I will get it all sorted out."

Wait. Wait. Wait. WHAT? What will we get sorted out?

I didn't understand a single word that just came out of that woman's mouth. Am I even in the right classroom? This is debate, right? It's not the German club, is it?

What the heck was she just going on about? Inherency issues? Topicality? I don't remember hearing any of those words when I was *debating* with Izzie about who gets to sit by the window on the plane ride up to Grandpa's house.

Perfect. What on earth did I get myself into now?

Or better question, what on earth did *they* get me into?

This is sounding like a whole lot more work than just picking a fight with someone. So much for finding my true calling.

Ms. Rich finishes up her announcements, which once again

I barely understand, and tells us all to "get to work." Brian scoots his desk toward mine so that our tabletops are touching.

"So? You pumped?" he asks.

"Um . . ."

"Hold on," he says, popping up from his seat. "Let me get the files."

I watch in horror as he scampers to the corner and proceeds to lug a truly ginormous, trunk-size plastic bin across the room, plopping it down next to me with a frightening thump. He pries the lid off to reveal hundreds upon hundreds of tabbed file folders, all carefully labeled with some kind of complex, coded filing system: "2N," "1A," "1N-CX."

I sit and gape, openmouthed, at the sheer mass of this container and the contents inside. "What *is* that?"

Brian looks as if he doesn't really understand the question. Or rather, he doesn't understand why I'm asking. "It's half of our debate files."

"Half?" I nearly choke on the word as it stumbles out.

"Yeah," he says as though it was obvious, and before I can respond he's already back in the corner, heaving another identical bin across the room. He sets it down next to the first and pops it open. Hundreds more meticulously organized folders.

"But . . . what are they for?"

He laughs as though I'm making a joke. But when I don't share his amusement he says, "They're for our debate next Saturday. All the teams have them."

Just when I thought my eyes couldn't open any wider. "We have to carry these two huge crates with us?"

Brian laughs again, this time with a bit of endearment. "Of course not." And I breathe a sigh of relief and fall back against my chair. That is, until he points toward a metal fold-up contraption in the corner. "That's what the carts are for."

So much for debate being *fun*.

"I don't get it," I say, still unable to tear my eyes from the plastic bins. "Why do we *need* all this stuff? Don't you just, you know, get up there and . . . debate?"

Brian tilts his head to the side and regards me like I'm a small child who's lost her mother at the mall. "What's the matter, Brooks? Afraid of a few harmless file folders?"

I don't really appreciate the mocking tone in his voice and I do my best to communicate my discontent through my rigid body language. "No," I shoot back snidely. "I'm not *afraid* of them. It's just . . . you know . . . not really what I expected."

Brian chuckles. "Don't worry," he teases, covering the bins back up with their respective lids and standing protectively between me and the files. "I'll make sure they don't hurt you." Then something snags his attention and he leans in closer to me, scrutinizing my face. "Although," he says, studying my left eye from various angles. "Judging from that shiner you've got there, I'd say you can probably take care of yourself."

My hand immediately reaches up and touches my cheekbone. Damn it! My foundation must be wearing off. Up until now, I've managed to successfully cover up the bruises from my unfortunate knee-to-face encounter with Parker High School's first-string rugby hooker. (I swear that's the actual name of the position— I'm not just being bitter.)

"Oh," I say, trying to play off my embarrassment. "Right."

"Did you get in a bar fight?"

I shake my head. "No. Just, you know"—I lower my voice and speak under my breath—"tried out for the rugby team."

For a moment he seems to contemplate my statement, trying to figure out how to respond to it. And then, without warning, he breaks out in hoots of laughter. "You? Play rugby?"

I immediately get defensive. "Yeah? What's wrong with that?"

He shakes his head and throws his hands in the air in the universal sign of surrender. "Nothing. Sorry. I just didn't peg you as the rugby type."

"Well," I say, crossing my arms over my chest. "Maybe you shouldn't go around pegging people."

"You're right. Maybe I shouldn't," he concedes. Then the corner of his lip quivers slightly before curving into a sly smile. "So, did you make the team?"

He knows I didn't. He knows I wouldn't be here if I'd made the team. Because I'd be at practice right now. Instead of chilling out in Debate Central with a zillion pounds of files to go through.

"It wasn't for me," I say dismissively, turning my nose slightly upward.

To which he nods meaningfully like he understands, even though we both know he's just making fun of me. "Yeah, I know what you mean. They wanted me to be captain of the football team this year and I was just like, 'Yeah, you know, I think I'm gonna pass. I've got some other commitments on my plate. Thanks for thinking of me, though.'"

I scoff at his joke, which really shouldn't even be called a joke because in order to deserve that title, it technically is supposed to be *funny.*

"Oh, shut up," I say, shoving him aside and flipping the cover off the nearest bin. "Just tell me what all these labels mean."

MY LIFE UNDECIDED

LAST CHANCE TO DO
THE RIGHT THING!

Posted on: *Saturday, October 30th at 7:21 am by* BB4Life

Well, tonight's the big opening at Rhett Butler's dad's club, and so far, the general consensus among you is that I shouldn't go. That I should just stay home and be a really big loser and spend the evening drawing big fat letter L's on my forehead in permanent marker.

But I would like to take this opportunity to appeal to you all right now. To offer you the chance to take another hard, dutiful look at the situation, just in case you want to change your mind. You know, because you might have voted too quickly the last time. Didn't give the circumstances enough thought and reflection. Hey, we all make mistakes. We all act rashly and impulsively from time to time. And no one is judging that. I'm just saying that maybe you need to give this particular question a second consideration.

With that being said, I'm launching a brand-new poll and leaving it open until the very end of the day in case any of you do have a change of heart.

But before you make your final decision and cast that fateful vote, let me just leave you with a few details about Rhett Butler that you might not already know:

1) He has the most amazing crystal blue eyes you've ever seen. They pull you in and hold you captive and make you never want to leave.

2) His hair is the most beautiful shade of dark blond and it's longish and insanely sexy and sometimes it falls in his eyes and I nearly forget to breathe.

3) When he pronounces simple words like "again" they sound like they're dipped in chocolate. *"Agaaaayn."* (Sigh.)

4) He drives a shiny new Mustang convertible that he looks totally smoking hot in.

So there you have it. Consider yourself informed. As always, I swear I will follow whatever the final vote dictates, so *pleeeeease* don't take this decision lightly. Be sure to think long and hard about your vote before pressing "Submit." This one result could drastically change the course of my life. I'm counting on you to make the right decision.

Okay, I'm off to service the community.
TTYL!
BB

FINDING NICHOLAS

Mrs. Moody is asleep when I enter her room. And since I don't really feel like hanging out in the activity room during Parcheesi hour, I figure I'll just chill in here until she wakes up and see if she wants me to read to her. But since there are not many exciting things to do in an old lady's bedroom, I decide to explore, hoping to get a better idea of who Mrs. Moody is and what makes her quite so . . . well, moody.

I don't really find all that much. The top of her dresser is crammed with miscellaneous knickknacks that look like the result of a long career as a garage sale scavenger. Her picture frames are filled with photographs of what appear to be the same yellow dog and her bookshelf, as we already know, houses nothing but *You Choose the Story* novels, with a dinged-up copy of the Bible thrown in among them. So I abandon my search, grab one of the books from the shelf—a title I haven't had the privilege of reading yet—sit down in the plastic visitor's chair, and examine the cover. This one is about a mission to Mars and fighting evil aliens. I dive in, eager to finally have a chance to choose the story myself, without Mrs. Moody's bad judgment getting in the way.

I prop my legs up on the edge of the bed and start reading.

Within the first two pages, I've already blasted off into space toward the red planet and made the prudent decision to send my rover craft down to explore before I disembark. But my spaceship is soon sucked into the gravitational force field of an invisible enemy ship and I have to make the choice to get into my space suit and jump ship or let the force pull me to wherever it's going.

I turn to page twenty-three, electing to get the heck out of there, but instead of discovering my fate as a lost soul in space, I discover something else.

A photograph.

It looks rather old and discolored but I can still see the subject clearly. It's a young blond boy dressed in red overalls and a white T-shirt. He's standing in the middle of an open field, holding out a freshly picked daisy in his hand, as though he's offering it to the camera.

I study it curiously before flipping it over and reading the back.

In tidy cursive, the following is written:

Nicholas, age 4.

This must be the mysterious Nicholas Townley who Mrs. Moody refuses to talk about. Why she refuses to talk about him or why just the mention of his name nearly sent her into cardiac arrest, I still have no idea, but I have a strong feeling he's *not* just some guy she bought books from on the Internet.

Mrs. Moody stirs in her bed and I quickly slip the photograph back in the book and slide the book into my bag. When she opens her eyes, I greet her with a bright "Good morning, Mrs. Moody!"

"Humph," she grumbles groggily. "You again, huh?"

At least now she remembers who I am. I suppose that's an improvement.

"Yep," I reply cheerfully. "It's me."

"Whaddya want this time?"

I do actually have something in mind, but I realize that I'm going to need to put her in a better mood (if such a thing even exists for this woman) before I can execute my plan.

"This dog is really cute," I remark, picking up one of the framed photographs on her dresser and bringing it over to the bedside. "What kind is it?"

The subject matter appears to put her at ease right away. "It's a mix," she grumbles, but this time, with noticeably less bitterness in her voice. She takes the photograph from my hand and gazes into it. For a second there, I almost think I see longing in her eyes.

Figuring I must be on the right track, I press on. "What kind of mix?"

"Golden retriever and poodle." The crinkles around her mouth soften just a fraction as she stares at her former companion.

"Oh, a golden doodle!" I say, excited that I actually know the name of the breed thanks to Brian and his little Heimlich maneuver pinecone story.

But my fortuitous knowledge seems to have the opposite effect as she drops the frame, photo-side down, on her bed and grunts. "Those mamsy pamsy dog breeders have to have a name for everything. Back when I had Ruby here, we called her what she was. A mutt."

"Ruby. That's a cute name. I like that."

"Humph. Wouldn't let me keep her."

"Who wouldn't?" I make an obvious show of my astonishment.

"The losers who run this place. Had to give her up."

I sit down on the edge of her bed, thinking that I might have just made some kind of breakthrough. "I'm sorry," I offer in a somber tone, hoping my sympathy will open some doors and possibly lead me to some answers.

But any semblance of a mood shift is already long gone. "Doesn't matter anymore," she growls. "I'm sure she's long dead by now."

I opt not to even go there as it's clearly a dead end (no pun intended) and instead move forward with my plan. "Well," I say, looking pensive. "I was hoping you might be able to help me with something."

She grunts again and pulls the covers up under her chin. "Doubtful."

I locate a piece of paper and a pencil on her desk and bring them over. Then I hold up my right hand and twist my wrist in a circle, feigning discomfort. "I think I sprained my wrist the other day playing rugby and I really need to document my hours and activities for Gail. Would you mind writing them down for me?"

I can tell from the way Mrs. Moody wiggles her lips around that she's contemplating my request. After a few moments pass, she finally scoots herself up and mutters an unenthusiastic "Fine."

I breathe out an exaggerated sigh of relief. "Oh, thank you! That would be *so* helpful."

I maneuver her food tray over the bed so that it acts as a

desk, then I set the paper down on top of it and hand her the pencil. She grips it so tightly between her fingers I'm worried she might snap it in two.

"Okay," I say. "Please write: Saturday, four hours, helped Mr. Nichols with his luggage."

She starts to scribble and I tilt my head to watch her shaky letters appear on the page.

Saturday, four hours, helped Mr. Nichols . . .

"Actually," I interrupt, pointing to the page. "I need you to write the number 4, not spell it out."

"What the heck for?" Mrs. Moody protests.

I shrug and roll my eyes. "Don't ask me. Gail is just so anal about stuff like that."

"Fine," she concedes with a scoff and erases the word "four," replacing it with a numeral. Then I repeat the remainder of the sentence as she finishes writing.

. . . with his luggige.

"Oops," I cut in again. "You spelled luggage wrong. It's actually *a-g-e* not *i-g-e*."

She gives me the stink eye and I throw my hands up in surrender. "I'm telling you. She's a stickler for the details."

Once again, Mrs. Moody erases her text and rewrites the word.

"Thanks!" I exclaim, sliding the paper out from under her hand and relieving her of the pencil. "You're the best!"

She peers at me with suspicion. "That's all?"

"Yep," I reply, folding up the page and stuffing it into my pocket. "That's it."

The intercom screeches to life just then and Carol's annoying voice (made even more annoying by the scratchy effect of the dilapidated old PA system) comes on. "Brooklyn Pierce. Please report to the activity room." As usual, her disdain for me is evident in the way she pronounces my name. As though it's riddled with disease. And she does little to hide it.

Regardless of Carol's feelings toward me, I'm grateful for an excuse to exit. I gather up my book bag and sling it over my shoulder. "Well, I better turn this in and get to the activity room. Gail probably needs help setting up Family Feud for game show hour."

Mrs. Moody slumps back down into her bed and turns to look at the wall. "Humph."

I stop just short of the door and glance back at her, studying her closed-off body language. I take a shot in the dark. "Do you want to play Family Feud with us?"

Her body tenses up even more. "Ha!" she quips sarcastically. "Like I would *ever* want to do anything with those old clowns."

I study her taut mouth and white fingers gripping the sheets around her chin and wonder if she really does mean that. Somehow I don't think so. But who I am to psychoanalyze a ninety-year-old lady? So I just shrug and go, "Okay, suit yourself," before disappearing out the door.

As soon as I'm in the hallway, I remove the photograph from my bag and the piece of scratch paper from my pocket. I squat down against the wall and balance each item on opposite knees. I carefully compare the last name "Nichols" to the first name "Nicholas" on the back of the photograph, then I look at the letters "age" in "luggage" and compare it to the "age" in "age 4." And last, I study the two fours, noticing how each of them has a unique arch to its edges with short, curling tails ticked at the bottom.

The cursive on the page is definitely shakier and a bit more fragile than the writing on the back of the photograph, but there's no doubt in my mind they originated from the same hand. And that can only mean one thing: Mrs. Moody has a secret that she refuses to talk about. A secret involving someone named Nicholas Townley.

Dead End

I head down the hallway toward the front desk, careful to duck past the activity room so that Gail doesn't spot me. Once I reach the lobby, I look for someone besides Carol to approach, but she appears to be the only one around. So I take a deep breath, cringe, and walk up to her. "Good morning, Carol," I say, trying to sound friendly and upbeat.

"Aren't you supposed to be in the activity room?" she snarls back at me with an exasperated sigh. "I paged you there ten minutes ago."

I conceal my annoyance with a beaming smile. "I know. I'm heading over there. I just had a quick question."

She opens her eyes wide at me, as if to say "And your question is?"

I force out a laugh. "Sorry. I wanted to know if Mrs. Moody in 4A has any relatives named Nicholas Townley."

She flips a page in the magazine that's lying open across her desk. "I don't know," she replies dismissively. "I'd have to check her file."

I fight the urge to roll my eyes and shoot back some kind of snotty remark and just maintain my smile until my cheeks start to ache. "Well, would you mind checking her file?" I ask as politely as I can.

"Why? What is this regarding?"

"Oh, I'm just curious."

"Well," she huffs. "I'm not really at liberty to start rummaging through confidential patient files just to satisfy *your* curiosity."

Jeez, I think. Apparently Mrs. Moody isn't the only person around here with an attitude problem. What did I ever do to this woman?

I struggle to keep grinning through gritted teeth as I turn on my heels and mutter, "Thanks, anyway." Then I head for the activity room.

"Brooklyn," Gail says, sounding relieved to see me. "I'm glad you're here. Will you take over the Family Feud game? I have to make a phone call."

"Sure." I shrug and take her place at the front of the room. She shuffles out the door as I pull the next card from the deck and read the question aloud to a room full of semi-eager faces. "Name something you do when it snows."

A lady in the front shouts out, "Pick it!"

A man toward the back yells, "Blow it!"

A third answer comes from somewhere in the middle. "Smell things!"

Confused, I study the card in my hand. "No," I announce with sudden realization. "Something you do WHEN IT SNOWS. Not *with your nose.*"

"Sledding!" the lady in the front answers without missing a beat.

I nod, referencing the card. "Yep, that's number two."

"Skiing," someone else shouts.

"Number three," I reply.

"Poh-uh," the mumbling man with the eye patch ventures from somewhere in the middle.

I force a smile and look down at the card. "Yep. That's the number one answer!" Even though I have no idea what the heck he just said.

The rest of the hour passes by much like this, and when Family Feud is over I put away the game and return the box to the shelf. Gail hurries back in, looking a bit flustered. "Oh, thanks so much, Brooklyn. How did it go?"

I shrug. "Fine, I guess."

"And how's Mrs. Moody doing?"

"Fine," I say again.

"You know," she says after a moment of reflection, "I definitely had my doubts about you when you first got here, but I think you're really starting to show signs of improvement."

I glance at her skeptically, waiting for the "but." When it doesn't come, I ask, "Really?"

She nods. "Really. You've come a long way in just a few short weeks. I think you show promise. Mrs. Moody has definitely taken a liking to you. And as you can imagine, she doesn't like most people."

"About that," I begin cautiously, "do you have any idea why she's like that?"

Gail flips on the TV and navigates through the channels until she arrives at one of those courtroom shows—a late-morning favorite around here. "Oh, who knows," she says forlornly. "Most of our residents are dealing with some form of regret at this stage in their life. You know, they're thinking about death, taking inventory of their life, wishing they'd done things differently. Some people react by getting depressed. Some people by getting angry. Mrs. Moody is clearly one of the latter."

The mention of regret definitely piques my interest. "What would she be regretting, do you think?"

Gail sighs. "It's hard to know. She's certainly never told me."

"Does she have any family?"

She purses her lips in contemplation. "Mrs. Moody? No. As far as I know, she doesn't have anyone."

"But then who brought her in? And who pays for her to be here?"

"She checked herself in and she pays the bills. Or, rather, the lawyer in charge of her estate does."

"So she has *no* visitors? Ever?"

"Besides her lawyer—and you, of course—not that I've seen."

"Oh." My face falls into a frown as I feel like I'm nearing a dead end. "Well, does the name Nicholas Townley mean anything to you?"

Gail shakes her head as she starts stacking up chairs—preparing the room for the next activity. "Doesn't ring a bell. Why?"

For a moment, I consider telling her. Divulging the story of the name written in all the books, Mrs. Moody's reaction to it, and the photograph I found between the pages with the matching handwriting on the back. But something is nagging at me to keep quiet. That if Mrs. Moody truly *has* taken a liking to me (regardless of how she may act when I walk into the room), then keeping her secret would be the right thing to do. So I just mutter, "Never mind," and get to work stacking chairs.

DAILY POLL RESULTS SUMMARY

Date: Saturday, October 30
Username: BB4Life
Blog URL: www.MyLifeUndecided.com

Second Chance: Should I go to the kick-ass, once-in-a-lifetime club opening that Rhett Butler's dad is hosting?
(75 total votes)

Yes! Go! Be fabulous! Have a fabulous time with other fabulous people! ☺   (7 votes)

 9%

No. Stay home. Do nothing. Be a loser and watch the 11:00 news with your parents. ☹   (68 votes)

91%

Comment 1:
Sorry, BB, I stick by my original assessment.

Comment 2:
I'm new to the blog, so I didn't vote in the last poll about this, but from reading your archives, staying home sounds like the better bet.

Comment 3:
You're not a loser! You're just being smart. A fifteen-year-old at a downtown club? Sounds like a recipe for trouble.

Comment 4:

There's nothing wrong with watching the news. Believe it or not, it's cool to know what's going on in the world. And I wouldn't advise choosing a guy just because he has a sexy accent.

Comment 5:

What's going on with Heimlich? Is he still in the picture?

DOWNER TOWN

I give up.

I seriously do. I tried really hard to talk some sense into these people but they appear to be a lost cause. All of them. Well, except those seven people who had the right mind to actually vote for me to go to the club tonight. Who are *these* people? Where do *they* live? I'd like to meet them. Hang out with them. Follow them on Twitter. The world could use a whole heck of a lot more people like that.

As for the rest of them—the *sixty-eight* readers who think I'm better off staying home tonight—I just don't know what to say. I feel sorry for them. I honestly do. They obviously live very sad, pathetic, frustrated lives in which nothing fun ever happens and the eleven o'clock news is the highlight of their day. And there's nothing I can do about that.

But a promise is a promise. And I *am* still grateful that seventy-five people took time out of their day to actually read what I had to say and vote on it.

So I'm going to follow what they say. Just like I swore I

would. I'm not going to go to the club. I'm not going to dance all night with Hunter in the cute, (slightly) too-short miniskirt that I picked out especially for the occasion. I'm not going to get lost in the thrumming music and feel the pressure of Hunter's arms wrapped tightly around my body as we get close and hot and sweaty from the MTV-style gyrating on the dance floor. I'm not going to feel his lips brush against my skin as we share some steamy stolen moment in a dark back corner of the club. I'm not going to do any of that.

I'm just going to stay here, dressed in my boring jeans and a pastel green I LOVE CUPCAKES graphic tee, and maybe even go out to dinner with my parents later.

Yes, I'll keep my promise to the blog-reading population of the world.

But I'm not going to like it.

And allow me to just state for the record—in case there's any doubt left in *anyone's* mind—that I am completely, one hundred and *fifty* percent opposed to the notion. And that this is *not* my idea of a good time. Which is why, in a silent act of protest, I don't even bother to change my clothes before sulking into my dad's car to go to dinner at some "hip" new bistro that just opened in town. And the reason that word is in quotation marks is because I think my parents and I have very different ideas of what constitutes "hip."

As we drive north on I-25, passing familiar landmarks and miles upon miles of green, open space, I stare out the window, feeling pathetically sorry for myself and wishing I were anywhere else but here. My self-pity party is so intense and intricate, in fact, that I don't even notice my dad hasn't gotten off on any of the streets that we usually exit when we go out to dinner. And as

I crane my neck to look farther ahead on the freeway, my heart starts to thump loudly in my chest as I realize that we're heading straight for . . .

"Wait, where are we going?" I ask hastily, my tone just bordering on rudeness.

"To the restaurant." My dad glances at me briefly in the rearview mirror.

"Yes, but *where*? I thought you said it was 'in town.'"

My dad chuckles, clearly thinking I'm being ridiculous. "Yes," he states matter-of-factly. "*Down*town."

Oh, no.

No, no, no, no, *no*.

"As in downtown Denver?" I ask, clinging to some rapidly unraveling string of delusional hope.

Now it's my mom's turn to chuckle at my seeming antics. "No," she mocks. "As in downtown Detroit."

Oh God. This can't be happening.

I cannot be anywhere *near* that club. My heart can't take it. My self-esteem will never survive. Downtown Denver is not a big place. In fact, it's small. Extremely small. WAY TOO SMALL. Just a handful of main streets. The chances of us getting off the freeway and driving past . . .

But, looking out the window, I can see it's already too late. Because my dad is veering down the exit, flipping on his blinker, turning right on 15th Street, and before I can even process what's happening, we slow to a stoplight and there it is. Right in front of me. With its red carpet and velvet ropes and black-clad bouncers. Club Raven. Hunter's dad's latest investment.

Without thinking, I hit the deck. Clicking off my seat belt and diving onto the floor of the car. And trust me, there's not really that much room down here. Especially given how tall my dad is and the fact that he has to adjust his seat all the way back so that his long legs can fit under the steering wheel. But here I am, regardless. Crouched in the most uncomfortable of positions, attempting to poke my head up just enough to see what's going on beneath the crisscrossing searchlights but not enough to actually be noticed, or worse . . . recognized.

"Brooklyn, what on earth are you doing?" my mom screeches, turning her entire body around to scrutinize my unusual behavior.

"Nothing," I whisper, which in actuality is pretty stupid since it's not like the people waiting in line behind the velvet ropes out there can *hear* me. "I'm just . . . um . . . I dropped my lip gloss."

"Well, find it quickly and get your seat belt back on," my mom commands, sounding irritated. "The light's going to turn green any second."

But I don't even respond. I'm far too concerned with stealing just one tiny peek at the spectacle going on outside the window. I tilt my chin a half an inch higher and strain my eyes to see through the glass. But despite all the chaos, the lights, the pulsating music, the commotion of people trying to get past the bouncer, I only see one thing.

Or I guess I should say, one *person.*

And that's Shayne.

Dressed to the nines in whatever super trendy, super flattering, super expensive outfit her dad just purchased for her no questions asked, surrounded by all her little I-heart-Shayne groupies, standing at the very front of the line, and flashing those irresistible baby blues at the burly bouncer.

My whole body turns to ice.

Of course she's there.

And why wouldn't she be? It was foolish of me to think that I'm the *only* student at Parker High that Hunter would invite. I guess in reality I'm just the only one who was stupid enough not to accept the invitation. Or rather, stupid enough to listen to the sixty-eight people who *told* me not to accept.

"Oh, jeez. Where is that god-awful sound coming from?" my mom says with a scowl.

"Looks like a new club just opened up," my dad replies, glancing out the window.

My mom groans. "Perfect. Just what we need. Another club. I swear this town is turning into New York City."

But I'm barely listening. I'm far too obsessed with what's going on outside my window. With what I'm missing out on. With Shayne Kingsley stealing *my* night, right out from under me.

The whole wretched situation just makes me feel sick to my stomach. Thankfully, I don't have to stare at it for much longer. Because a few seconds later the light turns green, my dad steps on the gas, and the sights and sounds of Club Raven and everything it represents in my sad, pathetic life fade away in the rearview mirror.

Unfortunately, though, no matter how far we drive, it doesn't fade from my memory.

EMOTIONAL FUSION

"So how's the community service going?" my dad asks as soon as we're seated in the restaurant with menus.

Just what I need right now. To be stuck in a romantic, candlelit heart-to-heart . . . with my *parents*.

I mumble out some kind of noncommittal response as I scour the menu for something that looks even halfway edible. Since when did *fusing* foods from two different ends of the globe become an acceptable form of cuisine? I don't want my Mexican food *fused* with my Japanese food. And I'm not sure the Mexican traditionalists would appreciate it much either. If I want Japanese food, I'll go to a Japanese restaurant. Let's not try to kill two birds with one stone here, okay? Is it so much to ask that my burrito *not* be filled with seared Ahi tuna?

"Are they still having you read to that one lady?" my mom asks, trying to carefully reel in the information like a fisherman with a faint tug on the end of his line.

"Yep, still reading."

"What else do they have you do?"

I shrug and close my menu, settling on the safest-looking item I can find: chicken flautas (wasabi guacamole on the side, please). "You know, just the usual. A little bingo. A little Family Feud. Rummikub. Whatever."

"Oh, we used to play Rummikub in college," my dad says, getting this dreamy kind of nostalgic grin on his face. "Remember, Camille? My roommates and I would have these huge Rummikub tournaments on the weekends. Boy, would those get competitive. Sometimes downright nasty."

"Wow," I muse sarcastically. "Life without TV must have *really* sucked big-time, huh?"

My mom feigns offense. "Brooklyn. Your father and I aren't dinosaurs. We *had* television in the eighties. We just valued quality time with our friends. You know, before everyone communicated via text message and Twitter, human beings actually interacted with one another face-to-face."

I raise my eyebrows like I'm sincerely interested in taking this trip down pre-technology memory lane with my parents. "Sounds thrilling."

"Well, aren't you in a surly mood tonight," my dad remarks.

"Sorry," I mumble, turning away. Even though I don't really know what "surly" means, I can pretty much surmise from the way he's glowering at me from across the table.

"What's that about?"

I almost feel like telling them. Spilling it all out on this Mexican fusion tabletop. That I put my trust in the world and the world failed me. That I placed my life in the hands of the blog-reading population and they let me down. And that if it weren't for them, I'd be the one standing in that line, giving my name to the bouncer, being admitted into the most exciting night of my life.

But I know I can't. For two primary reasons.

1) They would never understand.

2) If I admit now that I had every intention of sneaking out of the house tonight to attend the opening of some hot new club that my parents would have *never*, in a million years, allowed me to attend, I know I would just get myself into more trouble. And I really don't want to give them any reason to extend my grounding. Because even though I *didn't* ultimately end up sneaking out of the house, I'm pretty sure they'd find me guilty by consideration.

So I just shrug and say, "Nothing."

And my parents press on with the questioning, asking me about school and homework and teachers, until they finally land on the topic I've been avoiding for the past three weeks.

"How's Shayne doing?" my dad asks. "We haven't seen her in a while."

"Because I'm grounded, remember? I'm not allowed to do anything or see any*one*."

My dad laughs. "Yes, I know. But what I meant was, we haven't heard you talk about her in a while."

I haven't exactly *told* my parents yet that Shayne and I aren't friends anymore, and I definitely don't feel like getting into it now, so I just say, "She's been really busy with her stuff and I've been really busy with mine. You know, debate team and all."

"That's right," my mom says, her face perking up with interest. As if the words "debate team" were the secular equivalent of me announcing that I'm joining the seminary. "How did that come about?"

I sigh and slouch in my seat. What is with the twenty questions tonight? Is today National Drill Brooklyn Day and I just forgot to mark it on my calendar? No wonder I'm in such a surly mood.

"I don't know," I say, taking a sip from the virgin strawberry daiquiri the waiter just delivered and trying not to think about the fact that had I been at Hunter's dad's club tonight, the word "virgin" wouldn't have been anywhere near the name of my drink. "I guess I just wanted a change of pace. And, you know, I thought it might be fun."

My dad opens his mouth to comment, but thankfully, I'm spared from further scrutiny when the waiter appears to take our order. And I don't know if it's the anticipation of their teriyaki salmon enchiladas and lobster spring roll taquitos that has distracted them or just some unexpected consideration for my sour mood that keeps them from pressing the issue, but by the time the waiter leaves with our order, they've moved on to other topics of conversation.

MY LIFE UNDECIDED

LIFE GOES ON . . .
IF YOU CAN CALL MINE A LIFE

Posted on: *Sunday, October 31st at 8:14 pm by* BB4Life

My first debate competition with Heimlich is coming up this Saturday. Heimlich says the debate team always goes to the same diner in town on Saturday nights and he's invited me to come along after the tournament. My parents have okayed it since technically it's "school-related." Now it's up to you.

That's all.
BB

Buried Beneath
the Rubble

As soon as I publish my latest post, I feel just a teensy bit guilty for my brusque tone. For a minute I even consider going back in and sprucing it up with some fun phrasing and exclamatory punctuation, but I'm far too depressed to muster the energy. So I just close my laptop, mope around my room for a few minutes, and finally just collapse on my bed.

To be honest, I'm a little bit pissed off at my blog readers right now. Okay, I'm a *lot* pissed off. I recruited them to help *improve* my life, not make it worse. But that's all they seem to be doing lately. I have no doubt they'll be totally gung ho about Saturday's highly unpromising night out with the debate team because the majority of them seem to *live* for dull stuff like that.

Raging Saturday nights at a hot new guest-list-only club? Nah, I'll pass. But hitting the local diner that's been here since the Depression? All right! Rock on!

I'm so miserable I don't even do anything for Halloween. Although it's not like I *can*. I'm obviously still grounded and usually fun Halloween activities involve leaving the house. So instead I'm forced to stay home and hand out candy to the neighborhood kids. But my mood doesn't exactly make me the world's best candy distributor, because every time I see one of their smiling, carefree faces peeking out from underneath a princess tiara or cowboy hat or prairie girl bonnet, I find myself bitterly dolling out little nuggets of advice with each Snickers bar that I drop into their awaiting sacks. "Live it up while you're young." "Have fun now. Because it's all downhill from here." Or my personal favorite, "Make wise choices with your life because the rest of the world certainly isn't going to do it for you."

The first snowstorm of the year hits on Monday morning. As if Halloween was some kind of trigger to the weather gods to get their butts in gear and stop messing around with this Indian summer business. That means the bus is probably going to be late. Of course, *I* still have to be at the bus stop on time. Just in case it's not.

I zip up my coat, slide on my mittens, wrap my scarf tightly around my neck, and start the ten-minute trek to the bus stop. When our school budgets were slashed last year they had to merge some of the bus routes, which meant longer rides and fewer stops. The bus route goes *right* by my house every morning but does it stop there? Of course not. It stops half a mile down the road. Because apparently the extra five seconds it would take to stop at my driveway is not in the budget. And if I'm running late and Mrs. Gore *happens* to drive past me on my way to the stop, do you think she has the compassion to slow down and let me on? Of course not. She just drives right by.

This is why one of my parents has always taken me to school. Because they felt sorry for me that I had to walk so far to catch the bus. But apparently they stopped feeling sorry for me about the time they heard the words "burned down model home." And what's that thing they say about not knowing what you have until it's gone? Yep, that pretty much sums up how I feel about my morning commute right about now.

Today I get to the stop with time to spare. In fact, I stand out there for a good ten minutes freezing my butt off while I wait for the big yellow tank to round the corner. Then I hunker down for the forty-five minute ride to school . . . which, by the way, is five miles away.

At least I'm not waking up at the crack of dawn anymore to follow my former Shayne-approved preparation routine. And I have to admit, this plain, solid-colored long-sleeved shirt that I found at the back of my closet is pretty darn comfy. Roomy. And not at all binding. And it's kind of nice not to walk around with two pounds of makeup on my face. Plus, now that I'm getting so much sleep, I no longer have to wake up early to apply complicated treatments to fight the bags under my eyes that I used to get from lack of sleep.

Hmmm . . .

At school, I do everything in my power to avoid both Hunter and Shayne. I fear that if I get anywhere near Shayne I'll be forced to overhear some full or partial retelling of how totally amazing her Saturday night was. And with Hunter, I don't want to have to try to come up with some pathetic excuse to explain why I wasn't there. Of course, that's assuming he actually *noticed* I wasn't there. He was probably too busy bumping crotches with Her Royal Heinous all night to even realize I never showed up. Maybe in my former life when I was still popular and glamorous and worthy of being noticed by someone as fabulous as Hunter

Wallace Hamilton III he might have missed me. But not now. I mean, he just moved here a month ago and already he's king of the school. The kind of guy people flock to. Basically a male version of Shayne Kingsley.

Me, on the other hand, well, I'm pretty much a has-been.

Because look what I've become. A member of the debate team who spends her lunch hour in the library. Yes, I've returned to my little back table in the library. After my near-death experience in the cafeteria two weeks ago, I don't think I'll be returning to the world of public meal consumption anytime soon. But it's not like I'm cheating or anything. The poll specifically asked about *that* day and that day alone. It didn't make any reference to any subsequent days.

At least the librarians are letting me bring food in now. Honestly, I think they feel sorry for me. Even *they* can recognize a loser when they see one.

To add insult to injury, my mom informed me this morning before I left for the bus stop that the permits and paperwork have been cleared and construction on the replacement model home starts today!!! Can you sense the sarcasm in those exclamation marks? Trust me, it's there.

She picks me up right after school to bring me over there for my first day of manual, underpaid labor. So apparently, now you can add "construction worker" to my résumé as well.

I'm stuck out in the middle of the frozen tundra, shoveling charred rubble and debris into a wheelbarrow and then wheeling it to a Dumpster that they *easily* could have parked right next to the construction site, but instead it's positioned a good two hundred feet away, behind a massive hill. Because before they can start rebuilding the fire-damaged portion of the house, they first have to clear away the leftover debris. And let me just say, pushing a wheelbarrow full of burned wood and seared metal up a steep, icy incline is by far the hardest thing I've ever had to do in my life. Not to mention the fact that charred rubble pretty much smells like crap. I mean, it's like nothing you've ever smelled before. And the dust mask covering my nose and mouth isn't helping much either. Plus, the ashes from the debris are disgustingly filthy and get *everywhere*. After only twenty minutes, I'm covered from head to toe in black soot.

On the plus side, I did stumble across my missing cell phone. Although it's not exactly in working order.

About halfway through my slave labor shift, my mom gets off a phone call and announces, "Good news! The contractor says the fire damage was contained to only the front portion of the house and it didn't reach the foundation. So once we get this debris cleared away it should only take about four weeks to rebuild the model."

I pull off the mask, revealing a white oval in a sea of black soot around my mouth, and then collapse into a nearby chair. I'm sure in my mom's mind this is incredible news. But for me, it's just the opposite. Her words echo hauntingly in my mind like a death sentence. Four weeks. Four weeks. FOUR WEEKS! It may not sound like much. But in this hellhole, it might as well be a lifetime.

When I get home later that night, I run a bath and soak my tired, blackened bones in a tub of hot, soapy water. I swear I'm finding ash in places I don't even want to talk about. As I lie there marinating, trying to wash off the remnants of the day, I realize that I can keep fighting—bitching and moaning and complaining about the way my life is turning out—or I can surrender.

Resign myself to the fact that Hunter and I are just not going to happen. That Shayne is going to get her way like she always does and I'm going to spend the next month working at a construction site.

And really, what's the use of fighting when I never win? When I'm pretty much destined to lose no matter what I do? Maybe it really *is* in my DNA. Could there be such a thing as a *loser* gene?

As I sink deeper into the bubbly water that has turned a murky shade of gray from all the soot, I feel somewhat liberated in my admission of defeat. Relieved, even. I guess all I can do now is accept my inferior fate and try to make the best of it.

By the Dashboard Lights

My first debate competition is this weekend and I'm feeling massively underprepared. Even after Brian's explanation of the colossal file bins and how the debate is structured, I'm still totally lost. So for the entire week, Brian and I meet almost every day to practice. The topic is illegal immigration in America and what to do about it. Or if we even *should* do something about it. As much as I hate to admit it, all the articles and research Brian has collected on the subject (enough to fill two gigantic plastic bins) are pretty interesting. I've read almost all of them now and it's crazy how much information there is supporting both sides of the argument. I mean, I'll be sitting in Debate Central, reading one article about how big of a problem illegal immigration is and how it poses such a serious threat to our society and proceed to get totally riled up about it and then Brian will flash me this smug smile as he plucks the article from my hand and replaces it with another one that convinces me of exactly the opposite. Then the process starts all over again.

I suppose that's the very essence of debate.

By Saturday morning the decision is made. Eighty-three percent of my now ninety-two blog readers are in favor of a night out on the town with the Parker High School debate team. Excuse me for not fainting from the surprise. I *was*, however, surprised to see that a whole *seventeen* people thought it was a bad idea. Maybe my readership is finally branching out, expanding beyond lame science nerds. This week, at least, I seem to have attracted some people who are sensitive to the social rules of high school. Not that it matters. They're still a minority. And I'm still a has-been.

Brian is picking me up from my house to take me to the meet. It's at Arvada High School, which is about an hour's drive from here. The first round starts at eight a.m. so he's coming to get me at six-thirty. A little too early for the weekend if you ask me, but whatever. Not my choice, right?

At least I got out of community service today. Because technically debate is a "school-related activity."

But the worst part about this whole thing is that I have to wear a suit. Yes, as in a full-on matching jacket and skirt . . . *with* nylons. And Brian already warned me about skirts that are too short. Something about offending the more conservative judges. So basically my entire closet is out. My mom had to take me to the mall on Thursday night to pick out something more . . . "appropriate." And believe me when I say I'm not the *least* bit happy about wearing it. First of all, it's the most boring shade of gray ever. The skirt goes down to my kneecaps, the cut of the jacket is completely unflattering, and I'm going to need some hydrocortisone cream to get rid of the itch from the wool turtleneck thing I have to wear underneath.

It's no wonder everyone on the debate team is still a virgin.

I pull my hair into a tight, smooth ponytail—because that's how the girls in the debate videos Brian made me watch wore their hair—and spritz the top and sides with extra-firm hair spray to keep flyaways from popping up.

Brian arrives at six-thirty on the dot and I gather my things, take one last look in the mirror, and step outside, bracing myself for the cold. As soon as I open the door of his truck, I can't help but do a double take. I mean, it's still really dark out, and for a minute I actually wonder if I'm getting into the right vehicle. Because the person sitting behind the wheel is hardly recognizable. He only bares a *slight* resemblance to my debate partner.

His brown curly hair, which is usually fairly unruly and all over the place, has been gelled back. His standard attire of black jeans and white T-shirt has been replaced by a really sharp navy blue suit that makes him look kind of prestigious and important. Like he's going to start rattling off stock prices at me or something.

His glasses are gone. I assume they've been replaced by contacts. And maybe it's just a trick of the lights from the dashboard, but are his eyes actually sparkling? For a few seconds, I can't stop staring at him. He just looks so . . . so . . . *different.*

"Get in," he grumbles, sounding annoyed. "You're letting the cold air in."

"Oh, sorry," I say with a start, hopping into the passenger side and closing the door behind me.

Without another word, Brian shifts into reverse and backs out of the driveway.

"Are you all right?" I steal a sideways peek at the scowl on his face.

"Yeah," he mutters, seemingly trying to shake himself out of a funk. "Sorry. I had a really bad fight with my dad before I left. I guess I'm still sorta out of it."

"Do you want to talk about it?"

He continues to face forward, focusing intently on the road. "Not really."

"Okay," I reply swiftly.

"I'll be fine," he assures me. "Just give me a few more miles to cool off." Then after a brief pause and a deep breath, he peers at me out of the corner of his eye and adds, "You look good, by the way."

I scoff at his compliment. "Yeah, right. I look like a stuffy politician's wife."

"No," he's quick to correct. "You look like a debater."

I roll my eyes. "Great. My lifelong mission. Accomplished."

He ignores the jab as he comes to a stop at a red light and gives my ensemble another inspection. This time his eyes linger much longer. His gaze is more intense. I can feel it pulling me in. I bite my lip and am about to turn away when he hits me with "I'm glad you wore your hair up." Then he reaches out and gently touches the hairline above my left temple.

His statement is so unexpected—not to mention his touch—that any response gets caught in my throat.

"I like it that way."

"You do?" I manage to get out. But it's weak. It's small. It's barely audible. Actually, I'm starting to wonder if he even heard me—if maybe I only asked the question in my head and the words never made it to my lips—because he doesn't answer. The light changes and he turns his attention back to the road. I turn mine out the window, watching the sky slowly morph into a beautiful canvas of pinks and grays. I'm somewhat grateful that the sun is finally starting to rise. Because clearly there's something about being in the dark with Brian that's messing with my head.

Text Messages and Crabs

We won!

We actually won. Our very first debate tournament and we officially *kicked ass*! We were victorious in all *three* of our rounds and it feels positively *ah-mazing*. Especially after how hard we've been working over the past week. I mean, besides the never-ending, daunting task of keeping my operating system "Shayne-compatible," what else have I ever worked this hard for in my entire life? Not much, really.

I admit, Brian helped me through a *lot* of it. Passing me notes during my cross-examinations, holding up cue cards during my rebuttals, and giving me encouraging pep-whispers before I had to go up and speak. But in the end, whatever we were doing obviously worked because we went 3 and 0. Something Ms. Rich says I should be extremely proud of for my first tournament. And you know what? I am!

After the long day is finally over, Brian and I are back in his pickup truck, on the way to the diner to meet everyone. I'm still gloating about our victory and reliving all the best moments, while he tries to sneak in a few veiled critiques about my performance along the way. You know, small stuff like standing up straighter at the podium, not getting so defensive when the other team cross-examines me, and not shouting "aha!" when my opponent fails to answer one of my questions. I do admit I got a little carried away with that one.

"Remember, no matter how many times we win," he begins in earnest, "there's always room for improvement."

And although I nod my head with equal earnestness, as if I truly do agree with him, really all I can continue to think is *We won! We won! I can't freaking believe it!* If someone had told me three months ago that I'd be driving home from a school-sponsored debate tournament at nine o'clock on a Saturday night, I would have laughed in their faces. Actually, no. I probably would have just walked away before they finished talking because they would have lost me at "school-sponsored."

But here I am. Thanks to my blog readers. And I have to say, despite the fact that I'm still totally pissed off at them for not letting me go to that club last weekend with Hunter, I have to give them props for this feeling. Winning is pretty awesome. I mean, even if it is at debate.

About halfway home, however, the exhilaration of victory slowly starts to give way to the drowsiness of fatigue. I had no idea how completely exhausted I am until my eyelids start to feel like rocks and my head starts to flop forward like a rag doll's.

Brian just laughs at me like he's been through this progression of emotions before and he knows exactly how I feel. "Go ahead. Get some sleep," he tells me as he glances out the window. "We still have about forty minutes until . . ."

But I don't hear the last part because I'm already out like a light.

I wake up to the sound of a far-off beeping noise. I'm not sure how long I've been out. My eyes slowly heave themselves open as I try to figure out what my head is resting on. Something kind of hard, yet cushy at the same time. With the texture of scratchy wool.

I look upward and my face immediately flushes with color as I realize that I totally passed out on Brian's shoulder. And there's even a small puddle of drool on his jacket to prove it. I quickly wipe my mouth and push myself back up to sitting. "Sorry about that," I say with a humiliated chuckle.

But Brian, who's fully focused on the road, just shrugs like he didn't even notice. "It's no biggie. You were really tired."

"What was that beeping noise?" I ask, glancing around.

"I think it was your cell phone."

I look at him like he's clearly on something. "My cell phone?" Since when does *my* cell phone make any kind of noise?

"It wasn't mine."

I reach down into my bag and remove the phone from the front pocket. I'm still slightly unfamiliar with the device since it's new and, let's be honest, it's not like I use it all that much, except to call my parents. I know, really frigging exciting. But I don't need the user's manual to decipher the message on my screen.

New text message from 720-555-9098

A text message? Who on earth would be sending *me* a text message? Especially at nine-thirty at night. The only person who actually speaks to me these days, besides my parents, is sitting right next to me. I don't recognize the number although I know from the area code that it's local.

Curious, I click "OK" to read the message and then I let out the loudest, most obtrusive gasp in the world.

> Hey, it's Hunter. Missed you at the club last weekend.
> Haven't seen you around school. Where you been?

I look up to see that Brian is staring at me with this really worried expression on his face. When he slows at a stoplight, he leans over and attempts to read the screen. "What happened?"

I pull the phone possessively to my chest, instantly feeling foolish for making such a big deal about a stupid text. "Oh, nothing," I say with a wave of my hand. "Just . . . um . . . my parents. They texted to tell me that . . . uh . . . my grandmother is coming to visit."

Brian looks dubious. "Your grandmother elicits that kind of reaction?"

I force out a strained laugh. "Yeah . . . well . . . no one really likes her. She's kind of . . . you know . . . crabby. We call her Crabby Granny. My mom says she came up with the nickname. But I'm pretty sure I'm the one who said it first."

Okay, time to stop talking.

"Uh-huh," Brian finally says, stepping on the gas and refocusing on the road.

Checking to make sure that his attention is thoroughly occupied, I hastily tap out a response to Hunter.

> Sorry about Saturday. Couldn't escape the 'rents.

I hit "Send" and hold my breath, vowing not to release it until I get a reply. Thankfully for my lungs, it comes thirty seconds later.

What are you doing tonight?

Oh my God, oh my God, oh my God!

Hunter Wallace Hamilton III just asked me what I'm doing tonight!

I try to restrain my excitement but clearly I don't do a very good job because Brian glances over at me again and raises his eyebrows inquisitively, as though he's expecting a play-by-play of my text conversation. "Good news?"

"Oh," I trill, nodding to the phone. "Yeah. Um. Grandma's staying at a hotel." And then for an extra ounce of credibility, I pretend to wipe sweat from my brow. "Phew! What a relief."

He smiles politely and I start typing furiously.

Not much. Just hanging out.

Of course I'm going to lie to Hunter. It's not like I can tell him the truth. "Oh, yeah, hi, Hunter. Just hanging with my debate partner. You know, heading back from the meet. Good times. Good times."

Heck no! How stupid do you think I am?

Actually, on second thought, don't answer that.

Hunter's next message comes even faster than the last.

Let's do something. Where should I pick you up?

Seriously, did someone slip caffeine into my water? My heart is beating so fast it no longer feels like a distinct rhythm. More like just a constant hum. And I have to fight *so* hard to keep my reaction under wraps because I'm running out of make-believe details about my grandmother. Not to mention how guilty I feel about lying to Brian. But I can't tell him the truth because . . .

Well, I'm not really sure why. I just can't. He wouldn't understand. He doesn't seem like the kind of guy who can relate to the thrill of receiving late-night text messages from sexy Southerners with roman numerals after their name.

"We're almost there," Brian informs me, exiting the freeway and veering left onto Parker Road.

"Oh!" I exclaim, with sudden realization. "Right. The diner."

He laughs. "Did you forget?"

"No. I didn't forget."

Okay, I *kind of* forgot. But only for a second.

"It's just that . . ." My voice trails off as I look longingly at my cell phone which is still clutched between my fingers.

I know that I said I would go.

I know that my blog readers chose *this* as my Saturday night activity and that I vowed to do whatever they said.

But I also know this new opportunity that's presented itself is simply too good to pass up. The debate team get-together is just a casual, whatever sort of thing that they do all the time, after *every* meet. A night alone with Hunter, on the other hand, is a once-in-a-lifetime chance.

And besides, even if I did have time to run home, type out a blog, post a new poll, and wait for a response (which I totally don't), it's not like I don't already know what that response would be. What my blog readers would advise me to do. It doesn't take a Harvard degree to figure that one out.

But you know what? I don't care. Forget them. They already ruined my last weekend. I'm not about to let them ruin this one, too.

"It's just that . . . ?" Brian prompts me, interrupting my thought flow.

"Well, it's just that," I continue, gaining confidence and allowing my anticipation of the night to come to overshadow the guilt I feel for being dishonest, "you know, now that my grandma's coming tomorrow—Crabby Granny—my parents need help getting the house ready. Vacuuming, dusting, changing the sheets in the guest room and everything—"

Brian's forehead furrows in confusion. "I thought you said she was staying in a hotel."

"Well, yeah . . ." I stumble, feeling ridiculous. "She is! But she likes to inspect the house every time she comes over. You know, make sure it's clean. Now you can understand why no one likes her."

I swear I see just the slightest trace of disappointment on Brian's face, but before I can be sure, it's quickly replaced by a shrug and his usual carefree smile. "Okay, then. Do you want me to take you home?"

"Oh, no!" I say, a bit too fervently, causing Brian's eyebrows to pull together in what can only be interpreted as suspicion. I glance out the window and catch sight of a 7-Eleven coming up at the next intersection. "I mean, I don't want you to have to go out of your way. You can just drop me off up here and I'll have my parents come get me."

It's a brilliant plan, if I do say so myself. My parents already think I'm going to be out with the debate team. Plus, I can slip into the store bathroom and change out of this ugly suit before Hunter arrives.

Brian turns on his blinker and changes into the right lane. "Are you sure?"

"Absolutely."

The truck pulls into the 7-Eleven parking lot and stops in front of the entrance. I unbuckle my seat belt, grab my bag from the floor, and hop out of the truck. Brian rolls down the passenger-side window.

"Thanks for the ride," I say cheerfully.

"I can wait with you until your parents get here."

"No, no," I tell him, zipping up my jacket. "You don't have to do that. I don't want to keep you from your friends. You go. Tell everyone I said hi and sorry I couldn't make it."

"Okay . . ." he says reluctantly.

"Go," I insist, trying to sound light and jokey and not in the least bit how I really feel (which is totally desperate). "Have fun. Eat pancakes. I'll be *fiiiine.*" I purposely elongate the word in hopes that the extra syllables will add some much needed conviction to my case.

"All right," he finally agrees. "Well, we'll miss you tonight."

"Yeah," I reply absently. "I'll miss you guys, too." But I'm barely even paying attention, because I'm already tapping away on my phone, telling Hunter to pick me up from the 7-Eleven parking lot in twenty minutes.

INCONVENIENCE STORE

The 7-Eleven bathroom is not exactly my idea of the perfect
first date prep location. The lighting is dreadful, the mirror is
lined with milky streaks of I don't even want to know what, and
it's extremely difficult to change without my bare feet touching
the grimy floor. Evidently that yellow bucket and mop in the
corner are there purely for decorational purposes.

The outfit I brought was intended for a casual night at the
Main Street Diner and is nowhere near the caliber of what I
would normally pick out for a date with someone like Hunter
Wallace Hamilton III, but when it comes down to that or the
option of wearing this hideous suit, the choice is pretty obvious.

My hair is still up in that tight ponytail, and because I didn't
bring any product with me it's going to have to stay there. But
I manage to extract a few wispy layers from the top and frame
my face with them so that the hairstyle doesn't look quite so . . .
severe. Then I pull out the tubes of mascara and lip gloss that I
brought with me and do my best to touch up my face a bit.

But I nearly jam the lip gloss wand up my nose when a loud

crashing noise resounds from outside the door, causing me to jump. It sounds like one of the stockers just knocked over a huge rack of soda cans while he was refilling the refrigerators. That's gotta suck.

I take one final glance in the mirror—not the masterpiece I would have liked, but I suppose it'll have to do—and cram my stuff back into my bag. When I first step out of the bathroom, I'm surprised by how quiet it is. Ten minutes ago this place was bustling with activity and now it's deathly silent. Not even the ding of the cash register.

Then I see the woman on the floor. She's lying facedown, her arms huddled up underneath her chest and her forehead resting against the tile. She appears to be crying.

Oh God, I think. *Was that the noise I heard? Did she fall and hurt herself?*

I take a step toward her and that's when I see the rest of them. About ten in total. All on the floor. And before I can even comprehend what's going on, the barrel of the gun is three inches from my face and the shouting has started.

"Get down! Get down on the floor NOW!"

Without a second thought, I drop to my knees and sprawl out onto my stomach. Now all I see are feet. Dirty white tennis shoes with mud caked to the bottoms. Thankfully, they're moving away from me. Back in the direction they came from. The cash register.

There's more yelling, but I don't dare look up. I keep my face down, finding it extremely ironic how just seconds ago I was dancing around the bathroom trying to avoid extended contact between my bare feet and this dirty floor, and now I'm practically making out with it.

"The money! In the bag! Don't think! Just do it!"

I turn my neck to the side and make eye contact with a woman around my mom's age. She appears to be hyperventilating. The guy to my other side is mumbling whispered prayers under his breath.

I know I should be scared—making bargains with God like everyone else—but for some reason, all I am is annoyed. This really couldn't have come at a more inconvenient time. I mean, seriously. A holdup? In Parker, Colorado? What are the odds?

"Nobody move!" The white tennis shoes are all over the place now. Unable to stand still. From this angle, it almost looks like there's some kind of routine going on here. The tango, perhaps? Or maybe a nice fox-trot.

Just then, a shrill ringing sound blasts through the air and I hear several people gasp. The woman next to me actually buries her head in her hands, as though she doesn't even want to witness what happens next.

Crap.

"Whose cell phone is that?" the gunman thunders.

I know for a fact that it's mine because I can see the light from the screen through the fabric of my bag, but it's not like I'm going to raise my hand and volunteer so I stay quiet.

The phone keeps ringing, which seems to be totally pissing off the white tennis shoes because they're galloping around the store now, searching for the source of the noise. "I want everyone's cell phone out and on the ground where I can see them," he commands.

Fortunately the ringing stops the moment I pull my phone out of my bag, but I can see on the screen that I have one missed call from Hunter's number. And just as I'm placing it on the ground in front of me, a text message dings through.

I strain my neck to see what it says, but before I can decipher any of the words, a giant calloused hand swoops down and yanks it out of sight.

Damn it! That was from Hunter! And now I'll never know what it says.

He's probably wondering where I am. Wondering why I'm not in the parking lot where I said I would be. What if he gets tired of waiting and leaves? What if he thinks I stood him up again?!

If only White Tennis Shoes would hurry up with whatever he's trying to accomplish here, I still might be able to get ahold of Hunter before he writes me off forever. I consider trying to appeal to the shoes' common human decency and ask if I can be excused from this little "situation," but even *I* know that wouldn't be a smart move. No matter what, gun always trumps cute guy. Even Hunter.

Plus, the shoes are really starting to look annoyed. I mean, I know they're only a pair of dirty sneakers, but they seem to have taken on a personality of their own. And right now, that personality is "ticked off."

So I guess it's adios to my romantic evening with Hunter Wallace Hamilton III. It's too bad. I was *so* close this time.

I hear the slam of the cash register drawer closing and I feel my hopes lifting. Maybe this means it's almost over. Maybe I'll be able to go on my date after all! But my dreams are quickly dashed the moment I see the now-familiar red and blue lights reflecting in the store windows. The sirens come shortly after. And judging from the fact that the sound seems to be emanating from every direction, I'm assuming we're surrounded.

And now all I can do is groan and rest my cheek on the cold tile floor as one thought filters through my mind. *Oh, great. Not again.*

HELD HOSTAGE

I'm being punished, aren't I? The universe is punishing me for breaking my promise. For defying the wishes of my blog readers and making a choice on my own. And I think we can *all* agree at this point that it was a pretty crappy one.

As usual.

One spur-of-the-moment decision and I'm back where I started. Surrounded by the flashing lights of emergency vehicles and camera crews. And to make matters worse, it doesn't look like I'm getting off this dirty floor anytime soon. The arrival of our little disaster entourage has really seemed to piss off the guy with the white tennis shoes and now he's refusing to leave the store. He's also been shouting something about "having hostages" (I'm assuming that's us) and that therefore he doesn't need to listen to anything the police are saying.

The cops have brought in a negotiator who keeps calling the store with various offers, but judging from the obnoxious grunting sounds the gunman keeps making every time he takes one of these calls, I'm guessing the offers aren't what he was hoping for.

Minutes pass followed by hours and my back is starting to cramp from lying here. The only thing I can do to pass the time is think about Hunter and how he's probably home by now, cursing my name and vowing never to speak to me again. I also think about Brian and wonder how his night chowing down on pancakes is going. If only I had listened to my blog readers and followed the poll results as I swore I would, I could be at that diner right now. Instead of sprawled out on this disgusting floor.

And just the thought of those syrup-drenched pancakes is making my stomach growl. Did I mention how hungry I've been getting down here? It's actually quite torturous because I'm lying right next to a full rack of Hostess snack cakes. The whole darn product line from Twinkies to Ho Hos to those yummy little Mini Muffins. Do you know how many times I've thought about grabbing one of those, tearing the wrapper off, and stuffing it in my face? It would be so easy, just a *slight* reach and the delicious sugar rush would be mine.

But the white tennis shoes tend to get kind of irritated when any of us so much as breathes too hard. And I guess I can understand that. He seems to be under a ton of stress right now. He's been eating a *lot* of candy up there in the front of that store. And last time he walked by here, drops of sweat actually trickled off his face and splashed on the floor next to me. Plus, he's started muttering things in a language I don't understand. Yep, the pressure is definitely starting to get to him. I'll tell you one thing. I certainly don't envy him right now.

Well, I mean, except for the eating part.

After three long, muscle-cramping hours on the floor, a deal is finally made. Actually, it's not so much a "deal" as a surrender. I guess the white tennis shoes figured he just couldn't win and, around two in the morning, he walks out of the store and into the blinding light of the news vans and camera crews.

None of us really knows what to do at this point and we all kind of look at each other, waiting for someone to make the first move and get up. But I think we're still paralyzed from fear. Not to mention the fact that my legs are so stiff I don't think I'll be able to move them for a week.

Three police officers burst through the doors a few seconds later and assure us that the nightmare is over and we can get up and leave. With a sigh, I push myself up and grab on to the Hostess rack for balance as I struggle to my feet.

As soon as my legs stop wobbling and I feel like I'm standing on solid ground again, I look to the uniformed policemen and immediately recognize one of them as Officer Banks, the man who released me from the station less than a month ago. He obviously recognizes me, too, because his lips curve into a grin and he walks up to me and throws an arm around me. "Baby Brooklyn," he says, giving my shoulder a squeeze. "Rescued again."

I offer him back a weak laugh and a halfhearted "Yeah, how do you like that?"

"You seem to have a knack for being in the wrong place at the wrong time, don't you?"

What a canny observation.

"You better get outside," he tells me. "Your parents are waiting. I'm sure they'll be happy to see you."

I brush off my shirt and grab my bag from the floor. "Thanks."

As I step outside into the frenzy of media, I'm happy to find that my parents aren't the only ones who are waiting for me. Hunter is there, too. And instead of looking pissed off that I stood him up and didn't answer his call, he actually looks *worried*. After my parents have fawned over me for a good ten minutes, Hunter pulls me into a deep hug and holds me close enough that I can smell his aftershave. It's so amazing, it makes me wonder if I should get held up at gunpoint more often.

"Hi," I murmur bashfully as I watch my parents' reaction to our exchange out of the corner of my eye. "I'm sorry I messed up our plans."

"You're sorry?" Hunter repeats dubiously. "That a madman decided to hold up a convenience store while you were in it?" He laughs and gives my shoulders a squeeze. "Brooklyn, this was *not* your fault. I'm just glad you're okay. I was *so* worried about you."

"You were?"

He laughs again and shakes his head. "Yes! I kept thinking about what would happen if—" He stops short and pulls me into another embrace. "You know what, never mind. It doesn't matter."

A few minutes later, my parents say something about getting me home to rest and lead me to the car. As I'm ushered through the crowd of photographers, news vans, and family members of the other victims, I think about what Hunter said. That I'm not to blame for what happened to me tonight. That none of this is my fault.

But as hard as I try, I just can't bring myself to accept that.

Because although I know the man, who has now been identified as Viktor Dolinsky, will go down in history as the responsible party for this evening's events, although I know everyone in this parking lot—from the police, to the EMTs, to the eleven o'clock news—will mention *his* name when doling out the criticisms about judgment and poor choices, I will always know the truth.

I will always know where the fault really lies.

MY LIFE UNDECIDED

GRATEFUL

Posted on: *Sunday, November 7th at 8:20 pm by* BB4Life

My dear blog readers. I just want to take this opportunity to thank you for your time, thoughtful feedback, and dedication to this blog. Not only did Heimlich and I win our very first debate, but I had *the* most amazing time last night at the diner afterward. It surpassed *all* of my expectations. It was the most fun I've had in *years*! Today I am walking on air. Floating on a cloud. So thank you for pointing me in the right direction.

Now, on to today's order of business:

1) We're almost finished with *The Grapes of Wrath*. Now it's time to choose a Shakespeare play. So what do you think? *Twelfth Night* or *Julius Caesar*? Once again, I know nothing about either of these plays except that Julius Caesar has a salad named after him. Please vote!

2) Because Heimlich and I won our debate yesterday, we're now qualified to compete in some big upcoming tournament next weekend. It's an overnight thing where we get to stay in some hotel. Sounds interesting. Any thoughts on whether or not I should go?

3) *Contempo Girl* magazine is asking if I'd like to renew my
   subscription. Hey, it's a choice! So please make it.

Thanks again, everyone! The blog readership has now
grown to 105 people and I'm grateful for every single one
of you.

Signing off . . .
BB

Same Old Brand-New Me

Okay, so I lied. But only about the going-to-the-diner part. The rest of the blog is absolutely true. But I couldn't admit that I disobeyed them. That I blatantly ignored the results of my last poll and ended up the victim of a three-hour hostage situation as a result. Mostly because the news of the crisis has been playing on a continuous loop on every local television station for the past twelve hours along with video footage of me leaving the store and being reunited with my parents. Apparently the fact that "Baby Brooklyn" found herself trapped in yet another disaster thirteen years later makes a much better story than any of those other poor people who had to suffer through the same fate. And if I write about what *really* happened last night, my cover will definitely be blown. Someone is bound to put two and two together and figure out who I am.

So I lied. To protect my own identity. And *maybe*, just a teensy bit, to protect my pride as well. I mean, I'm not exactly *pleased* with myself after last night's mistake. Do I wish I could take it back? Yes. Do I wish I had just stayed in Brian's truck and gone to the stupid diner like I promised I would? Yes. And did I learn my lesson about defying my blog readers? Absolutely.

No more detours. No more last-minute modifications to the plan. From now on, what they say goes.

On Monday morning I'm out of bed at the crack of dawn. Today is very important because it's the first time I'm going to see Hunter since that embarrassing fiasco on Saturday night. I mean, he *was* there when I came out, which is great and all, but it also means the last time the guy saw me I looked like a total zombie after lying on a dirty floor for three hours with a gun pointed at my head. Not exactly the image I want him to remember me by.

Plus, the news is *still* running the story with my picture on it. Chances are, people are going to notice me at school again. And *not* in a good way.

So today I have to look incredible. No. Not just incredible. *Breathtaking.* Like someone who just stepped off the set of a *Vogue* photo shoot.

My former camera-ready glam routine may have fallen to the wayside a bit ever since Shayne ejected me from her coveted co-pilot seat, but now it's time to get my act back in gear and reinstate my old beauty regimen.

I take my time showering, making sure to shampoo *twice* and leave the conditioner in for the full *three* minutes as directed on the bottle while I meticulously run a razor over every square inch of my legs, paying special attention to the hard-to-reach nooks and crannies.

All the while I can hear Shayne's voice in my head, like a drill sergeant, keeping me in line, making sure I don't cut corners. *"It doesn't matter that it's too cold outside to wear a skirt. You should never be caught with furry legs. NEVER. The consequences far outweigh the extra few minutes it takes to shave daily."*

I hop out of the shower, dry myself off, and rummage under the sink for my old supplies, freighting out armfuls of different-size containers filled with various popularity-enhancing products that I recently deemed pointless in my current social condition. I diligently apply *two* different moisturizing lotions to my entire body—the first intended to turn my paling, sun-forsaken skin a shade and a half darker by lunchtime and the second intended to give said darker skin a silky, glowing effect.

"Just because we live in Colorado doesn't mean we can't look like we just stepped off the beach," I can hear Shayne say. *"Even in November. Year-round sun-kissed skin isn't only for Orange County reality stars. After all, God created sunless tanning lotion for a reason: to even out the playing field."*

Next, I pull my wet hair back with a headband and start on my face. With the masterful strokes of a well-trained artist, I transform my plain eyes into piercing, seductive portals framed with luscious, velvety shades of mocha and cinnamon and dramatic lashes the color of midnight. I apply a thick coat of lip-plumping gloss that stings like heck as it is slowly absorbed into my skin and gets to work giving me that highly sought-after Hollywood pout look.

"Real beauty—at least the enviable kind—doesn't come easy. And it often involves pain. Do you think the celebrities on TV became sex symbols because of the way they look when they wake up in the morning?"

Normally I get annoyed by the haunting memories of Shayne's dictatorial commands and her strict codes of conduct and simply do my best to tune them out. But this morning I listen intently. Welcoming the harsh guidance. Thriving off the callous yet effective encouragement. And for the first time in a long time, I'm actually grateful for my five long, hard years of Shayne Kingsley's popularity boot camp. Because although I may no longer be a soldier in her precious pink-clad platoon, the information is still useful. Especially on a day like today.

Two hours later, I emerge from my bathroom, the picture of perfection. Like a magazine cutout. From the soft waves in my hair to the trendy shoes on my feet. And I have to admit, when I look at the final product in the mirror I feel good about what I see. Empowered. Confident. Not to sound totally full of myself or anything, but the person staring back at me right now is actually pretty darn cute.

Honestly, it's been so long since I've seen her, I guess I kind of forgot what she looked like. Or that she even had the ability to look like *this*.

Like someone who *belongs* on the arm of a hottie like Hunter.

And I have to say, it's nice to be back.

After the traumatizing events of Saturday night, my parents felt pretty sorry for me and agreed to release me from my grounding. I still have to work at the construction site twice a week but I'm no longer bound to the house every night. And they promised they would start taking me to school again in the mornings so I don't have to take the smelly old school bus anymore.

My new/old "look" must be working because as soon as my mom drops me off and I walk through the front doors, people are already starting to stare. Or maybe it's working a bit *too* well because I don't even make it down the hallway. Within two seconds, I'm suddenly surrounded by a mob of people. They're calling my name and asking me questions, and I'm so overwhelmed I'm rendered utterly speechless. All I can do is stand there like a deer caught in headlights as strange stuttering sounds come out of my mouth.

"Oh my God, Brooklyn. I saw you on the news. Are you okay?"

"Did he ever point the gun right at your head?"

"Did you think you were going to die?"

"Are you really the same Baby Brooklyn who fell down the mine shaft thirteen years ago?"

I try to push through the crowd, but I'm trapped. There're just too many of them. This is insanity! I've backed myself up so far against the row of lockers behind me, a combination lock is jabbing into my spine.

I see an arm reach through the mass, grab me by the shirtsleeve, and yank me out. It isn't until I'm clear of the wall of people, dragged into an empty classroom and the door is shut behind me, that I lay eyes on my savior. It's Hunter.

"Thanks," I say, somewhat breathless. "That was crazy."

"How are you holding up?"

"I'm fine!" I say, waving away his concern. "Totally, one hundred percent fine."

"We really don't have much luck with this whole hanging-out thing, do we?" he asks.

I laugh nervously and shake my head. "No, not really."

"I'm afraid if I ask you out again you'll end up locked away in a South American prison or something."

"Oh, I doubt that," I say hastily.

"Well, then, how about this," he suggests with a flirtatious grin. "Let me take you to the winter formal next month."

My mouth flies open and I'm ready to shout "Yes!" at the top of my lungs but then I think about the blog. How I'm not at liberty to answer that kind of question on my own. Especially after what happened the last time I tried to defy the wishes of my blog readers. So instead of saying what I really want to, I respond with "Thanks. I'll think about it."

And then I pray he doesn't get offended, turn around, and walk out the door mumbling something like "Don't bother."

But Hunter just laughs, like it's part of some elaborate game that he's more than happy to play, and gives my waist a squeeze. "Okay, Brooks, you do that."

I'm about to walk out the door and face the daunting crowd of people, when I'm stopped by a thought. Actually, it's a memory. I remember the night of the club opening. And how I saw Shayne waiting outside to get in. And then I hear myself asking, "What about Shayne?"

Hunter appears surprised by my question, but not put off. "What about her?"

"Did you hook up with her?" I blurt out, before I can think of any creative ways to veil the bluntness of my question. "I'm sorry if I'm not supposed to be asking that but I need to know."

He presses his fingertips against his temples, like he's fighting off some massive headache that's brewing. "Um . . ." he starts, sounding baffled and thrown.

"I mean, it's an easy enough thing to do. I know *plenty* of other guys who have done it."

"No," he finally says, grabbing my hands and holding them in front of him. "Definitely not. Nor do I have any interest in doing so."

"But . . ." I begin, biting my lip, "she was there. At the club that night. She went and I didn't."

Hunter looks positively lost. Like I'm speaking a whole other language. "No," he says again. "I know for a fact, she wasn't there."

"Are you sure? Because—"

But Hunter interrupts me with a squeeze of my hands. "I know for a fact she wasn't there because I never put her name on the guest list."

Puzzled, I think back to that night when I was ducked down on the floor of my dad's car, peering out of the window like some kind of inept spy. I saw Shayne twinkling her big blue eyes at the guy with the clipboard and then I saw her go inside. Or did I?

Wait, maybe I *didn't* see her go inside. Maybe I just *assumed* the bouncer had let her in.

"So you mean, if she wasn't on the guest list—" I begin.

"Then she didn't get in," he finishes the thought.

By lunchtime, I've been inundated with various proposals on how I can most effectively share my powerful story with the world. The school newspaper kids want to interview me for an upcoming feature they're planning about my brush with death. One of the religious groups wants me to come speak to their church group about near-death experiences and how it's changed my view on Jesus. Even the drama club wants to produce a reenactment of my three-hour hostage situation. They've already given it the working title "Trapped in Terror. The Brooklyn Pierce Story."

I don't understand. This is definitely *not* the reaction I was expecting. I thought I'd be pitied. I thought people would flash me hurried, fake smiles and then gossip about how pathetic I am behind my back. I never, in a million years, predicted I'd become some kind of school hero.

My plan is to hide out in the library at lunch again and blog about Hunter's invitation to the winter formal, but a dozen or so people intercept me on the way and practically drag me to the cafeteria. Everyone is begging for me to sit with them. I really don't know how to choose so I finally settle for the same lonely table in the back and the remainder of the seats fill up like a championship game of musical chairs.

It feels so strange and I'm not sure how to respond to it. I watch everything in a total daze. Like I'm living in someone else's dream.

Hundreds of people stop by to tell me how inspired they were by my bravery. Halfway through lunch, someone from the yearbook committee approaches and asks if I'd be willing to be photographed for a special page they're planning dedicated to local heroes. And then when I'm eating the turkey sandwich that I packed for myself this morning and a bit of it seems to go down the wrong tube and I start coughing, I'm not kidding, *ten* people rush over to pat me on the back and ask me if I'm okay.

Ten people!

Three weeks ago I nearly died at this very table from choking on a piece of melon because no one even remembered I existed, and now I've got people lined up to save me.

I need some time to think. To process this. It's all happening too fast and I can't decide how I feel about it. As much as I once wished people would remember my name again, recognize me in the hallway, notice when I'm choking in the cafeteria, now that it's happening, it's kind of freaking me out.

I'm grateful when fifth-period English starts and I can collapse in my seat and do nothing but discuss *The Grapes of Wrath* with Brian. He's the only thing that feels normal in this new tripped-out world of mine—the only person who noticed me *before* all of this craziness began—and I'm looking forward to talking about something else for a change. But as soon as I fall into my seat like I've just run a marathon, the first thing out of his mouth is "Oh God, Brooks. I'm so sorry about what happened on Saturday night."

"It's fine," I assure him hurriedly. "Let's not talk about it."

"No," he protests. "I feel horrible about it. Like it's my fault. If I had just stayed with you at that store until your parents came. Or—"

"Really," I insist. "It's fine. And totally *not* your fault so don't worry about it. Now can we please talk about something else?"

He looks hesitant to change topics, but after I toss him another pleading glance, he holds up his copy of Steinbeck's novel and asks, "Maybe we should talk about the book?"

"Yes! Please!"

Brian immediately launches into the first question on today's list of discussion topics and it's not until then that I notice he's not wearing his glasses again.

"Did you just get those contacts?" I ask, pointing the tip of my pen at his eyes.

He self-consciously touches his face. "Uh, no. Why?"

"Because I'd never seen you wear them before the tournament on Saturday."

"Oh. I rarely wear them," he replies hurriedly.

"Why are you wearing them now, then?"

He starts flipping his pen around his fingers again, this time extremely fast. "I don't know. I just, you know, felt like wearing them again."

"Well, they look good," I tell him.

His face reddens slightly as he bows his head down and mumbles something that sounds like "Thanks."

"How are things with you and your dad, by the way? Were you able to patch everything up?"

But the second the question is out of my mouth, I wish I could take it back. It's like someone turned off a light inside him. The corners of his mouth dip into a frown and he won't even look at me. "Not really," he mutters. "But it's nothing."

"Okay," I say quickly. "We don't have to talk about it."

But apparently Pandora's box has already been opened and now it's impossible to shut. "According to my dad, I'm a huge failure."

"Why?" I ask hotly. "Just because you don't want to do Bird Scouts?"

Brian cracks a smile. "*Eagle* Scouts."

"Whatever," I hiss. "It's ridiculous. You're a straight-A student, captain of the debate team (as a sophomore!), a shoo-in for any college you want to go to. What else could your dad possibly want from you?"

"To be more like him."

I snort. "And what does *that* entail?"

He releases a heavy breath. "My dad's the wrestling coach at this school."

"He is?" Evidently my surprise was a bit too loud, because Mrs. Levy peers over her reading glasses at us and I bow my head and pretend to be studying a passage from my book until she goes back to her paper-grading.

"Yes, he is," Brian replies. "And he's been trying to get me to join the team for two years. But wrestling just isn't my thing. I like debate. I'm good at debate. But my dad went to CSU on a wrestling scholarship, so according to him, that's the only path to college. They don't normally give out debate scholarships."

"But they have academic ones, don't they?"

He shrugs. "Yes, but they're harder to get. There's more competition. And the schools I want to go to are all academic schools so it's virtually impossible to get one."

"Oh," I say, feeling discouraged, even though it's not even *my* life we're talking about.

"So," he continues, his voice still fraught with anguish, "my dad's trying to get me to quit the debate team and try out for wrestling next semester."

Suddenly there's a lump in my throat and I have no idea where it came from. It makes my voice come out sounding wobbly and broken. "But you're not *going* to quit, right? You *can't* quit!"

"Of course not," he responds, sounding determined, which makes the lump shrink a little.

"Good," I say. "Stand your ground. Remember, this is *your* life. Not his. And he needs to deal with that."

Brian nods and runs his fingers through his thick curls. "You're right. Thanks, Brooks."

I offer him a broad smile. "Sure."

He looks like he's going to say something else on the subject, but Mrs. Levy chooses this moment to stand up and walk by our desks and we both pretend to be deep in discussion about the ending of *The Grapes of Wrath*—a title that is slowly starting to make more sense to me.

DAILY POLL RESULTS SUMMARY

Date: Wednesday, November 10
Username: BB4Life
Blog URL: www.MyLifeUndecided.com

Which Shakespeare play should I read for English?
(105 total votes)

Julius Caesar   (42 votes)

40%

Twelfth Night   (63 votes)

60%

Should I go on the overnight debate tournament?
(105 total votes)

Yes   (79 votes)

75%

No   (26 votes)

25%

One more year of *Contempo Girl* magazine?
(105 total votes)

Contempo on!   (71 votes)

68%

Contempo off!   (34 votes)

32%

MELTING DOWN

I've been meaning to get on that blog post about going to the winter formal with Hunter but I've had absolutely *zero* free time. I'm booked solid this entire week. Not only do I have interviews lined up with the school newspaper, the school TV station, the yearbook committee, and a few school activist groups, but *Good Day Colorado* called and wants me to come on their show on Thursday morning to talk about my experiences going from Baby Brooklyn to Brooklyn the Hostage. According to them, it's a very compelling story.

Also, I still have to work at the construction site after school. This week, my job consists of taxiing large pieces of wood from the lumber pile to the guy running the table saw and then from him to the guys working on rebuilding the garage portion of the house. It's about as fun and stimulating as it sounds.

And now that I'm back in the public eye and people are actually taking notice of me again, I have permanently reinstated my early-morning prep routine. So I'm once again waking up at the crack of dawn to get picture-perfect ready for school, because these days, I really *am* having my picture taken on a daily basis.

And to be honest, I'm not exactly chomping at the bit to post a poll about the winter formal. My blog readers have not proven to be huge fans of Rhett Butler in the past and I really don't think I can stand to reject him again. So I figure I'll wait it out for a few days and see if I can't come up with some clever way to convince them of his worthiness.

Because I missed an entire day of community service last weekend and this weekend I'm going to be on that overnight debate tournament in Colorado Springs, Gail agrees to let me make up a few hours on Friday afternoon.

By the time I finally get there, I'm mentally and physically drained. I've forgotten how tiring popularity can be. I mean, to be on stage 24/7 like that, to know that someone is always watching you, someone is always listening to what you say—it's exhausting. I'm looking forward to my no-frills afternoon reading to Mrs. Moody, away from the insanity.

But as I walk the long hallway to her room, I'm stopped halfway there when I hear a loud commotion originating from the other end. It doesn't take long to realize that the noise is coming from room 4A. It sounds like a full-on riot with screaming and thrashing and expletives. A projectile object, which I immediately recognize as one of Mrs. Moody's many garage sale knickknacks (this particular one in the shape of a four-inch lawn jockey), comes flying out the door and clinks against the tile floor of the hallway before sputtering to a halt under the fire extinguisher. Then Carol storms out of the room, looking extremely pissed off (even more than she usually does), holding a blood-soaked tissue against her left hand and mumbling something about the last straw as she stomps right past me and disappears around the corner.

As I approach the room there's more yelling, followed by another projectile object—one of Mrs. Moody's framed photographs of her dog, Ruby—that clatters to the ground by my feet. A second person exits the room in a huff. I immediately recognize her as Harriet, the nursing director of the home.

She stops for a moment just outside the door to collect herself and take a deep breath.

"What's going on?" I find the courage to ask.

She shakes her head. "Mrs. Moody is having another one of her meltdowns. I'm afraid she's gone too far this time, though. She bit Carol's hand."

My eyes grow wide. "She did what?" Although inside I'm kind of chuckling to myself because it's not like that nasty woman didn't deserve it.

Harriet nods solemnly. "I don't know how to control her. She's beyond my expertise now. We're going to have to find a new home for her. We just can't tolerate behavior like this."

"Really?" I ask in a weak voice. I mean, Mrs. Moody's not my favorite person in the world and she's certainly not known for her pleasantries, but the thought of her being kicked out actually makes me feel really sorry for her.

"I don't know what else to do. And I can't have her injuring anyone else." There's a certain finality in her tone that resonates with me as she steps past and continues down the hall. I'm not sure what to do at this point, so I simply stand there, two feet outside of Mrs. Moody's doorway, and strain my neck to see if I can catch a glimpse of the destruction inside.

I have half an idea to just turn around and retreat to the

safety of the quiet activity room where normal, subdued residents are getting ready to play Name That Tune with Gail, but something stops me. It's not something that I see in the room, but rather something I see at my feet. As I stare down at the yellow dog in the wooden frame, with her frizzy tufts of fur, long whiskered snout, and round, expressive eyes, I'm struck with a sudden idea. It may be a shot in the dark, but it's the only shot anyone seems to be taking around here.

I turn on my heels and head straight for the nurses' station where Harriet is already on the phone, presumably finding another permanent home for Mrs. Moody.

"Wait!" I plead, coming around the corner. "Don't kick her out yet."

Harriet eyes me apprehensively. "Frankly, Brooklyn, this doesn't concern you."

I bite my lip, feeling insecure and slightly in over my head, but somewhere deep down, I find the strength to press on. "I might have another solution. Will you let me try something first?" I ask, surprised by how assertive I sound when I could have sworn my words would come out garbled and shrouded in doubt.

Harriet looks reluctant, as do the rest of the nurses at the station, especially Carol, who's currently having a series of bite marks on her hand cleaned out with disinfectant.

"I can't risk you getting hurt," Harriet begins, looking apologetic. "Our insurance company would have my head."

But in the end it's *her* voice that seems to carry the uncertainty, so I waste no time taking advantage of her hesitation, whipping out my cell phone and dialing before she can stop me. "Just give me thirty minutes," I tell her.

EVERY DOG HAS HIS DAY

I wait outside, pacing the sidewalk and obsessively alternating between checking my watch and checking the entrance of the parking lot. I hope my directions to the nursing home were okay. I was kind of in a hurry when I dished them out, racing through the details at warp speed and rattling off turns like there was a potential terrorist attack with a ticking bomb about to go off.

And in all honesty, there kind of is. Except in this scenario, the ticking bomb would be Mrs. Moody.

I hug my jacket tighter around me to edge out the cold and hop around to keep myself warm. The sun is starting to set and the windchill is picking up. Fortunately, I don't have to wait much longer because a few seconds later I see a small, blue, beat-up truck pull into the parking lot and veer into a spot. The door swings open and Brian hops out, giving me a quick wave before running around to the passenger side and opening the door. I see him reach inside to grab the end of a leash before a bouncy and eager golden doodle springs onto the pavement, sniffing the ground curiously with his wispy ears perked up and his bushy tail wagging vigorously.

I run over to them and the dog greets me warmly with a lick on the hand.

Brian laughs and smooths back his dark curly hair. In a way it kind of matches the dog's. At least in terms of its thick, wiry texture. "This is Dudley. Dudley, meet my new debate partner, Brooklyn."

I kneel down and give Dudley a quick head ruffle. "Hi, Dudley!" Then I pop back up. "Thank you so much for coming on such short notice. I hope you two weren't doing anything important."

"Just the usual. Chasing fire trucks, digging up flower beds, defacing people's front lawns. You know, the Dudster and I like to live on the edge."

I try to laugh but I'm clearly too distracted.

"So what's going on?" he asks, sensing my distress. "You sounded panicked on the phone."

I huff out a heavy sigh. "Well, it's a bit of a crisis situation. C'mon, I'll explain everything."

By the time we make it to the hallway that leads to Mrs. Moody's room, Brian is entirely caught up to speed. Dudley is trotting happily beside us as if he understands exactly what he's been called in to do and has accepted his challenge dutifully, ready to serve mankind—his universally acknowledged "best friend."

"I had no idea you volunteered here," Brian says, taking in his surroundings.

"Well, it's complicated," I divulge guardedly. "Let's just say the whole *volunteering* aspect wasn't my idea."

We're nearly at Mrs. Moody's door when Carol seems to appear out of nowhere, stepping in front of us and blocking our path. "You can't bring that dog in here," she snarls.

"He's here to help Mrs. Moody," I explain, having no patience to deal with her right now.

"We have a strict no-animal policy at this facility."

"I know," I begin with an exasperated sigh but Brian is quick to cut me off.

"Dudley is a service dog," he says smartly, nodding toward his eager companion who appears to be wondering why we've stopped in the middle of this hallway when clearly there's a job to be done.

She eyes both of us with skepticism. "He is?"

Brian nods. "Absolutely. Brooklyn called me in a panic, and I was in such a hurry to get here I forgot to bring his service vest."

Carol's eyes narrow. She's obviously deciding whether or not to believe us. "What kind of service dog?"

"A therapy dog," Brian replies confidently without missing a beat. "Yeah, we do this kind of stuff all the time. In fact, Dudley *loves* coming to nursing homes. It's his specialty."

We look down at the dog and, as if sensing something is being desired of him, he drops to his haunches and stares back at us expectantly, as if to say "Okay, now what?"

Carol mulls over the situation for an awfully long time until the overhead PA system squawks to life, interrupting her thoughts. "Carol, please come to the front desk. Carol to the front desk, please."

Out of the corner of my eye, I see Brian cringe at the awful sound of the corroded speaker, but he manages to keep smiling.

Carol looks down the hall toward the reception area, then back at us, and finally, seeming to tire of this argument, she mutters, "Fine. Just keep him away from the other residents. Some are allergic." Then she spins on her heels and stomps away.

As soon as she's gone, I whisper, "Is that true? Is he really a service dog?"

But Brian just laughs and shakes his head. "Nah." He nods his head down the hall and gives the dog's leash a small tug. "Come on. Dudley's getting antsy."

Once we've reached the door to room 4A, I make Brian and Dudley wait outside so they can be formally introduced, then I step hesitantly into Mrs. Moody's room. The place is still in shambles, evidence of her aversion to unwanted visitors, and I immediately wonder if I should have worn some type of protective headgear.

"Mrs. Moody," I say delicately as I hover close to the far wall. Although judging by those items still lying in the hallway, Mrs. Moody may be old and fragile-*looking*, but she has an arm that could pitch game seven of the World Series.

She doesn't answer and for a moment I think that she might be sleeping. But as I tiptoe closer to her bedside I see that her eyes are open and her nostrils are flaring angrily with each inflamed breath. Like a dragon ready to burn the place down with one fiery exhale.

"Mrs. Moody, it's me, Brooklyn." Then just in case she really *has* lost it, I throw in, "You know, *Baby* Brooklyn."

The room is silent apart from the sound of her ragged breaths.

"I brought someone who might cheer you up."

The breathing quickens and I notice her knuckles start to

blanche again, indicating that she *has* heard me and she's reacting with her usual tenseness.

I extend my arm and beckon toward the open doorway.
"He's been waiting in the hallway and he's been absolutely dying
to meet you."

On cue, Dudley prances into the room, leash-free, and with
a quick sniff of the air he veers left and heads straight for Mrs.
Moody's bed. His snout plops down atop the covers as he waits
to be noticed and fawned over.

I watch Mrs. Moody's reaction very carefully, and as soon as
she catches sight of Dudley's large black nose and matted yellow
fur around his snout, she hoists herself up to get a better look.

"Ruby!" she cries wistfully. "Ruby, you've come to see me.
Here, girl!" She pats the bed and Dudley eagerly obeys, hopping up and stepping around Mrs. Moody's frail little legs until
he's able to position himself next to her. It's almost as though he
can somehow sense her fragility. Maybe he really *should* be a
service dog.

He lies down against the wall and allows Mrs. Moody to
wrap her wrinkled and vein-covered arms around his neck like a
teddy bear. "Am I dead?" she asks the dog, having clearly forgotten that I'm even in the room. "Are you here to take me to
Heaven? Oh, I just knew they'd send you, Ruby. I just knew it!"

Dudley pants contentedly beside her, and although I'm quite
enjoying this brand-new side of Mrs. Moody, I really don't think
it's healthy to allow her to continue to think that she's dead, so I
have to interrupt the tender moment between them and set the
record straight. "No, Mrs. Moody. You aren't dead. You're still
alive. This is Dudley. He belongs to my friend Brian."

It's then that I turn around and see Brian standing behind

me, next to the bookshelf. I flash him a grateful smile and a quick thumbs-up to let him know that it's definitely working.

"Oh," she replies, sounding eternally disappointed. For a moment I worry that the new Mrs. Moody is going to vanish instantly and disappear out the door like a ghost and the old Mrs. Moody is going to take over again and start barking out obscenities and throwing stuff, like she never left.

But she simply leans back to get a better look at the dog that's lying next to her, with his head resting on his paws. She repeats the name Dudley quietly to herself, trying it on for size, and begins to stroke his shoulders.

"That's a good dog, Dudley. You're a good boy, aren't you? Yes, you are."

I watch in complete astonishment as Mrs. Moody continues to purr quietly to herself, running her hands mindlessly across Dudley's shaggy coat, as though she were momentarily in a world all by herself. A world without anger, without hostility, and without an ounce of moodiness.

And then the most amazing thing happens. As she sits there, caressing the dog and murmuring to him in a soft, almost sing-songy voice, the corners of her mouth start to curl, her lips begin to part, and before I can even comprehend what is going on, a joyful gurgle of laughter echoes throughout the room.

I turn to Brian and beam. He beams back at me even though I'm certain he can't possibly understand how huge this is. I mean, he doesn't even *know* Mrs. Moody. The only background he has on the woman is the thirty seconds' worth of information I dumped on him while we were walking from the parking lot to the building. There's no way he can really grasp how truly significant this breakthrough is.

But even so, I can't help thinking that on some level he *does* get it. Or at least he gets how it makes me feel. And for that reason, there's no one else in the world I'd want to share this moment with.

As our eyes meet, I'm struck by an incredible warmness that soaks through my entire body. Like tomato soup when it's too cold or rainy to go outside. His smile is loose but knowing. His gaze delicate but penetrating. And his eyes are a truly remarkable shade of greenish hazel. They seem to twinkle even without the help of dashboard lights.

Brian steps toward me and slowly reaches his hand to my face. I stand perfectly still and close my eyes. For some reason, I *want* him to touch me right now. I want him to be close to me. I want to share this warmth I feel with someone living, breathing, approaching. Someone who will appreciate it, absorb it, and return it back to me with the same intensity.

With my eyes closed, I can feel his proximity. I sense him moving closer to me. The heat from his body radiates off his skin and attaches to mine. The hairs on the back of my neck stand up. My pulse quickens. My breathing follows suit.

And then, I feel it. The tip of his index finger making contact with my cheek. The cool prick of moisture. I open my eyes to see Brian dabbing at a tear that has trickled down my face. Until then, I hadn't even realized that I'd been crying. Embarrassed, I lower my head and wipe hastily at both cheeks, feeling foolish and childlike. Then, like houselights illuminating a theater at the end of an enthralling movie, I remember where I am. *Who* I am. What I'm doing. Then I blink and turn back to Mrs. Moody.

Go Fish!

Colorado Springs is a beautiful town, nestled right up against the Rocky Mountains with Pikes Peak as an exquisite backdrop. Izzie went to tennis camp one summer at the nearby Air Force Academy but I've only ever been down here a handful of times. Unfortunately we won't have much time to see any of the city because our schedule for the debate tournament is jam-packed. Three back-to-back debate rounds today, an overnight stay at the Holiday Inn near the hosting school, and then it's back in the morning for more debating.

It takes about an hour to drive down to Colorado Springs. So just like last weekend, Brian picks me up super early on Saturday morning. I'm still half asleep when I toss my overnight bag on the floor of his truck cab and climb into the passenger seat.

Despite my fatigue, I'm actually really happy to see him this morning. After Harriet witnessed firsthand what a difference Dudley made on Mrs. Moody's notorious disposition, she agreed not to evict her as long as we could arrange to have a therapy dog visit her on a regular basis. Brian immediately volunteered to bring Dudley in once a week. The gesture really touched me. I mean, he totally didn't have to do that. And now every time I think about it, I find myself smiling.

The first day of competition doesn't go as well as our last meet. We win only one of our three rounds. That's probably because, as Brian explains, this is an advanced level meet that you have to qualify for to enter in so the competition is naturally going to be tougher.

Even though he assures me that I'm doing extremely well, I'm starting to feel very discouraged by the results.

The first day ends at around eight and we stop for a fast-food dinner before retiring to the hotel. Because Katy "Huffy" Huffington and I are the only girls on the team, we're forced to share a room, which, trust me, I'm *not* thrilled about since Katy pretty much hates everything about me, but as soon as we get to the room she dumps her stuff on the bed and disappears to an undisclosed location, so now I pretty much have the whole place to myself.

I take off my stuffy debate suit, shower, and slip into a comfy pair of sweats and a tank top. With wet hair and a clean face, I lie back on my double bed, grab the remote and flip on the TV, searching for something to distract me until I fall asleep.

I'm just settling in for a rerun episode of my favorite sitcom when there's a knock on the door. I peer through the peephole to see Brian's face on the other side, distorted like in a fun house mirror.

"Hey, what's up?" I ask, opening the door and leaning against the jamb.

"You busy?" He glances apprehensively over my shoulder,

as if he expects to see me entertaining a group of foreign dignitaries or something.

I look back at the TV. "Not really, why? Did you want to go over the inherency issues again?"

He stuffs his hands in his pockets and kind of teeters back and forth from his heels to his toes. For a minute, he almost looks *nervous* about something. "No. I'm tired of talking about debate."

I laugh. "I didn't think that was possible."

He jerks his head in the direction of the hallway. "A couple of us are getting together to play a game. Do you want to join?"

"What kind of game?"

He shrugs, looking kind of sheepish. "Nothing fancy. Just, you know, the usual. Monopoly, Uno, maybe a little Go Fish if we're feeling especially rebellious."

I touch at my wet hair and glance down at my sweatpants and tank top. "I'm not really dressed."

"Oh, you're fine," he assures me. "Totally casual. We're just hanging out in Jake and Dave's room."

I shrug and grab my hotel key off the dresser. "Okay. Let me put on my shoes."

I follow Brian a few doors down until we arrive at room 202. He pushes the slightly ajar door open and that's when I come face-to-face with something that is definitely *not* a game of Go Fish. Unless they totally changed the rules to include making out with someone when they fail to produce the card you're asking for.

Our entire debate team is scattered around the room and they're all cheering and counting backward in a unified chant like they're getting ready to kick off the New Year or something.

And smack-dab in the center of everything is Jake, a junior on the team, totally swapping spit with Katy "Huffy" Huffington.

"What is this?" I yell to Brian over the noise.

"Twenty-one! Twenty! Nineteen!"

"Truth or Dare," Brian yells back, once again looking totally uncomfortable and embarrassed. "They were dared to make out for ninety seconds."

I stare at him in disbelief. "Truth or Dare? I thought you said we'd be playing Uno!"

"Truth or Dare is a Colorado Springs Overnight tradition. We play it every year."

"Ten! Nine! Eight!" the room chants.

"You lured me here under false pretenses," I say, looking outraged, although I'm really just in shock. The debate team playing Truth or Dare? Who would have guessed?

"Sorry," he offers, even though it's clear from the coy smile on his face that he's not.

"Three! Two! One!" The room erupts in loud cheers as Katy and Jake finally break apart and wipe their mouths before plopping back down into their respective seats.

Jake catches my eye and grins. "Newcomer!" he shouts and suddenly every pair of eyes is on me.

I instinctively take a step back toward the door but Brian holds me in place. "Think of it as an initiation process," he whispers into my ear as he places his hand on the small of my back and guides me farther into the room. He presses down on my shoulders until I'm sitting on one of the beds. I grab his arm and yank him down next to me. "Don't you dare leave me in here."

He chuckles as he scoots closer to me. "I wouldn't dream of it."

"Truth or dare?" Jake launches into the question of the hour.

Seeing that I barely know any of these people, apart from Brian, I take the easy road. "Truth," I say, prompting a series of disappointed boos.

Brian reaches over and gives my arm a squeeze. "Just ignore them."

"Okay," Jake says, rubbing his hands together sinisterly. "Truth."

"Hey," Brian warns. "Go easy on her. It's her first time."

I turn and give him a grateful look that he acknowledges with a wink.

Jake rolls his eyes, clearly disapproving of his captain's orders. "Fine. How many guys have you slept with?"

My eyes grow wide. "That's an *easy* question?"

Brian laughs. "You probably should have picked dare."

I slump on the bed and glance around at the nine pairs of inquiring eyes directed right at me. I think about Shayne and all the times she lectured me about the power of perception. About all the times my experience in the bedroom was alluded to yet never confirmed. This is the way it was designed. For my personal life to appear shrouded with mystery. Because according to Shayne, mystery is always better than truth. I can hear her voice in my head now. *"Don't destroy the illusion. Who cares if you lie to these losers?"*

But suddenly, I *do*. I care. I'm tired of lying. Tired of living my life by Shayne's rules. I've spent the last five years trying to fit into her cookie-cutter mold of popularity. She's not even my friend anymore and I'm still listening to her imaginary advice!

And for some reason, I feel like I can trust these people.

That I don't *have* to lie to them. I don't have to rely on flattering façades to get their approval. I mean, here I am sitting in a hotel room with them at eleven o'clock at night with wet hair, sweatpants, and no makeup. As far as I'm concerned, the façade has already been destroyed. I've already been stripped clean.

The room is waiting. Every pair of eyes is on me, including Brian's, who somehow seems more vested in my response than anyone else. I take a deep breath and deliver my verdict. "Zero."

"Zero?" Jake repeats skeptically. "As in none?"

I confirm with a nod. "As in none."

Katy echoes the sentiment of disbelief. "Are you telling me Brooklyn Pierce, the official co-captain of Queen Kingsley, is a virgin?" It's probably the nicest tone she's ever used to speak to me.

"That's what I'm telling you."

The room has gone dead silent. I'm honestly surprised. I had no idea my sex life was such a topic of interest for everyone.

"But," she argues softly, "I thought for sure you'd . . . At least with Kyle Logue or Mike Paisley, or—"

I shake my head resolutely. "Nope. Never."

It's strange how good it feels to say it aloud like that. To shatter the illusion once and for all.

There's another dead silence and I gaze around the room. Brian looks genuinely confused, Jake looks kind of turned on, and Katy flashes me a small, totally unexpected smile, as though she's finally found *something* to like about me. I feel extremely uncomfortable under this spotlight so I clap my hands together in an attempt to break everyone from their stunned trances and exclaim, "Okay! My turn, right? Jake, right back at you. Truth or dare?"

The focus is instantly shifted, and within minutes everyone is laughing and jeering again as Jake peels off his pants and sets out to fulfill my dare of running to the end of the hallway and back in only his boxers. And before long, everyone has forgotten about my moment of truth.

That is, everyone but me.

DANCING IN THE DARK

The game continues into the early hours of the morning and I can't remember ever having so much fun. Over the course of the evening, I've learned that Jake has nightly fantasies about his physics teacher; Brian walked in on his parents having sex when he was seven, thought they were wrestling, and asked if he could play; and during those two weeks when Katy was supposedly on a cruise with her family, she was actually getting a boob reduction.

As the night goes on and we all get a little loopier from the lack of sleep, the dares get more and more outrageous, and despite my better judgment, at about two-thirty a.m., I find myself answering, "Dare," when the question comes back around to me.

"Ha!" Katy squeals in delight. She appeared to have magically forgotten about her grudge against me hours ago. "I gotta come up with something really good now."

I watch her face as she plots my demise and I'm fully expecting to have to shed at least one item of clothing.

"Okay, I've got it," she finally says, tickling her top lip with her tongue. "You have to go into the bathroom, lock the door, and turn out the lights for a full five minutes."

"That's it?" I ask incredulously, thinking I've gotten off easy.

"Oh," she adds nonchalantly, as if this next detail were just a casual afterthought, "and you have to take Brian with you."

The room erupts with whistling and catcalls as I look over at Brian and feel my face get hot. "Katy . . ." I try.

"Nuh-uh," she stops me. "A dare is a dare."

So I reluctantly stand up and beckon for Brian to come with me. "All right, let's get this over with," I say, rolling my eyes and heading for the bathroom. Brian enters right behind me and closes the door. The tile is cold against my bare feet. "This is so stupid." I cross my arms and lean against the counter.

He nods but doesn't say anything.

"Lights off!" I hear Katy call from the other room. "We can see the light from under the door."

Brian looks to me as he rests his hand on the light switch.

"Whatever," I say with a shrug, and he hits the switch.

Darkness instantly surrounds me. The only sliver of light comes from the crack under the door, not enough to light Brian's face or any of the fixtures around the bathroom.

There's an awkward silence that falls between us, and for a second I wonder if he's even still there. Then I hear a creak in the floor and I realize that he's repositioning himself. To where, I have no idea. I can't see a freaking thing.

"This is so stupid," I say again, knowing full well that I'm just repeating myself. "What do they expect us to do in here?"

Brian chuckles. "Make out, I guess."

This makes me laugh. Hard. Like I'm seriously keeled over.

I've never heard of such a crazy notion. Make out with Brian Harris? *Heimlich?* Yeah, right. Why would I want to do that? I mean, he's my debate partner. And . . .

And . . .

Well, that's enough. Everyone knows you shouldn't mix business with pleasure.

"Is it really that funny?" Brian asks. I can't see his face but from the tone of his voice, it almost sounds like he's offended. It's then that I realize I'm still laughing. But it's not like an uncontrollable fit of giggles. It's more like this nervous, drawn-out stutter of a laugh. An empty sound with absolutely no emotion behind it.

Because in reality, it's not that funny.

I'm just trying to fill the space.

"This is stupid," I say for a third time. "I can't even see you. I don't even know where you are!"

I reach my hand out into the void and it lands on the soft fabric of Brian's T-shirt. Evidently, he was closer than I thought. I can feel his loosely defined chest muscles under the cotton. And despite the fact that I've now successfully established exactly where he is, for some reason my hand doesn't move. Or rather, I can't *seem* to move it. It stays there, planted on the front of his chest, as though it has a mind of its own. The proximity shoots tingles up my arm, across my shoulder, and right into my heart.

I can't really explain what comes over me next. Maybe it's the darkness. Or maybe the darkness has absolutely nothing to do with it. But I feel my fingers start to curl, the fabric snagging into my grasp until I'm literally clinging to his shirt. Then I just pull.

Despite the pitch blackness, his lips land right on mine. Like a magnet to metal. Drawn together by an invisible force. Our mouths are dancing. A perfectly choreographed routine. And yet it's our first time performing it. Some things don't require practice. Some things simply work on the first try.

I reach up and touch his hair. You would think, from the way it looks, it would feel coarse and wiry, but it's nothing like that. It's soft and thick and amazing.

His hands wrap around my hips and slip under the back of my tank top. His fingers dig into my sides and suddenly I'm in the air, being lifted. My butt lands on the countertop. I can feel the hard porcelain of the sink basin digging into my left thigh. All the while, his lips never leave mine. Our dance never stops.

He leans into me and I wrap my ankles around the back of his legs, pulling him closer. His hands are still tightly clasping my exposed waist, pressing into my skin so hard that I can feel the white imprints of his fingertips start to form.

I am completely lost. I can't remember where I am or how I got here. My body feels separate from my mind. In fact, I can't even remember what my mind is for. Time no longer exists.

I don't even hear the click of the bathroom door as it opens. I don't even see the light from the hotel room as it floods the room. I don't even feel the eight pairs of eyes on us. That is, until the heckling starts. Followed by the catcalls and the whooping sounds and the laughter.

Brian pulls away from me with a chagrined laugh and I untangle my legs from around him and attempt to hide my face behind his shoulder, mortification paralyzing my entire body.

Meanwhile the jeering never stops. I have a feeling it won't for a long, *long* time. I guess I should have known that any good dance routine is eventually going to attract an audience.

BFF, WTF

Truth or Dare is *not* cheating.

It's only a game. A bunch of people, milling around in a hotel room in Colorado Springs with nothing better to do than dare each other to steal away into darkened bathrooms. Besides, it's not like Hunter and I are officially a couple or anything. I mean, we haven't even gone on a first date! So really, I have *nothing* to feel guilty about. Absolutely zilch. Especially because that little escapade with Brian was completely insignificant. It didn't mean a thing. If you place any two people in a darkened room—whether it be a coat closet or a supply room or a hotel bathroom—something is bound to happen. It's only natural.

I chalk up the whole thing to simple biology. And peer pressure. Lots and lots of peer pressure. We were practically *expected* to make out.

But I do think it's probably best that I quit the debate team. For everyone.

I know I didn't poll my blog readers or make an official "choice" about it, but I'm just not sure the debate team is really what I should be doing right now. And let's face it, it's not like I joined because I was actually interested in debate. I joined because I was given the *choice* to join and my blog readers thought it was a good one. And I fulfilled my obligation to them. I went for it. I tried it. I had some good times in the process and now that's that. I'm grateful for the opportunity but I don't see why I have to continue doing something I was never really all that keen on doing in the first place. There's nothing wrong with trying new things, but eventually there comes a time when you have to take a step back and be perfectly honest with yourself and say, "Yes, that was fun, but it's really not for me."

I have no doubt Brian will understand. In fact he'll probably even be somewhat relieved. I can't imagine this has been very fun for him. I mean, the endless hours of coaching he's had to do. I'm sure I've been quite a burden over the past couple of weeks. He deserves a debate partner who will help him move forward, not hold him back.

When I get downstairs on Monday morning, I find a note from my mom explaining that she and my dad both had early meetings and I'm going to have to take the bus to school. With a frustrated sigh I grab a granola bar from the pantry, sling my bag over my shoulder, and tromp out the door. I pull my jacket tight around me to stave off the mid-November chill and the small flurries of snow that have started to fall and brace myself for the long walk to the bus stop.

But I don't get very far. In fact, I don't even make it to the curb. Because idling in the driveway, with the motor running, is a car I've never seen before. A shiny silver SUV (one of those expensive kinds) with tinted windows and dealer license plates that indicate it's fresh off the lot. I squint into the windshield, trying to make out the identity of the mysterious driver. I see flashes of long blond hair and before I can try to match them to a name and a face, the driver's-side door swings open and a pair of designer red leather boots clack onto the pavement.

And there's only one person I know who owns shoes like those.

"Brooks!" Shayne choruses as she flounces around the front of the car and pulls me into this very awkward, zero-body-contact hug. I stand there with my arms hanging limp at my sides and my mouth slightly agape as she air kisses my left cheek.

"How do you like my birthday present?" Shayne bubbles as she turns around and motions to the oversize vehicle in my driveway like one of those bikini-clad spokesmodels standing on a revolving platform at a car show.

"But your birthday's not until next month," I point out because it's really the only thing that's coming to mind right now. Even though "What the bleep are you doing here?" would probably be the more appropriate combination of words.

She shrugs at this and giggles mischievously. "I know, but my dad bought it for me early. And I'm allowed to drive it as long as my mom doesn't find out."

"But you don't have a license yet" is the next lame thing that exits my mouth.

She shrugs this off, too, as though it's just a technicality. A typo. As insignificant and unremarkable as accidentally adding an extra period to the end of a sentence. .

Although, honestly, I'm not surprised by the fact that

Shayne's dad bought her a car even though she's too young to drive it. Her father indulges her every desire. It's his way of winning her over. One-upping his ex-wife. Buying his daughter's love. And he certainly can afford it.

What *does* surprise me, however, and what I still can't figure out, is why she's chosen to drive this particular indulgence *here*. Although I have a sneaking suspicion it has something to do with my instapopularity around school lately.

"So, do you want a ride?" she asks, strutting back to the car and nodding her head in the direction of the passenger seat.

She asks the question as though it's nothing. As though we're still the very best of friends—the high-ranking general and her second in command—and nothing has ever happened or *could* happen to tear us apart.

I continue to stand there, my shoulders slightly hunched, feeling like the world around me has been translated into Japanese and I don't have a dictionary.

"Come on," she urges me, making a shivering sound. "It's cold out here. Get in. We have *loads* to catch up on."

I look up right in time to see the big yellow bus drive by, effectively leaving me with very few other options than to obey the order Shayne has cleverly disguised as a request. Because now it's either this or walk to school. And that would probably put me at the front entrance around the end of lunch . . . with a mild case of hypothermia.

I shuffle hesitantly over to the passenger-side door and reach out to test the handle for booby traps. You know, just to make sure this is not some kind of hidden-camera prank designed to humiliate me on YouTube. But apart from the frosty metal stinging my fingertips, the door appears to be relatively harmless. So I open it, toss my bag on the floor, and climb up into the seat. Like Alice in Wonderland tumbling down the rabbit hole, I allow myself to be lured into this strange upside-down dimension. If for no other reason than genuine curiosity.

BROOKLYN IN WONDERLAND

"So, how have you been?" she asks as soon as she's backed out of my driveway.

I shrug and glance out the window, still not sure what to make of the fact that I'm sitting in Shayne Kingsley's car. "Fine."

"You look good," she says, peering at me out of the corner of her eye. "I like your hair that way."

As much as I hate myself for it, the compliment feels good. Comforting. Like when you get a phone call from an old friend you haven't talked to in years.

"I heard about you and Hunter," she continues, flipping on her blinker and taking a left out of the subdivision. "I think it's awesome."

I turn and gape at her. *What is she talking about?* I tell myself to just ignore the comment. Not to engage myself in whatever game she's playing. But my mouth speaks without permission. "What did you hear?"

"That he asked you to the winter formal," she explains.

"He's really hot. You know, for a high school guy. You two make a cute couple."

She turns and flashes me a smile. What astonishes me most is not the smile itself, but the fact that it doesn't appear in the least bit fake. It's not the same one I saw a month ago in the cafeteria when she dismissed me in front of everyone. And believe me, if anyone can recognize the difference, it's me. As hard to believe as it is, her smile appears to be genuine. The kind I used to see on her, back when we were just two friends hanging out in her room, gossiping about boys. And suddenly I feel a pang of nostalgia. Because despite the fact that she totally ditched me without a second thought, despite the fact that she can be manipulative and conniving and completely insufferable, we did have some really fun moments together over the years. And Shayne is not all evil. There are some good parts about her, too. For instance, if someone wrongs you—like a teacher, or a parent, or another student—you can always count on Shayne for sympathy. She's the first one to make you feel better by calling the offender dirty names and telling you why they're not worth your time. Or if you're having a bad day, Shayne's the first person to offer to ditch class with you and treat you to a mani/pedi or spa treatment compliments of her dad's platinum Amex. I mean, she's certainly not perfect, but she was still my best friend. And I still feel her absence.

"Thanks," I hear myself saying.

"Look," Shayne says, her expression turning serious, "I'll stop beating around the bush. I owe you an apology."

My jaw drops and I gawk at her in silence.

"It's true!" she vows, reacting to my disbelief. "This whole hostage thing really got me thinking about our friendship.

When my mom and I were watching the situation unfold on the news that night and they announced your name as one of the people trapped inside, I totally started to panic. I didn't know if you were going to live or die. No one did. And then I started to think about what would happen if I lost you. If you never came out of that store. And . . ." Her voice cracks, and when I glance over, I can actually make out moisture forming in her eyes. It's like watching a fish jump out of the bowl and start walking around. In five years, I don't think I've *ever* seen Shayne Kingsley cry. I can feel my own eyes prick with tears and I quickly blink them away.

"I've been a really bad friend," she continues, her voice still heavy and fractured. "And I feel *awful* about it."

My mouth remains wide open. But not because I'm using it to speak. Quite the opposite, actually.

Fortunately, Shayne is quick to fill the silence. "That whole party at the model home. And the fire and everything. I handled it completely wrong. I started to think about my parents' reactions and I freaked out. Like totally *freaked* OUT. I'm really sorry. I should have been there for you. I should have taken half of the blame. Or all of it, really. Because you know, the party *was* my idea."

I simply can't believe what I'm hearing. Shayne Kingsley. Apologizing. Admitting a mistake. Admitting *flaw*. I didn't know that "I'm sorry" was even in her vocabulary. I'm really not sure what to do with this information. I don't know how to process it. It's like trying to run a Mac program on a PC. Does. Not. Compute.

I turn and look out the window. Her voice continues to drift through the car as she speaks, but it sounds like it's coming from a million miles away. Another world. Another lifetime. Not across the mere two feet that separate us now.

"I want us to be friends again," she finally concludes as the car rolls to a stop at a red light and she twists to face me. "I want to go back to the way things were. Life without you royally sucks. It's like a martini with no olives. It just doesn't taste right."

Her tone is so soft, so defenseless, that I have no choice but to face her, too. Because I simply *have* to know what that tone looks like. I *have* to know what kind of expression accompanies a confession like this. And what I find is something I've never seen before. At least, not on the face of Shayne Kingsley.

Vulnerability.

Weakness.

Anguish.

"Uh . . ." is the only thing I manage to utter. And although I know it doesn't sound like much, it accurately sums up everything I'm feeling right now.

"What do you say?" she asks, her voice still small like a child's. Like a human *being's*. "Do you think you can forgive me? Do you think we can be friends again?"

Friends? With Shayne Kingsley? Just like old times?

As much as it pains me to admit it, I actually *want* to believe her. To believe that she's truly sorry. That she's seen the error of her ways and wants to make amends.

On the other hand, though, what she did was pretty freaking horrific. I mean, she totally dissed me. In front of everyone. Threw me out like I was a bottle of expired cold cream. Can you really forgive something like that? Can you ever be sure that she wouldn't do it again just as quickly? Is Shayne Kingsley really capable of change?

"I don't know," I finally tell her after a very long moment and two more intersections. And I *don't* know. I don't have a flipping clue. But what I really want to say is "I don't know, but I know about a hundred people who will."

MY LIFE UNDECIDED

HEINOUS NO MORE?

Posted on: *Monday, November 15th at 8:59 am by* BB4Life

You'll probably notice from the time stamp on this posting that I'm supposed to be in class right now because the bell is about to ring in less than a minute. But the news I have is SO big, I felt it was worth the extra tardy on my school record to be able to share it with you right this very minute. You know, CNN Breaking News–style.

This Just In . . . Her Royal Heinous has apologized! Yes, you read that right. As in, "I screwed up. I was wrong. I'm *sorry*." I mean, she was *this* close to getting down on her knees and begging for my forgiveness. And trust me, Her Royal Heinous does not beg. To *anyone*. So you can imagine my reaction. Just imagine cartoonlike eyes popping out of their sockets and jaw on the floor and you'll pretty much have the entire picture. And to top it all off, now she wants us to be friends again.

Needless to say, I have absolutely NO idea what to do. I don't think I've ever been more grateful for all of you because I definitely would *not* want to make this decision on my own.

So what do we think?

Oh, and in case you missed the posting fully detailing exactly *what* Her Royal Heinous is apologizing for and how she received her fitting nickname, be sure to check it out <u>here</u> before you vote.

Okay, it's off to learn about American history for me!

Your friend,
BB

Blog Error in
Your Favor

The bell rings right as I hit "Publish" and I leap up from my chair at one of the library computers and toss my bag over my shoulder. I lean over and hastily click the "X" on the corner of the screen to close the window. But just as the image of my blog disappears, something unusual catches my eye.

I know it was probably a trick of my imagination and I should be bolting from the library right now and trying to slip into my seat at the back of my history classroom before Mr. Marshall notices that I'm not there, but for some reason, I find myself falling back into the chair and reopening another browser window so I can get a closer look at what I saw. Or what I *thought* I saw.

I mean, it *has* to be a mistake. There's no way it could be real. It's beyond all logic. Light-years outside the realm of possibility. That's why when I log back into my account and click on "View Blog," I fully expect the information in front of me to confirm that I *was* only seeing things.

But it doesn't.

In reality, it confirms exactly the opposite. That I am *not* going crazy. That my mind is *not* playing tricks on me. And that the impossible thing that I thought I saw just moments ago actually *is* real.

In fact, it's clear as day.

Under the words "Number of Blog Visitors" it reads "782,764."

I blink at the screen. Twice. Then I actually rub at the corners of my eyes to make sure there's no sleep left in there from this morning and hit "Refresh" on the Web browser. But the number does not change. Actually, it goes *up*. By about two thousand visitors.

Two thousand more visitors in *twenty* seconds?

But how is that possible? And where are they all coming from? Or more important, *why* do they all care? Before I went to bed last night that counter was at 125.

Suddenly it's very hard to breathe. Or move, really. I feel like my butt is cemented to the chair and my hand is glued to the mouse and my eyes are frozen in place. In fact, the only thing that *does* move is my index finger as I obsessively hit "Refresh" over and over, watching the staggering number continue to rise with each click of my finger.

786,975.

789,085.

793,468.

797,101.

What the heck is going on here?

I scroll back up to the top of the page, trying to make sense of this insanity. Then something else catches my eye. A little yellow bubble on the top of the screen that says "The system will be down for repairs today from 10:00 a.m. to 12:00 p.m. We apologize for the inconvenience."

I breathe out a heavy sigh and sink down into my chair, feeling like an enormous weight has just been lifted.

Well, that explains it!

There must be some kind of glitch in the program. A system-wide failure that's causing the whole site to go cuckoo. And now they have to shut everything down to fix it. That makes *so* much sense! I mean, how else can you explain an 797,000-hit spike *overnight*?

You can't.

This is the only plausible explanation.

I navigate over to the Help section, tap out a quick e-mail to the support team listing out the details of my issue, hoping it'll help them in their quest for a solution, and book it out of the library to my first-period class.

I can just picture the site's IT team, somewhere in Silicon Valley, California, running around the office like headless chickens, shouting out orders to one another, trying to sort out this embarrassing technical hiccup that's causing everyone's blog to go haywire. It almost makes me laugh. But I have faith that they'll figure it out. That this glitch will be fixed. And when I come back to the library at lunch, all will be right again.

Monday, November 15

Dear BB4Life,

Thanks for notifying us regarding the unusually high volume of traffic on your blog. After further review, we have not found any functionality issues in your account and we can attest that your blog hit counter is, in fact, working correctly.

Please let us know if we can be of any further assistance.

Sincerely,
Your Blog Support Team

Where There's Smoke . . .

22,980.

That's how many comments have been left on my latest blog posting.

Twenty-two *thousand* nine hundred and eighty people have felt the need to remark on my decision to forgive or not forgive Shayne Kingsley. My head is spinning so fast, I can barely focus on the screen long enough to read a single one of them.

I take a second look at the hit counter. It's over a million and a half now. A million and a *half.* As in the population of Idaho. As in the amount of money it would require to buy a house in my mother's new subdivision development.

And it's not stopping there. It just keeps going up. Every time I refresh the screen.

Like a wildfire.

It starts with a basic match. Struck innocently enough to light the way through a dark clump of trees and then it slips from your fingers, and before you can react the entire forest is ablaze.

Maybe I really am an arsonist.

I quickly close the window. As if making it disappear from my screen will also make it disappear from my life. Obviously, it doesn't work. Because the image is seared into my brain. So I open it back up again and stare numbly at the screen.

My heart is hammering in my chest. My fingers are cold and clammy against the buttons of the mouse.

Who are these people? Where did they come from? How do they know about *my* little, insignificant blog?

Last week this blog was nothing and today it's the toast of the Internet. How long will it take people to figure out who wrote it? How long will it take them to put the pieces together and deduce that, like BB, I *also* joined the debate team and tried out for the rugby team and chose to read *The Grapes of Wrath*, and nearly choked in the cafeteria?

My estimate: not very long.

Which means I have little time before all hell breaks loose.

A hand lands on my shoulder and I nearly jump out of my skin.

"There you are!" Shayne's voice echoes through the entire library, despite the "Quiet Please" signs that are plastered on every wall. "What are you doing in *here*?"

There's a clear disdain in her voice as she glances around the room, taking in her surroundings as if she's seeing them for the first time. A secret chamber discovered in a house you've lived in all your life.

I dive for the mouse, trying to close the window before Shayne catches sight of it. But it's too late. "Oh," she says, glancing at the screen and rolling her eyes. "That. *Please* don't tell me you're into that thing, too?"

Way too late.

My breath catches in my throat.

Shayne Kingsley knows about the blog.

Shayne Kingsley has read it.

It's already happening. I'm already doomed.

There's no way she doesn't know it's her I'm talking about. She has to at least recognize herself. Could this be the real reason behind her apology? Could she have read the blog and now be setting me up for some kind of retaliatory revenge scheme?

"Everyone is talking about that stupid blog," she continues.

"They are?" I manage to say. But it's barely a squeak.

"I think it's totally overrated."

I search her face for a clue. A flash of accusation. But I don't see anything.

"Have you read it?" My voice is trembling now.

She stares down at her manicure, as if even the maintenance of her fingernails interests her more than the topic at hand. "Yeah, I read some of it last night after DishnDiss posted it. But I really don't see what the big deal is. So some girl needs help figuring out her life. What else is new?"

"Wait a minute." I rewind her words until I reach the part that strikes me as odd. "DishnDiss? As in DishnDiss *dot com*?"

She looks at me like I'm clearly stupid. "Um, yeah."

"They posted it on their site? The site that's read by millions of people *a day*?"

"Duh," she says, clearly getting bored with this conversation. "How else would you have heard about it?"

I scramble for words but they're coming out in short, incoherent clumps. "Uh . . . I . . . don't . . ."

"Whatever." She spares me from having to finish. "*So* not interesting. Let's go to lunch."

I don't know if it's the shock, or the fact that I'm still just trying to find my footing in this overturned world of mine—like a
baby horse trying to walk for the first time—but I don't argue. I
let myself be led down the hallway and into the cafeteria. And
before I know it, I'm right back at the center table, occupying
the coveted spot next to Shayne Kingsley.

As if I never even left.

Under the Radar

Everyone **is talking about my blog.** And debating about the
fate of BB and Her Royal Heinous's friendship like it's a feud on
an MTV reality show. Meanwhile, I just sit there, listening to
people go back and forth, trapped in the constant fear of expo-
sure. Convinced that any minute now someone is going to walk
up to the table, point to me, and go, "Hey, you're BB4Life, aren't
you?" And then everyone else will turn and stare at me in astonishment as the gears in their heads start turning and the puzzle
pieces start falling into place.

Thankfully, "that stupid blog" is the very *last* thing Shayne
wants to talk about. And she makes her objections very clear
about five minutes after we sit down.

"Can we *please* talk about something else?" she whines.
"This is *such* a waste of brain activity. Besides, BB is a loser for
even contemplating forgiveness. If her ex–best friend really dicked
her over that badly, then why is this even a decision to make?
Her Royal Heinous is clearly a major biatch. End of discussion.
Let's talk about something else. Like the winter formal. Ooh! Or

the fabuloso sweet sixteen my father is planning for me next month."

And for the first time in my life, I'm actually grateful when everyone obeys her command like sniveling dogs following their alpha leader and the subject is promptly changed.

I duck out of lunch early, claiming to have to print something out before English class, and make my way back to the computer terminals in the library. I go straight to DishnDiss.com and rapidly scroll past the custody battles, eating disorders, and stories of leaked sex tapes, until I find what I'm looking for.

It's not long. It's not complicated. And yet, after reading it, everything about the last few hours makes perfect sense.

How lazy have teenagers gotten these days?

When I was fifteen, we didn't have blogs and online polls. We actually had to make our *own* decisions. And we had to walk to school . . . uphill both ways . . . in the snow.

Click here to vote on a hopeless girl's life.

This is bad. This is very, *very* bad. This could be the end of me. For heaven's sake, it's listed under the "Diss" column! I've been publicly dissed by the most well-known gossip site in America! If people find out that this blog is mine, I'll never be able to recover.

It's no wonder I didn't see this until now. I haven't looked at DishnDiss.com since Shayne dissed *me*. Because there was no reason to. Staying up-to-date on all the latest gossip was always Shayne's thing. Not mine. I honestly couldn't care less which celebrity was knocked up and which one was caught red-handed in a fashion faux pas. But Shayne did. And therefore, I was expected to as well.

And in that moment I realize why no one can identify me as the mysterious blogger behind MyLifeUndecided.com. Why I seem to be the only person at this school who actually knows the blog belongs to me and not "some random person in Ohio" as a few of the readers have speculated. Because after I was officially excommunicated from the United Church of Shayne (and before I became a local hero), I was invisible. I was no longer a subject of public speculation. I was no longer talked about, observed, analyzed, studied, or emulated.

And now with the details right in front of their eyes, the evidence all lined up for everyone to examine, the answer couldn't be more obvious. And yet, in the shadow of Shayne Kingsley, no one can even see it.

Well, almost no one.

Believe it or not, there is *one* person who knows that I joined the debate team. That I tried out for rugby and got my butt handed to me. That I went on an extra credit field trip to see chopped-up human bodies for health class. And that I nearly choked and died in a hidden back corner of the cafeteria.

There is one person who knows the real *me*.

Not as an extension of Shayne Kingsley, but as an entity in and of myself.

Brian "Heimlich" Harris.

My debate partner. Or soon to be *ex*–debate partner.

I slow to a stop outside the door to my English classroom and think about the implications. *What if he knows? Will he be upset? Or will he think it's kind of funny?*

And then, as though I've telepathically summoned him, suddenly he's standing right next to me.

"Hey, you," he says, poking me in the arm.

I jump nearly a foot in the air.

Brian chuckles. "Sorry, didn't mean to scare you."

I force out an uneasy giggle. "Hi." And then I simply stare at him and wait. Wait for the bomb to drop. Wait for him to confirm my worst suspicions.

"What?" he says, wiping his nose and mouth. "Do I have something on my face?"

I hastily shake my head. "No, I'm just . . . I'm just wondering if you have anything to tell me. Or talk to me about."

He raises his eyebrows inquisitively and then a flash of realization settles onto his face. "Oh," he says, lowering his voice and dropping his head closer to me. *"That."*

Just as I suspected. He *knows.*

"Yeah," I say, cringing. "That."

"Actually, I do want to talk to you about that."

I take a deep breath and prepare myself for the worst. "Okay."

"But not here," he declares, glancing around. "Meet me outside Debate Central after school."

My whole body slumps. I really just wanted to get this over with. I don't want to have to go through the rest of the day with this hanging over my head. But I suppose he's right. Class is starting in less than a minute and this conversation is going to take much longer. So I nod and say, "Okay. That sounds good," before following him into the classroom.

DISHED AND DISSED

As soon as the final bell rings, I don't even stop off at my locker, I just head straight for Debate Central and I wait. Brian shows up a few minutes later with a playful grin on his face.

Well, I think, *if he's pissed about this blog, he certainly has an interesting way of showing it.*

"So," I prompt anxiously.

Brian motions to the open door of the debate room. "Shall we?"

I nod and step inside. Because Ms. Rich is at a faculty meeting we have the classroom to ourselves. Brian takes a seat at a desk and I quickly follow suit and collapse into the one next to him.

"What did you want to talk to me about?" I ask, reminding myself to take deep breaths and try to hear him out without totally freaking.

Brian suddenly appears very nervous. He keeps looking down at his hands and avoiding eye contact. "Well," he begins timidly. "I wanted to talk about this weekend."

"This weekend?" I repeat skeptically. "What about this weekend?"

"I mean, what *happened* over the weekend," he rephrases.

I furrow my eyebrows at him. "You mean, because this weekend is when you *read* it?"

He matches my confused expression. "Read what?"

And then I freeze and squint at him, trying to draw information from his eyes. "Is this about something you saw on DishnDiss.com?"

His face twists in more confusion. "What's Dishndiss.com?"

Oh my God. He doesn't know!

I should have realized. I mean, Brian is probably the least likely person in the world to read Dishndiss.com. He's too busy reading *Time* magazine and *Newsweek* for relevant illegal immigration articles. Why would someone like Brian Harris, bless his soul, care about celebrity gossip?

"So, this isn't about anything you've *read* recently?" I confirm, studying his face for clues.

"No," he replies, still somewhat lost. "It's about what happened at the overnight debate tournament."

And then it suddenly dawns on me.

He wants to talk about the kiss.

But I don't want to talk about the kiss. I don't want to even think about the kiss. Hopefully in a few weeks I'll be going to the winter formal with Hunter and that's all that matters. That kiss meant nothing. And there's no point in dwelling on something that doesn't mean anything.

I have to preempt him. I have to take control and change the subject.

"Oh," I reply, my face brightening. "Right. The tournament. Of course. I've been meaning to talk to you about that, too."

He exhales loudly, his face falling in seeming relief. "Oh, good. Maybe you should go first."

I take a deep breath and begin the speech I rehearsed in front of the mirror last night when I got home from Colorado Springs. "Well, I think we both know I'm not very good at this, you know, *debate* thing. And although I had fun and I'm grateful that you gave me the opportunity to try it, it's pretty obvious that it's not really for me. So it's probably best that I just bow out now."

I cringe inwardly and wait for his response.

"You're quitting?" he practically yells.

I bite my lip and nod timidly. "Yes."

"But you're just starting to get the hang of it. You can't quit now. The Greeley Invitational is coming up after Thanksgiving. It's one of the biggest tournaments of the year."

"Uh . . ." I stutter, trying to come up with something intelligent and convincing to say but failing miserably.

"Is this because of what happened in the hotel room?"

"The hotel room?" I repeat, playing dumb. Because truthfully, it's all I've got right now.

"The bathroom," he clarifies through gritted teeth.

"You mean the dare?" I ask, scrunching my forehead and feigning cluelessness.

He throws his hands up in frustration. "Yes, the dare!"

I laugh off his speculation. "Of course not. That has nothing to do with it. I just don't think I'm very good at debate. It's really not . . . you know . . . my thing. I think you'd be better off finding a partner who can be an asset to you as opposed to a liability."

Brian rises from his chair and starts pacing the length of

the room. Then he stops abruptly and his eyes narrow into a very suspicious glare. "Why are you really doing this?" he demands.

"I . . . I already told you," I falter, suddenly unable to meet his penetrating stare. "It's not my thing. And I'm not really enjoying it."

"No," he argues, taking a menacing step toward me. "That's not the real reason."

"Yes it is," I insist, starting to get irritated. Is he accusing me of lying? After I bared my soul to him and everyone on Saturday night?

"I think there's another reason."

I rise up out of my seat and face him with my arms crossed. "Well, there's not."

We're in total standoff mode now, each of us staring the other one down and neither daring to look away first. But after a few moments of heavy silence, he backs down. His posture loosens and his eyes soften. Then he looks right into me and with a quiet, vulnerable voice—almost like a child's—asks, "But what about us?"

I relax as well and reach out to touch his arm. "Brian," I begin gently. "Don't worry. I'm sure you'll find another debate partner. One who's ten times more qualified than me."

"No," he says, lowering his head half an inch. "What about *us*? As in you and me. What about the kiss?"

At first I think he's joking, which is why I chuckle. But once I notice he's not sharing in the amusement, I wipe the smirk from my face and nervously tuck a strand of hair behind my ear. "Um," I start uneasily. "That was a dare, remember? I was only doing what Katy told me to do."

"No," Brian says again, this time so quickly it makes me

blink. "You were *dared* to go in the bathroom with me. You *chose* to kiss me."

"Brian," I say, my voice measured and my palms starting to sweat. "It's pretty obvious what 'going into the bathroom together' is supposed to mean. It was just a *dare*."

"I think we both know that kiss was more than just a dare," he fires back. "That it meant something."

His comment renders me speechless. *More than just a dare?* No, I've already been through this. It couldn't have been more than a dare. This is Brian Harris we're talking about. Sure, he's cute and sweet and probably gets me more than anyone else in this school but he's a *friend*. Someone you goof around with. Debate illegal immigration with. Discuss John Steinbeck novels with. Not someone you go out with. Not someone you *make* out with. At least not unless it involves a harmless game of Truth or Dare.

So why is he trying to turn this into something it's not?

"Did *any* of it mean anything to you?" he asks, interrupting my silence. "The debate team? The field trip? The overnight?"

The question hangs in the air, dripping down on me like a leaky water balloon ready to burst. I can't answer it. Not because I'm afraid to, but because I don't know the answer. Up until this moment, Brian has been just a question on a blog. A possible option on a multiple-choice poll. I guess I never thought he'd ever turn into an actual person.

But my silence is apparently answer enough. Because his shoulders slouch and his head falls forward. He looks like a blow-up pool toy that someone has let the air out of.

"That's fine," he says, puffing himself up a bit. "You know what? You don't even have to quit. I'm kicking you off the team."

Then he storms out the door.

EMPTY SPACES

The public bus is crowded and somewhat smelly but it's the only source of transportation I have. I can't call my parents because I'm *supposed* to be waiting outside the school right now for my mom to pick me up and take me to the construction site. I can't ask Shayne to drive me in her new car because I know she would never approve of my destination request. And I definitely can't ask Brian to drive me because he clearly wants nothing to do with me anymore.

So the bus it is.

I have to change buses twice and sit next to a middle-aged man who's singing to himself, but an hour later, I finally arrive at the Centennial Nursing Home. Why did I choose this specific location? I'm not really sure. Maybe because it's far enough away to feel like I'm really escaping. Or maybe because it's pretty much guaranteed that no one in here has read my blog. Or *a* blog period.

Or maybe because Mrs. Moody is, ironically, the only person I want to see right now.

I decide to sneak in the back door to avoid having to deal

with Carol when I pass by the reception desk or Gail when I pass by the activity room. As I creep down the hall toward room 4A, I'm looking forward to curling up on that uncomfortable plastic chair with a copy of a *You Choose the Story* in my hands and watching as Mrs. Moody leads our adventure down every wrong path she can think of. I'm looking forward to focusing on someone else's choices for a change.

But when I push the door open and quietly announce myself, there's no answer. And the first thing I notice is the top of the dresser that stands by the door. It's usually covered with all her tiny knickknacks and figurines. Not today. Today, it's empty. Like someone cleared off the entire thing with one long sweep of their hand.

Worried, I step hesitantly into the room. "Mrs. Moody. What happened to all your—"

The breath flows out of me as soon I see the bare shelves on the bookcase, and my heart stops as soon as I see the bare mattress on the bed. The sheets have been stripped off. The room has been evacuated.

And that's when the anger comes.

I spin on my heels and march straight to the nurses' station. Harriet is bent over the back of the chair, showing a new nurse how to do something on the computer. I bang my fist against the countertop so hard it shakes the monitor and knocks a cup of pens to the floor.

"Where did you send her?"

Harriet peers up at me and her shoulders immediately fall. I can see it on her face. She knew she'd have to deal with me eventually and now that time has come. "Brooklyn," she begins, her voice pointed and patronizing.

"No!" I growl. "You told me you would let her stay. She was making progress. The dog visits were going to change everything. She just needed some more time."

"Brooklyn," she repeats, her eyebrows furrowing. "You need to listen."

"No, *you* need to listen!" I scream back. I have no idea why I'm getting so upset. Mrs. Moody isn't even very nice to me. But I know there is no one else in the world that is going to stick up for her. Because she doesn't have anyone else.

I guess we're kind of similar that way.

"You can't just give up on people like that! You can't just turn your back on them because they make *one* mistake. You can't send them away so you don't have to deal with them anymore!"

"Brooklyn, I didn't send her anywhere," Harriet says, her eyes focusing intently on mine. "Mrs. Moody passed away yesterday."

Suddenly my entire body is numb. I can't feel my legs. I can't feel my feet. My brain has turned to mush. My throat stings. Like someone poured acid down it. "Passed away as in . . . ?"

"I'm really sorry," she offers.

"But . . . she was . . ."

"She was old," Harriet explains. "And she was terminally ill. Most of the patients here are."

I nod weakly. I don't know what else to say. Or if there's even anything left *to* say. And I definitely don't want to hang around here while Harriet gives me pitying looks. So I turn and start walking. I don't know where I'm going. I just go. Gail appears from somewhere and asks me if I want to talk, but I don't hear anything. It's all white noise. Like static on the radio. The space between frequencies. The space between awarenesses.

The crazy one-eyed mumbler guy is suddenly in front of me. I'm not sure how he got there or where he came from, but he's there all the same.

"Hah yoh suh mah pah-puh swa-ha?"

"No," I tell him blankly, walking right by. "I'm sorry. I haven't seen your purple sweater."

I pass through the front doors and fall onto a wooden bench at the side of the parking lot. It's freezing outside but that's okay. I'm already frozen.

I have no idea how long I've been sitting here by the time my mom shows up. Time seems to have stood still. But I do know she's not very happy with me. I can tell from the tone in her voice. The way she grabs me by the elbow, leads me to the passenger seat, and shuts the door with a bang behind me.

I watch as she comes around the front of the car. I watch as Gail hurries out of the building and they exchange a few words. I watch my mom's face transform. Soften. Fall.

Then I listen to her apologies. The entire drive home. I listen to her speech about death and acceptance and grieving. It sounds like it's straight from a self-help book. *How to Help Your Teenage Daughter Deal with Loss*.

I listen, but I don't absorb it.

I don't absorb anything.

Why do I feel like I lost more than just a moody old lady today? Why do I feel like nothing in my life makes sense? Why do I feel like, despite every attempt I've made to relinquish all decision-making power in my life, I've still made a terrible choice?

As soon as we get home, I go straight to my room. I close the door. I sit down at my computer and I log on to my blog account. When it asks me if I really want to delete my blog, I don't hesitate. I don't second-guess. I just click "Yes" and then I slam my laptop closed.

BACK ON TOP

The phone rings at seven. The caller ID comes up "Unknown," but as soon as I hear the voice on the other end, I know exactly who it is.

"Hey, biatch."

"Shayne," I say numbly, feeling a strange mix of disappointment and relief. Disappointment because I kind of hoped it would be someone else. And relief because I'm not sure I could have dealt with anyone else right now.

"What are you doing?"

I glance around my room. I haven't left it since my mom brought me home from the nursing home. "Nothing much."

"Well, put on something cute 'cause we're going out."

I think about a lot of things in that moment. Some that matter and some that don't. Some that seem to make a difference in my life and some that seem pointless. I think about the party. The fire. The courthouse. I think about Shayne's heartfelt apology speech in the car this morning.

I think about Brian.

I think about Hunter.

I think about choices.

And then I hear myself saying, "Sounds good. Pick me up in fifteen."

Shayne arrives in her illegal indulgence mobile and we head over to Billy Jenkins's house because his parents are out of town and they left the liquor cabinet unlocked. The regular crew is there and it feels good to be back among them. Speaking their language, laughing at their jokes, valuing their values. It all comes so easily to me, it's almost as though I never even left. I guess some things are just in your blood. Some things you never forget.

And when Shayne and I walk through the front doors of the school together the next morning and begin our familiar catwalk down the main hallway, people notice. Heads turn. Lips murmur. Eyes stare. With Shayne's hand hooked into the crook of my elbow, bringing me up to speed on all the gossip that I've missed over the past few weeks, telling me how much she loves my accessories and whatever creative thing I've done with my eye shadow that morning, I feel safe. I feel content.

I feel like I've come home.

At first the deletion of my blog seems to upset people. Everyone has a theory about why it suddenly vanished. Some even go so far as to speculate that BB4Life has been assassinated, but after a few days people seem to forget all about it. Or at least they stop lamenting its disappearance. Plus, DishnDiss.com posted some site where you can play matchmaker to a bunch of cartoon characters and after that I'm pretty much old news.

Not that I mind in the slightest.

Hunter asks me to the winter formal again and this time I don't hesitate. I just say yes while Shayne claps ecstatically next to me and gushes about how perfect it will be for the four of us to go together: Hunter and me and Shayne and Jesse.

She assures me that I've made the right choice. That Hunter is a guaranteed stock booster. Beautiful and popular and highly sought after by every girl in the school. And according to Shayne, "What else could you ask for in a guy?"

I tell her I can't really think of anything.

But the truth is I don't really try. With Shayne, it's always a rhetorical question. It's never meant to be answered.

After that, Hunter starts to sit with us at lunch every day. And every time he leans over and whispers flirtatious things in my ear or plants delicious kisses on my cheek, I notice Shayne nodding in approval out of the corner of my eye. And there's always this comforting sense of satisfaction and relief that accompanies Hunter's displays of affection. Like a weight has been lifted. Like after so many detours, my life is finally back on track.

The struggle is over.

By the time school lets out for Thanksgiving break, I've managed to assimilate seamlessly back into my old life. I'm reinstated as Shayne's second in command. I've reclaimed my coveted seat next to her at the center table. Recovered my high-ranking status at our school.

And you know what? I've never been happier.

Life is more glamorous at the top. People respect you. They move out of the way when you walk by. They talk about what you're wearing and what you were seen doing the night before.

Things are much simpler here, too. There are fewer choices to be made. Shayne and I go to the mall and she picks out my next favorite pair of jeans. We go to the food court and she tells me what I can eat and still manage to fit into those jeans. We cruise the makeup counters and she tells me which colors bring out my eyes and which ones make me look dead. We see a table full of hot guys and she decides whether or not they're worth talking to.

There's less to think about. And I like it like that.

Maybe I was never meant to be a leader. Maybe I was never meant to tackle huge decisions all on my own. Maybe I'm just a natural-born sidekick.

And if I try hard enough, I can *almost* make myself believe that the past six weeks never even happened.

THE TOAST OF HARVARD

Brian is the exception.

Thoughts of him are like ghosts from my former life—my *temporary* life, as I've come to call it—returning from the dead to haunt me. To remind me of what I left behind. In ruins.

No matter how hard I try, I still can't seem to fully erase his presence. His voice lingers in my ears. His face appears around every corner. The pain in his eyes is still fresh in my mind.

"I think we both know that kiss was more than just a dare."

That sentence follows me wherever I go. Taunting me. Provoking me. Challenging me to refute it. Challenging me to debate the other side of the resolution. And as much as I want to, I can't do it. I can't find one convincing argument to support a contrasting point of view.

It's Truth or Dare all over again. Except this time, I don't want to play the game. I don't want to choose either one. The truth is too destructive. But the dare is too exposing.

And now all I'm left with is an answered question.

My sister's flight arrives at eleven a.m. on Wednesday morning and my mom insists the whole family be there to greet her when she steps off the plane.

Izzie looks so different, I barely even recognize her. She used to have this kind of bland, dishwater-colored, stick-straight hair that did nothing except lie there like a dead appendage. She wore barely any makeup and her clothes were always straight out of a JC Penney catalog. It never bothered me before because at least I never had to worry about her raiding my closet.

Now her hair is dyed honey blond and cut in cute layers. Her eyes are dramatized, her lips are lined, and her clothes are actually somewhat fashionable. She has this kind of hip, East Coast preppy look. And as soon as I see her walk out of the security doors, the only thing I can think is *Great. Now she's smart* and *stylish. What's left for me?*

"Did you join a sorority?" I ask as she wraps her arms around me and pulls me into a hug.

She laughs and ruffles my hair like I'm five years old. "Don't be preposterous, Brooks. When you go to Harvard, you don't have time for *sororities*." The way she pronounces the word makes me cringe. Like she just stepped in dog poo.

I want to say something to the effect that I would never go to college and not join the Greek system since Shayne and I have been planning to pledge the same sorority since we were twelve, but I'm not given the opportunity. Izzie starts blabbing the minute she steps off the plane and doesn't stop the entire ride home.

Seriously, the girl can't shut up. She's like one of those creepy talking dolls . . . on steroids. She uses words you'd only see in the verbal section of the SATs, and she switches subjects so rapidly I almost want to pop open the back of her head and check if she's running on batteries.

She yaps about how her art history class has given her such an in-depth appreciation of some French painter I've never heard of. She gripes about the socioeconomic climate of our country and how we're all to blame for global warming. And then she claims that her Judaic studies class has inspired her to take a tour around Eastern Europe to visit the concentration camps.

"But we're not even Jewish," I point out.

She turns toward me with this pitying look on her face and says, "*Nie wieder*, Brooklyn. Those who cannot remember the past are condemned to repeat it."

Did she just speak to me in German?

But before I can fully digest her last sentence, she's already chattering about something else entirely.

Her energy level doesn't falter for an instant. Even after we've arrived home. For a day and a half I don't think I see my sister sit down once. She's like a bee buzzing around from room to room. One minute she's helping my mom in the kitchen with food preparation, the next she's carrying firewood into the house with my dad, and then she's wandering around my bedroom, fidgeting with stuff and asking me questions about boys and life as if we're best friends.

If there's one thing my sister and I have never been, it's friends. Never mind *best* friends. I see all those movies where two sisters are inseparable and share everything, including their hearts and souls. Well, that's about as inaccurate a description of Izzie and me as you can get. We've been fighting for as long as I can remember. Now that we're older, we've matured a bit. Meaning that we no longer roll around on the ground and try to pull each other's hair out. Our fighting consists of shallow jabs and manipulative head games.

That's why I find it incredibly suspicious when she comes into my room on Thursday morning and bounces onto my bed while I'm trying to get through the first act of *Twelfth Night*.

"Hey, sissy. I'm bored. Let's go somewhere."

I give her a strange look. The lighting in my bedroom is making her pupils look huge. And kind of scary. This is definitely feeling like a trap. "That's okay," I say, shaking my head. "I think I'll just hang out here. I need to finish this."

"Oh, Brooks," she says, ruffling my hair again. I really hope this doesn't become a habit. "You're so obdurate sometimes."

"Whatever," I mumble, refocusing on my book.

She tilts her head to get a better look at the cover. "Are you reading that for school?"

I roll my eyes. "No, I'm reading it for fun. Of course it's for school."

She jumps off my bed, grabs my iPod from my desk, and starts scanning through my playlists. "That's so funny because that BB4Life girl was reading it, too."

Suddenly, *Twelfth Night* is no longer of any interest to me. It falls from my hands and plops onto the bed. "Who?"

"Don't tell me you haven't heard of that blog! MyLife Undecided.com."

"Oh," I say, chuckling weakly. "Right. *That.*"

"Everyone on campus was *so* into it."

"At Harvard?" I ask in disbelief.

"Yeah. When it got shut down, people went crazy. They were so pissed. Everyone on my floor was taking bets about who she was going to end up with."

"What do you mean?" My voice comes out almost in a whisper.

I watch as my sister discovers an underwater basketball game on my desk and becomes obsessed with trying to flip the submerged ball through the hoop.

"Rhett Butler or Heimlich," she says, as though it's obvious.

"Heimlich?" I choke out. "Why would she end up with Heimlich? She wasn't even dating him. I mean, she didn't even really like him. Not in that way, anyway."

Frustrated, she shakes the game and makes another attempt to steer the orange ball into the basket. "Yeah, but you know how girls can be. The guy you're really supposed to be with can be standing right in front of you and you don't even notice because you're too distracted by the one you *think* you're supposed to be with. It happens all the time. Sometimes the most obvious choices are the hardest to see."

I swallow. It hurts. Like a chicken bone pushing its way down my throat.

"They are?"

She sticks her tongue out in deep concentration and finally, with one swift jerk of the plastic, water-filled container, she gets the little orange basketball to sail through the red hoop. She throws her arms up in victory. "Score!"

"Izzie," I start, trying to sound as conversational as possible. "If you met BB, I mean, if she was your friend or something. What would you tell her to do?"

She places the game down on my desk and bounces back over to the DVDs. "I'd tell her to put her stupid blog back up so I'd have something to read during study breaks."

"No. I mean, about Heimlich and—"

"Oh my God!" she exclaims, yanking a DVD from the stack, causing the rest of them to topple over onto the floor. "I haven't seen this movie in ages! Remember how we used to watch it over and over again?"

"Yeah," I mutter. "I remember. But—"

"I'm going to go watch it now!" she resolves, hugging the case to her chest and waltzing out the door, leaving me with nothing . . . except a mess of DVDs to clean up.

Thanksgiving dinner in our house hasn't changed much over the years. It's always the same motley assortment. Me, my parents, my sister, my senile grandparents on my dad's side, and my crazy, middle-aged, and bitterly divorced aunt Linda.

By four o'clock, everyone is assembled around the table and the familiar sounds of a holiday meal fill the room. Silverware clanking against the good china. Slurping of wine. Bad jokes being told. Polite laughter.

It isn't until my plate is nearly empty that I notice that Izzie hasn't touched hers. And she hasn't said a word since she sat down either. She's been too busy fidgeting with her napkin holder. Sliding it on and off her fingers like a giant wooden ring.

"Izzie?" I ask, watching her questioningly. "Are you all right? You seem kind of restless."

"Of course I'm all right," she snaps, causing everyone at the table to halt their conversations and look up. This seems to piss my sister off even more. She groans and gives me an evil look. As though it's completely my fault that everyone is now staring at her. "Jeez. Chill out, everybody. I'm just stressed. Harvard is really hard, okay? Finals are starting as soon I get back to school and you have no idea how much pressure is on me right now."

"Izzie?" my mom begins tentatively.

"What?" she roars back. "What is everyone's problem?" Then, out of nowhere, she starts rubbing obsessively at her hands, as though she's trying to scrape dirt off. "And what's with all the bugs in this house? They're crawling all over me."

If the room wasn't silent enough before, now it's deadly still. My dad scoots his chair out and starts to come over to our end of the table. "Izzie," he says tenderly. "Maybe we should go get some fresh air."

But she's too quick for him. She violently pushes her chair back with a loud scrape against the hardwood floor and leaps to her feet. "I don't need fresh air," she insists. "I need everyone to stop nagging me."

I'm assuming from the way she throws her napkin down on the table that her plan is to make a dramatic exit from the dining room, but she doesn't get very far. She takes one step and collapses onto the floor.

Then I hear my mother scream.

THE PRICE OF PERFECTION

Since having children, my mom has had to endure three ambulance rides to the hospital. The first was when I was rescued from the abandoned mine shaft after having been stuck down there for two days. The second was when I was eight years old and a neighborhood kid dared me to take a swig from a bottle of 409 cleaner. And the third was two years ago when I stopped eating for three days so I could fit into a pair of size zero designer jeans that Shayne had handed down to me because she'd decided they were "too big" for her.

The common denominator in all of these tragic events, of course, is me.

I've always been the one lying on the stretcher. I've always been the one making the near fatal mistake. I've never once been in the car *behind* the ambulance.

Not until today.

My dad drives in silence, following the flashing lights in front of us. The large red and white van that holds my mom and my unconscious sister.

It's an entirely different experience sitting in this seat. The regret has been replaced with paralyzing fear. The shame for once again having disappointed my parents has been replaced with a mind-numbing panic. And the uncertainty of whether I'll be forgiven has been replaced with whether I'll ever see my sister alive again.

I'm not sure which side of the equation is worse.

The EMTs weren't able to tell us much. Except that her heart was beating abnormally fast and somewhat erratically. She has a fever of one hundred and two and her pupils are heavily dilated. We've been promised more information once we arrive at the hospital.

It feels like we've been driving for hours and I don't understand why they're taking her so far away. It isn't until I see the signs for Parker Adventist Hospital up ahead that I realize it's only been a few minutes. Time slows down in the shadow of sirens. I guess that's something I should know by now.

My sister is wheeled in through the emergency entrance and I follow her stretcher with my eyes until it disappears through a set of double swinging doors. My parents follow behind her while I wait in the lobby with my grandparents and my aunt. They try to talk to me, to keep me distracted, but I don't hear anything. They're like characters in a silent movie. I stand very still and watch the doors for signs of life.

I wonder if this is how Mrs. Moody went. If her last moments on earth were frenzied and chaotic like this. Doctors fighting to save her. Nurses running to and fro. Or if she just drifted away peacefully in her sleep.

I hope, for her sake, it was the latter.

My dad emerges a half hour later and I search his face for a hint of my sister's condition. For some reason I can't wait for him to speak. I need some indication of what to expect before the words start flowing. I have to have that extra split second to prepare myself.

"She's okay," he says, and I hear the sighs of relief from the rest of my family envelop me like a warm blanket. "She's going to be just fine."

But I can't exhale yet. I need more than that. "What happened to her?"

My dad collapses into one of the waiting room chairs and motions for me to sit down next to him.

"Your sister has been under a lot of stress at school," he explains. "Harvard is a lot harder than she expected—definitely harder than high school—and the pressure ended up being too much for her to handle. She started using a drug called Adderall."

My forehead crinkles. "The one they prescribe for ADD kids?"

He nods.

"I didn't know she had a prescription for that," I say.

My dad sighs. "She didn't. But according to the doctor, it's a very sought-after drug on Ivy League campuses. People manage to get prescriptions and then sell it to other students. They use it as a study aid. It helps you focus. And with the competitive landscape at Harvard, Izzie just found it too hard to resist."

"So what? She overdosed?"

My dad lowers his head. "Yes. Adderall does help you focus but it also speeds up your heart rate. And if you take too much of it, it can be very dangerous. It can also make you act erratically."

"But she's going to be okay?" I confirm.

My dad drapes an arm over my shoulder and squeezes. "She's going to be fine."

"Can I see her?"

He pushes himself back to his feet. "Of course. Come on, I'll take you."

I follow tentatively behind my father as he leads me through a series of long corridors. The smell of disinfectant is overwhelming and I'm reminded of the Centennial Nursing Home where I've spent so many of my weekends over the past couple of months.

My dad enters a patient room but I choose to linger in the doorway. My sister is awake and talking, but she looks so strange in her blue hospital gown with tubes hooked up to various parts of her body that I have trouble approaching her. Her skin is pale and her arms lie like limp strands of spaghetti by her sides.

One word flashes to mind as I watch her. And it's a word I've never used to describe my sister in all my life.

Defeated.

Suddenly I feel like the wind has been knocked out of me. Like the world has been turned upside down.

This can't be right. This has to be a dream.

Izzie doesn't make mistakes. She doesn't do things that land her in hospital beds or police stations or on the eleven o'clock evening news. That's *my* area of expertise. Izzie is the smart one. The one who makes *good* decisions. The perfect one.

But the beeping heart monitors are screaming otherwise. The scribblings on the chart that hangs on the outside of the door are spelling another story. The pink curtain that divides the room in two is pulled back to reveal a very different truth.

That no one is perfect.

That anyone can suffer from a momentary lapse of judgment.

Even Isabelle Pierce.

"Brooks." My mom beckons to me. "It's okay. You can come in."

Upon hearing my name, Izzie struggles to turn her head toward the door. A smile fights its way to the surface.

"I'm going to get some coffee," my mom tells us. "Dan, will you come with me?"

As my parents disappear out the door, I step hesitantly toward Izzie and reach for her hand.

"How you feeling?"

"Pretty stupid," she replies with a weak laugh.

I laugh, too. But only because I feel like I'm supposed to. Not because there's anything funny about this. "You scared me," I tell her in a scratchy voice.

"I know," she admits softly. "I'm sorry."

I squeeze my fingers around her hand and force out a smile. "It's okay. I'm just glad you're all right."

Izzie sighs and turns her head out the window. The sun is setting, leaving the sky a beautiful shade of coral pink. "No, I mean, I'm sorry I failed you."

My grasp automatically loosens and I shake my head at her, baffled.

"When we were little," she explains, "Mom and Dad told me that you looked up to me. I didn't believe them. But I always thought, you know, just in case, I should probably set a good example. So I've always tried to be this perfect role model for you. The perfect older sister. But tonight, I wasn't. And I'm sorry."

"Don't be," I assure her, glancing up at the IV bag hanging over our heads and reaching out to catch one of her tears on the tip of my finger. "I never liked you very much when you were perfect. You're much cooler now that you're human."

THE OTHER SIDE
OF MOODY

After Mrs. Moody's death, my mom offered to call Lawyer
Bob and have him request a transfer so I could complete the rest
of my community service requirement elsewhere but I refused,
insisting that all I needed was one weekend off and then I would
be fine to go back.

My sister was released from the hospital yesterday and is
now enjoying a relaxing day in front of the TV while I find myself walking back through the front doors of Centennial Nursing
Home.

Gail keeps me extremely busy for the first half of the day. I
think she feels obligated to distract me. And she's been doing a
pretty good job at it. She jam-packed the schedule with games
and special events and even a field trip to the park where we play
croquet with some of the more active residents.

But now things are starting to die down around here and
people are getting tired and retiring to their rooms for extended
naps. I've set myself up in the activity room with Rummikub,

but so far no one has wandered over to play. Jane, my regular Rummikub partner, is staying at her daughter's house for the Thanksgiving holiday and I've learned rather quickly that playing Rummikub by yourself is not only boring but nearly impossible.

After winning three games of solitaire, I finally decide to take a stroll down the corridor to see if the nurses need help with anything but I find the station empty. So I keep walking. I know exactly where I'm going, I'm just not sure if I really want to go there. But my feet seem to have a mind of their own, and before I can convince them to turn around, I'm standing in the middle of room 4A.

It's empty. Uninhabited. Apparently they've yet to admit any new residents.

I pull the orange plastic chair into the middle of the room and plop down into it. Then I wait. Except after five minutes, I realize I don't know what I'm waiting for. It's strange. How someone can be here one minute and then gone the next.

I've never known anyone who's died before. All of my grandparents are still alive. My mom is allergic to dogs and cats so we've never really had any pets. My sister and I got a turtle when we were younger but he died a few days later so I don't think that counts since I never really got to know him very well.

When I close my eyes, I can almost still feel her in the room. I picture her in the bed, her bony, vein-covered hands grasping tightly at the covers. I wonder where they took her. After she died. Was she buried? Cremated? Is it bad that I never thought to ask?

"Excuse me?" A voice startles me and I leap out of the chair.

I look up to see a middle-aged man standing in the doorway dressed in a pair of jeans and a sport coat. The kind with leather patches on the elbows. He's carrying a large box and a manila envelope.

"Sorry," I say, pushing the chair back into the corner. "I was just leaving."

He takes a step into the room. "Actually, I'm looking for someone named Baby Brooklyn. The receptionist said I might find her in here."

The mention of the nickname catches me off guard but I put my hand to my chest and say, "Um, I guess that's me."

He seems to find humor in this because his lips curl into a smile. "With a name like that, I didn't know what age to expect."

"Well, it's not really my name."

He looks at his feet. "No, of course not. I didn't think— Never mind. I'm here to deliver this to you." He heaves the box forward and sets it down at my feet.

"What is it?" I ask, eyeing it skeptically.

"It was left for you by Gertrude Moody."

"*Mrs.* Moody?"

He offers me a tight-lipped smile. "Yes." He removes a thick stack of papers from the manila envelope and flips to a page in the middle. "In her will, she asked that these be given to you. Well, to 'Baby Brooklyn,' rather."

"Oh, you must be her lawyer," I say, eyeing the papers.

"No," the man replies, looking extremely uncomfortable. "But her lawyer sent me."

I delicately lift the lid of the box and peer inside. Filling the box, all neatly stacked in rows, are the familiar blue and white bindings of Mrs. Moody's *You Choose the Story* collection.

"Oh my gosh," I cry, bending down to pull out a random title. "Thank you so much!"

He seems to find fulfillment in my reaction. "You're welcome. The nurses here said that you used to read these to her."

I nod, a prick of moisture stinging my eyes as I run my hand over the book's worn and weathered cover. I flip it open and catch sight of the "This Book Belongs To" sticker adhered to the inside.

My head pops up and I stare inquisitively at the man standing in front of me. "Wait a minute," I say, touching the sticker. "If you aren't her lawyer, then who *are* you?"

"Oh, I doubt she ever mentioned me." He dismisses my question with a disheartened smile. "My name is Nicholas Townley. I'm her son."

"*You're* Nicholas Townley?" I ask, giving the stranger another once-over. I'm not sure what I expected Nicholas Townley to look like and that's probably because I never expected to actually meet him. The only proof I had that he even existed were these stickers and a mangled photograph of a four-year-old boy in red overalls, holding a daisy.

He shifts his weight awkwardly. "So she did mention me."

I snort out a laugh. "Well, I wouldn't say that, exactly."

"Then how do you know about me?"

I flip the book around in my hand and show him the scribbled label. "Because your name is in all of these books. And when I asked her who you were, she nearly had a heart attack."

Recognition registers on the man's face and he nods solemnly. "Yeah, that sounds about right."

"If you're her son," I begin accusingly, "then why did you never come to visit her when she was alive?"

"I didn't know she was here!" he defends, pain shadowing his eyes and the deep lines around his mouth. "She refused to see me or take my calls or even tell me where she was living."

I cross my arms over my chest. "Why would she do that? And why did she react to your name like that?"

His shoulders fall in defeat and he looks to the ground. "We had a falling-out. Years ago. I told her I was getting married and she freaked out. Said she never wanted to see me again. That I was 'dead' to her."

Skepticism infiltrates my tone. "All because you were getting married?"

"All because I was getting married to a *man*," he clarifies.

"Oh."

"I tried to contact her. I tried to reconcile several times. But this was her choice. And when my mother makes a decision, that's the end. It's no use trying to change her mind."

I glance down at the *You Choose the Story* in my hand. Coincidentally it's the one about the island inhabited by vampires, the first title I ever read to her. I hug it to my chest. "I know," I whisper, a slight smile forming.

"And so we never spoke again. After my dad died about ten years ago, she changed her name back to her maiden name— Moody—and just like that, it was as if we weren't even related anymore. Until her lawyer called me to tell me that she had passed away and that her things could be collected at this address . . . if I was interested."

"I'm sorry," I mumble, fidgeting with the book in my hand, opening the cover and flipping through the yellowed pages. Then I eye the box by my feet, crammed full of adventures just waiting to be taken, and I think about the sticker inside each one of them, declaring their rightful owner. "These books belonged to you, didn't they?"

He leans down and pulls one from the cardboard box, laughing nostalgically as he reads the title. "They used to be my favorite," he tells me, fingering the binding. "She used to read them to *me* when I was little. Every night before I went to bed. She'd let me make all the choices. And when we'd reach a dead end, she'd always let me start over . . . until I found the ending I was looking for."

I laugh, too. Because suddenly everything about my long hours spent in Mrs. Moody's room at the nursing home makes perfect sense.

I return the book in my hand to the box and push it toward him. "You should really keep these."

But he shakes his head and takes a step toward the door. "My mom wanted you to have them. And I want to respect her choice. For once. Because God knows, there were many of them that I never could."

"Thank you," I whisper, hoisting the box of books into my arms. "For bringing these over here."

He gives me an awkward sort of wave. "No problem."

"Well, if it makes you feel any better," I try, "she wouldn't let me read anything else to her."

"Thanks. It does. A little." A strained smile appears as he turns to leave.

"Wait!" I call, struck by a last-minute thought. I dig through the box until I find the book I'm looking for, then I flip through its discolored pages until I arrive at the photograph.

Nicholas Townley, age 4.

"Here," I say, handing it over to him. "I found it in one of the books. For whatever it's worth . . ."

I can tell that he's no longer comfortable being here. He takes the picture from my hand, thanks me again, and is gone within a matter of seconds.

I'm alone again. And even though the majority of Mrs. Moody's mysterious secret past has finally been revealed, I still don't feel any better about her absence. She left behind a hole. A giant, gaping hole. And it's too late to fill it. It will always be there, casting a gloomy shadow on Nicholas Townley's life.

And I guess, in a way, casting a shadow on mine as well.

Because suddenly it dawns on me. Mrs. Moody and I are the same. We're built from the same mold. A mold of poor judgment and a propensity to make terrible choices. It's why she liked me. Why she trusted me and no one else. I was the "little girl who fell down the mine shaft." The little girl who became famous for her mistake.

In Mrs. Moody's eyes, I was safe because she saw me as a mirror image of herself.

The room is starting to feel claustrophobic. The walls are closing in, and if I don't get out of here, I fear they're going to squeeze me into pulp.

I dash from the room, down the hallway, and out the back entrance until I'm in the wide-open space of the parking lot. I take a deep breath, the frozen air chilling my lungs and awakening my cells.

I don't want to be like Mrs. Moody. I don't want to be a ninety-year-old woman with a life full of regret. I don't want to wake up one morning seventy-five years from now and discover that my life has been a series of bad decisions and wrong turns and heartbreak.

But what if that's just my destiny? What if I'm doomed to end up right here, in this very nursing home, bitter and irritable and biting the hands of nurses because I'm angry about all the terrible decisions I made? What if, ironically, I don't have a choice?

The moment I get home, I look at my computer and I know what I have to do. It's what I've always had to do, but somewhere along the way, my vision got cloudy and distorted and I strayed from the plan. I can't trust my own decisions. I can't trust my ability to lead myself in the right direction. And I know there's only one thing that will save me from becoming her. Or more important, that will save me from myself.

MY LIFE UNDECIDED

CAUGHT IN THE MIDDLE

Posted on: Saturday, November 27th at 11:01 pm by BB4Life

I know I owe you all an explanation. I know you probably have a lot of questions. And I know that some of you may even be mad at me. But I hope it will suffice to say that I'm sorry. I'm sorry for abandoning the blog. I'm sorry for abandoning you. I can't go into the full details of my previous decision to jump ship but I'm here now because once again I need your help. I need you to help steer me down the right path with your wisdom. To keep me from doing something I'll regret later.

Do you remember Rhett Butler? Do you remember how charming and beautiful and popular he is? Well, he's asked me to go to the winter formal next week and I've said yes. And I couldn't be more excited about it. Rhett is everything I ever thought I wanted in a boyfriend. He fits effortlessly into my life. Like white on white.

So what's the problem, you ask?

Well, remember Heimlich? My cute and somewhat dorky debate partner? He's exactly the opposite of anyone I ever thought I would fall for. In fact, before this blog, I never even gave him a second look (or a first look, for that matter). But now that I've seen him, I can't look away. Somehow he's managed to find a way into my thoughts and he won't leave. Somehow he's managed to *get* me, even when I don't.

And here lies my dilemma.

What are you supposed to do when one person makes you feel safe and another person makes you feel alive? It's like I'm caught between two versions of myself. The person I used to be and the person I'm too scared to become. I feel like I'm looking into a mirror and my reflection doesn't match. I just want to be myself again. Only, I'm not sure who that is anymore. Is it the girl in the mirror, the one I've struggled to be my entire life? Or is it this stranger living inside me who wants nothing to do with her? How do you decide between them? How do you know which one is really you? Especially when they're each in love with a different person.

So please, tell me what I'm supposed to do. Tell me who I'm supposed to choose.

I can't do it on my own. I can't see straight. I need your clarity.

Please vote.

Your lost and lonely friend,
BB

MISSING IN ACTION

Shayne hasn't stopped talking about the winter formal since we got back to school. It's all she can think about. Dresses and limos and hairstyles and the gorgeous necklace she found at the mall this weekend. Although I would never say it aloud, I'm honestly getting sick of hearing about it. I mean, does this girl really have nothing else to talk about but clothes and boys and updos? Has she always been like that or is this just the first time I'm noticing it?

"So anyway," she continues as we head to my locker after lunch on Monday. "We should probably go shopping together this week. To make sure we look good next to each other in pictures, but not too matchy matchy, you know?"

"Mm-hm," I agree wholeheartedly.

"My dad booked the limo, so that's all set. Jesse is going to drive down on Saturday afternoon. Tell Hunter that we'll meet up at your place. And then we'll have to keep our ears open for who's hosting the best after party and—"

"Don't forget that tryouts for the spring musical are coming up next week!" a bubbly thespian interrupts, thrusting green flyers into our hands. "We're going to be doing *Wicked*!"

"No way! Really?" Shayne trills, her phony public smile on full display. "That's totally my favorite musical."

The bubbly thespian beams. "Mine, too!"

"We'll totally be there," Shayne promises, and then three steps later balls up the flyer and tosses it into the nearest trash can. "Loser," she mumbles under her breath, relieving me of my flyer and subjecting it to the same fate. "Like I would ever be caught dead in a musical."

We arrive at my locker and Shayne continues to prattle on about some article she read in *Contempo Girl* magazine about the latest trends in eye shadow while I remove my copy of *Twelfth Night* and my English notebook.

"Omigod!" she exclaims in horror, interrupting her own diatribe and frowning at the inside of her sweater sleeve. I roll my eyes into my locker, fighting the urge to ask "Now what?"

But I don't even have to. Shayne thrusts her arm in my face. "Will you look at this stain?"

The fabric is about three inches from my face and I can't see what she's talking about. But of course I can't admit that because then I run the risk of the fabric being shoved two inches closer. So I scrunch up my nose to match Shayne's displeased expression and say, "Yeah, that's pretty bad."

She stomps her foot a little and scowls. "Damn it. I told Lupita to get that stain out. She is *so* totally useless! What on earth are they teaching those people down in El Salvador?"

"You know," I hear myself saying before I can censor it, "Lupita was probably a physicist or a doctor or something before she came here. A lot of immigrants give up much more prestigious jobs in their home countries to become housekeepers and gardeners here. All for the promise of a better life."

As soon as it's out, I immediately regret it. Shayne's eyes narrow and she takes a step toward me. I cower slightly into my locker. And then, just when I think she's totally going to lose it, she starts cackling with laughter. Kind of like a mentally unstable person.

"Oh my God, Brooks. You are *too* funny!"

I laugh, too. But mine comes out more like a stutter.

"Lupita? A doctor?" Shayne hoots. "That's hilarious. Can you imagine? She'd be like, 'This guy's coding. Hand me the Lysol!'"

"Right," I squawk uneasily, and spin around to close my locker door.

"Come on," Shayne says, linking her arm around my elbow. "I'll walk you to English."

As soon as we take off down the hall, a loud "Ding!" comes over the intercom, indicating that there's going to be some kind of all-school announcement.

Normally I would ignore any such broadcasts since they rarely have anything to do with me, but this time I hear the words "Parker High School debate team" and my ears perk up. I have to strain to hear the announcement over Shayne's blathering.

"We want to commend the team on their impressive showing at last weekend's Greeley Invitational Tournament and we want to congratulate all the key players who competed."

This was the big tournament. The one Brian was so excited about.

The announcer starts to ramble off the names of all the members of the debate team, starting with Jake Towers, Katy

Huffington, and Dave Shapiro, and I hold my breath as I wait for Brian's name to be called. I just want to hear it. Aloud. Over the PA speaker. So that for a brief, fleeting moment, I might indulge myself in the memory of what I used to be a part of.

But then I hear the announcer blabbing something about the winter formal this weekend and reminding everyone about the strict no-alcohol-tolerance policy that the school enforces and I realize that she's already changed subjects.

Wait a minute. What happened to Brian's name?

Why wasn't it announced? Was I so busy daydreaming about hearing it that I missed it completely?

"*Hello?* Are you even listening to me?" Shayne is clearly annoyed.

I blink back into the moment and unhook my arm from hers. "Yeah, sorry," I mumble. "Look, I have to make a stop first. I'll see you after class, okay?"

"Whatever," she replies with an eye roll before turning and sashaying away. I start in the opposite direction. Right toward Debate Central.

When I walk in, Ms. Rich is sitting at her desk in the back of the classroom grading papers. She looks up at me and greets me with a smile, which is much better than what I expected—a daggerlike glare.

"Hi, Ms. Rich."

"Brooklyn. How are you doing?"

I bow my head, feeling guilty for even being in here.

"Fine," I say weakly. "I heard the announcement. Congratulations."

She beams. "Thanks. The guys worked really hard for this. They deserved it."

"And Brian?" I ask, hoping this will be enough.

But clearly it isn't because her eyebrows knit together as though she has no idea what I'm referring to. "What about Brian?"

"Well," I stammer. "I just . . . didn't hear his name called. Was he sick or something?"

Her baffled expression doesn't change. "Brian didn't compete."

A very heavy sensation starts to build at the pit of my stomach. Like someone is shoving rocks into my abdomen. "Why not?" I manage to get out after a hard swallow.

"He didn't tell you?"

I shake my head.

Ms. Rich looks conflicted. Like she wants to say something but now she's not sure if she should. "He quit the team," she finally divulges.

"WHAT?" I scream. I didn't mean for it to come out so loudly. It just kind of emerged like that. Involuntarily. "Why?"

"He's starting wrestling next semester so he decided there was really no use in continuing."

"Wrestling?!" Another spontaneous outburst. "But he can't! He doesn't even want to wrestle. His dad is the coach and he's forcing him to. You can ask him yourself."

Ms. Rich surrenders her hands to the air. "I don't know anything about his decision. I just know what he told me."

I can see it's useless to stand here and yell at Ms. Rich about this. She's not the person I'm angry with. The recipient deserving of my fury is waiting in an English classroom down the hall. Waiting to pretend I no longer exist just as I've tried to do to him for the past two weeks.

But I have no intention of playing these silly avoidance games with him today. Today, I exist. And he's not going to be able to pretend otherwise. He's going to have to face me.

I thank Ms. Rich for the information, exit the room, and stomp my way to English, leaving behind only fumes of determination.

THE PUPPET SHOW

Class has already started when I storm into the room and Mrs. Levy reprimands me for being late.

I shoot dirty looks at Brian throughout the entire class. Like a mobster scoping out the guy who ratted on him to the police. He clearly knows something is up. Which is probably why he bolts from the room the minute the bell rings and I have to run to catch him in the hallway.

"Hold it right there," I say, yanking on his elbow and spinning him around to face me.

"What do you want, Brooklyn?" The cold sound of my full name rolling off his tongue chills me to the bone.

"Wrestling?" I ask. "Really?"

He yanks his elbow free of my grasp. "What the heck do you care what I do?"

The question stings. Like a slap in the face. Before you realize what's even happened, there's already a burning red hand mark forming across your cheek. "Because I care, Brian," I insist.

"I care that you quit the debate team—your passion—just because your *dad* told you to."

"You wouldn't understand," Brian growls back.

I hold my ground, my hard stare never faltering. "Try me."

"You don't know what it's like to live with him. To have to deal with him on a daily basis. Sometimes it's not worth the fight. Sometimes it's easier to simply roll over and play dead."

This infuriates me even more. "It's your *life*, Brian! You can't roll over and play dead on your life! You need to make your own decisions."

"Oh yeah? That means a lot coming from *you*," he sneers back.

I narrow my eyes. "What's that supposed to mean?"

"You don't make *any* decisions!" he cries. "You let Shayne Kingsley dictate everything you do. You have a lot of nerve criticizing me when you're just another brainless puppet in her manipulative little puppet show. Going wherever she goes. Saying whatever she tells you to say. Just lying around, waiting for her to yank on one of those invisible strings above your head and make you dance."

I'm seething now. The steam is seeping out through my clenched teeth as he mimes a dancing marionette.

"And you know what really gets me?" Brian continues, his voice quieter but his jawline still tight. "Is that you *have* the choice. You've always had it. And you *chose* to give it up."

"So do you," I whisper harshly.

"No," he says, raising one finger in the air. "That's where you're wrong. With my dad, there's never a choice. *Never.*"

"I don't believe that."

He scoffs at this. "Fine. If you don't believe me, ask my mom. She quit the job she loved to stay home and raise his kids. Or ask my older sister. She's getting married to a guy she doesn't love because he's the son of my dad's best friend. Or ask *Dudley*, even! He was trained to be a hunting dog even though he clearly hates it and whines every time my dad puts him in the back of the truck with a rifle. And now me. I want to debate. I want to graduate high school in two years and go to MIT. I want to major in environmental engineering and build facilities that don't pollute the country's drinking water. But it doesn't matter what I want. My life has already been decided. I'll wrestle for Parker High, I'll get a scholarship to a local state school, and that will be that. Why? Because I. Don't. Have. A. Choice."

Even if I could think of something to say at this moment, there's no way I would be able to get it out. There's no way my brain would be able to tell my mouth to form sounds or my tongue to form words. And so I'm forced to stand there and watch him walk away.

Again.

FROM THE GROUND UP

Construction on the rebuilt model home was finished the day before the winter formal. My mom gave me an exclusive tour after the decorators had moved in all the furniture. It was a very strange sensation walking through it because it was nearly *identical* to the one I burned down less than two months ago. My memory may have erased a few of the smaller details, but from what I could tell, they didn't change a thing.

The same dark red leather couches sat in the living room, with the same cream and brown throw pillows. The same brushed nickel hardware sat atop the bathroom sinks. They even remembered the same plastic vegetables to fill the bowl on the kitchen counter. The greenest green peppers you'll ever see and tomatoes without a single flaw.

Standing in the middle of that living room, I felt like my life had come full circle. That whatever had happened to bring this place to the ground had somehow been undone. Because here it stood. Once again. The same as before.

I'm just finishing up the final touches of my makeup when I hear the e-mail ding in my inbox. Call it sixth sense or whatever but I don't have to look at the screen to know what it is. The winter formal is tonight. The limo is arriving in twenty minutes and Hunter, Shayne, and Jesse will be here any minute to take pictures.

But *that* e-mail is the one that will tell me whether I'm going to be in any of them.

Slowly, warily, I lower myself into my chair and stare at the screen. I see the message—the one that says "Daily Poll Results Summary." It's just waiting to be opened. The subject line taunts me. Tempting me with promises of a resolution. Promises of a life without regret.

I place my hand on the mouse, and, inch by inch, I maneuver the cursor closer and closer to that promised salvation.

Hunter vs. Brian.

It's the question I've been asking myself for longer than I even realized.

And now the answer is here. My blog readers have decided. All two million of them. This time, the people really *have* spoken.

It doesn't matter what I want. It doesn't matter what I *hope* to see when I click that mouse button. The only thing that matters is what is there. What *they* have decided.

I've had more near-death experiences in fifteen years than most people have in a lifetime. I've had more "close calls" than I care to admit. But not during *one* of those times has my life ever flashed before my eyes the way it does in the movies.

I wouldn't call this moment a "near-death" experience, but I would definitely call it a "crossroads," and the images that are swirling through my mind right now are worthy of a movie montage.

There's my sister and the ambulance and the beeping heart monitors. There's Mrs. Moody and her son and her *You Choose the Story* books. There's the fire and the police station and the terrifying courtroom. And finally, there's Brian and his father and the wrestling team.

And that's when I realize.

If I open this e-mail, I'm just as guilty of rolling over and playing dead as he is.

If I click on this mouse button, I'm essentially opting out of my own life. And my only opportunity to live it.

Mistakes can be fixed. Bad decisions can be undone. Model homes can be rebuilt. And perfection is only a word that makes you feel bad about yourself.

My mom knocks on the door to tell me that Hunter and Shayne and Jesse are downstairs.

"Tell them I'll be right down," I say as I stand up, smooth my dress, and check my reflection one more time in the mirror. "There's just one thing I have to do."

As my mom disappears and the door closes behind her, I lean over the back of my chair and press the "Delete" key.

SHATTERED

The limo arrives at eight p.m. and after at least three dozen photographs, Hunter, Shayne, Jesse, and I all pile in and head downtown where the dance is being held at the Marriott. The limo is awesome on the inside. Plush leather seats, a flat screen TV, a fully stocked bar, and a rocking surround sound system. Jesse hooks up his iPod, pours us glasses of champagne, and pretty soon we're cruising down Highway 83 in style. The music is thumping. The booze is flowing. And I'm feeling good. Really good.

I've made my choice, entirely on my own, and I'm happy about it.

"By the way," Shayne tells me as we huddle together on the bench seat while Hunter and Jesse discuss their favorite bands on the other end. "We're making an extra stop."

"What for?" I ask.

"I told this new girl, Brianna Hudgens, that she could come with us."

"Who's that?"

"Oh, just some nobody," Shayne replies dismissively, taking a sip of her champagne. "Her family moved here from Kansas or something."

"If she's just some 'nobody,'" I ask suspiciously, "then why did you invite her?"

A mischievous grin appears across Shayne's lips. "Because her older brother was cast in the next season of *Reality Bites*."

I scowl in confusion. "The MTV show?"

Shayne nods, extremely proud of herself. "Yep. I got an inside scoop. So I figure we should probably befriend her now. You know, in case they come here to film anything."

The limo slows to a stop and I sit and stare at her in absolute astonishment. "Are you joking?"

She stares back at me as if she doesn't understand the question. "No."

"But—"

Shayne quickly shushes me as the limo door opens and Brianna's head pops in. "Hi, guys!" she says.

"Bree!" Shayne cries, like she's greeting a friend she hasn't seen in ages. Brianna climbs inside and Shayne gives her the obligatory air kiss before introducing the rest of us.

I wave and offer her the most enthusiastic salutation I can muster.

Jesse hooks her up with champagne before tapping on the glass divider and telling the driver we're ready to go.

"This is so cool," Brianna exclaims, glancing around the limo. "Thanks so much for inviting me to come along. It's really hard meeting people at a new school."

Shayne's eyes twinkle as her smile broadens. "Of course!" she says, her voice as bubbly as the champagne in her glass. "A party without you is like a martini with no olives. It just doesn't taste right."

Everyone in the limo simultaneously bursts into laughter.

Everyone except me, that is.

Because while they might be amused by Shayne's seemingly witty and creative use of metaphor, I've already heard that one.

About three weeks ago. Sitting in the passenger seat of Shayne's premature birthday present while she begged for my forgiveness.

If I remember correctly, she even *cried*.

And you know what? It worked.

I ate it up and then I asked for more.

It's all becoming painfully clear to me . . . painfully quickly. Shayne never *wanted* to be my friend again. She never *wanted* things to be back the way they were. She only wanted the spotlight. And the minute it was turned on me—the minute she felt even a hint of the cold darkness it left behind—she had to do something to direct it back to where she thought it belonged.

I was fooled. Just like everyone else, I was drawn into the fantasy. Lured by the bright, shiny light like an insect buzzing full-speed into an ultraviolet fly trap.

And that's exactly how I feel right now. Like I've been baited and zapped.

I should have known it was just another act. The tears, the apology, the vulnerability. She served up exactly what she thought I would respond to. What she *knew* I would respond to. And I was so desperate for things to return to normal—for things to feel safe again—that I completely ignored what was right in front of me the whole time. And the more I think about it, the more I realize that Shayne has built a façade so impenetrable, so impermeable that even *I've* never seen behind it.

It's almost as though Shayne Kingsley isn't even a real person. She's an illusion. As fake as the plastic vegetables decorating the kitchen of a model home. Designed to give off the perception of reality. The perception of perfection.

And with Shayne, there isn't anything *but* perception.

I turn and glance out the window. I can barely make out my reflection in the tinted glass. But the person staring back at me is a stranger. I'm not the girl I used to be. I'm not the insecure, overaccommodating sidekick who's too afraid to be alone. Who'd rather live in someone else's shadow than have to think for herself. And as hard as I've tried in the past three weeks, I can't return to my old life. I've seen too much. I've stood at a distance and watched my world from the outside. And once you've been given a glimpse of that perspective, you can't go back. Nothing on the inside feels the same anymore.

Everything is made of plastic.

"Who died?" Hunter says, scrambling across the car and plopping down on the bench seat next to me. "You look so serious."

Shayne lets out a lofty laugh and repositions herself next to Jesse. "I think Brooks is just being her moody self again."

Hunter leans over and kisses my neck. His muffled voice teases me. "Aww, are you in a bad mood? Do I have to cheer you up?" Then he lets out a vociferous growl that sounds like a hungry bear and pulls me onto his lap.

His lips press against mine. I use them to try to numb my mind. To try to smother this nauseating feeling that's overcoming my entire body. Hunter devours me. His hands are everywhere. I taste something funny in his mouth and I realize this champagne is not the only thing he's had to drink tonight.

The limo jerks to a stop at a red light and the champagne sloshes out of my glass and down the front of Hunter's suit jacket.

"Crap!" I yell, rolling off of him and reaching for a pile of napkins. "I'm sorry."

But Hunter waves it away. "Hey, no sweat. It's all part of the experience."

It's then that I happen to look out the window and see where we've stopped. And even though Parker is really just one stretch of road with a long line of stores and buildings down either side, I know this particular location is no coincidence. That some force greater than me has chosen *this* stoplight as the place to pause and pull my attention outside.

Because right beyond this glass, not one hundred feet from where I'm sitting, is the Main Street Diner, where Brian and his friends like to spend their Saturday nights.

And sitting in a booth next to the window, shoveling pancakes into his mouth, laughing at his friends' jokes, and having a grand old time . . . is Brian.

I know Shayne is talking to me. And I know there are going to be repercussions for not answering right away, but I can't help it. I'm no longer concerned with anything happening in this limo. All I can do is stare longingly at the little brown cabin—one of the oldest establishments in the town—and think about what it would be like to be sitting in that booth next to him.

"Brooks!" four voices yell in unison, and I finally pull myself away from the window.

I can hardly remember where I am. I can hardly recognize the faces around me. I think one of them was once supposed to be my best friend. And another slightly resembles my date. But my vision is blurry.

I glance down at the champagne in my hand.

How many glasses of this did I drink?

Everyone in the limo erupts with laughter. Hunter drapes his arm around my shoulder and pulls me closer to him, nuzzling his lips against the base of my neck. "God, you're such a lightweight," he teases with his sexy Southern drawl. "That's good, though. It'll make it much easier for me to take advantage of you later."

I laugh. But only because everyone else is. I'm honestly not sure what's so funny. But then again, I haven't really been listening to a word anyone has been saying. I've been too busy trying to solve a complicated logic problem in my head.

But really, when you break it down, it's not that complicated at all. It's actually quite simple.

I look over at Shayne. Perfect, beautiful, flawless Shayne. In her magazine cutout dress and makeup counter face and hair salon updo. Then I think about what's underneath and how far she goes to keep that hidden and I almost laugh aloud.

Then I look at Hunter. Perfect, beautiful, flawless Hunter. With his sexy accent and windswept hair and Roman numeraled birth certificate. Then I think about what else I like about him, what we have in common, what special, memorable moments we've shared together, and my mind fills with empty space.

Now I look out the window. My eyes focus right on Brian. On his untamed frizzy hair. On the friends who surround him—people who, at one time in my life, I never would have given the time of day. But I don't see any of those things. I only see *him*.

The person who makes me feel like I'm worth something . . . all on my own.

And then everything is clear to me.

Hunter is the illusion and Brian is the truth.

Hunter is the perception and Brian is the reality.

Hunter is everything I thought I wanted . . . for all the wrong reasons. The perfect guy . . . who's just not perfect for *me*. The choice I made for five years while I struggled to embody something that doesn't really exist.

And Brian is the choice I need to make now.

I glance at the intersection ahead of us and I see the light on the cross street turn yellow. I don't have any time for explanations. I lunge for the door handle and yank it toward me. The door flies open and I tumble out onto the sidewalk.

The cold December air slams against my bare shoulders like a knife slicing into my skin. It seeps effortlessly through the flimsy fabric of my dress, sending violent trembles through my body. As though someone has dumped a bucket of ice water over my head.

Note to self: next time you bolt from a stretch limo in the dead of winter wearing nothing but a formal gown . . . be sure to grab your coat first.

I fight to get traction in my dainty, bejeweled heels as they skid and slide along the icy concrete beneath my feet. I can hear the shouts behind me. The voices demanding to know what I'm doing. Why I've lost my mind. The jokes about my inability to consume alcohol. And then I hear Shayne. The voice of a dictator. Insisting that I get back in the car immediately.

But I don't pay any attention.

She can jerk on those strings as much as she wants. They're not attached to me anymore.

I turn and look at Hunter, whose face is one giant question mark. "I've made a mistake," I try to explain to him. "I said yes to you for the wrong reasons and I'm sorry. I really am."

The light up ahead turns green, I close the door, and the limo sails off into the night. I don't pause to say goodbye. I don't take a moment to remember the good times. I just head straight for the front door of the diner. And I don't look back.

CURTAIN CALL

I haven't been inside the Main Street Diner since I was a kid. It's one of those quaint and homey log cabin types of places that's been around forever. One of the few establishments left standing from the days before our little town was infiltrated by box stores. It's a local favorite. And when I say "local," I mean the people whose families have lived in Parker, Colorado, for generations. Like since gold was discovered. And, apparently, this is where they all come on Saturday night.

I burst through the door, breathless and still shaking from the cold.

I know I could dance around the subject for hours. Sidle casually up to Brian's table and make meaningless small talk about the diner and the town and how nice it is to see everyone again, but I don't. I've wasted enough time with things that have no significance and I don't want to wait anymore.

"It was more than just a dare!" I call out from across the restaurant.

The chatter from the various tables tapers off and sixty-five heads turn toward me. Like an audience settling into the theater as the orchestra starts up. Conversations halt. Cell phones are switched off. All eyes are on the stage.

And I have the floor.

Brian catches my eye and gives me an uneasy glance that clearly spells out "What are you doing?"

"The kiss," I explain, striding purposefully toward him. "It was so much more than just a dare."

Although I can feel the inquisitive stares from everyone in the restaurant—the steak-and-eggs locals, the gossipy, gum-chewing waitresses, Brian's stupefied friends—the only person I see is him. Brian's intense, soulful eyes penetrate me, digging deep into my subconscious, dissecting my thoughts, breaking down my ability to shield myself from the world.

"And *you*," I continue, allowing myself to be pulled into his powerful gaze, "you've come to mean so much more to me than I ever thought you could. Than I ever thought I could *let* you. I'm sorry I didn't see it before. I'm sorry I've been so blinded by stuff that doesn't even freaking matter. You were right. I've been living someone else's life. Playing by someone else's rules. Letting anyone else but myself make decisions for me. I was so terrified of making the wrong ones I figured the best thing to do was not to make any at all. That way I could never be held responsible when things went to hell. Because in my experience, when I'm in the picture, things *always* go to hell. I've been making bad choices my entire life and I'm through with it. I'm ready to make a good one. I'm ready to be with you." I pause and search his face for a reaction but I've yet to see one. And his blank stare is like a splinter in my heart. "That is . . . if you want to be with me," I whisper.

There are quiet murmurs emanating from every corner of the restaurant. Hushed voices questioning my identity, my integrity . . . and most of all, my sanity.

I guess it's not every night that a girl in an evening gown bares her soul to the whole diner.

I suck in a breath and hold it. The beautiful oxygen floods my lungs, calming my anxiety like a drug. I didn't realize how much air I'd used up in the last thirty seconds.

Brian stands up. He's nearly six feet and I have to look up to maintain eye contact, but his enchanting gaze never releases me. I can see the corners of his mouth start to twitch—the beginnings of a smile.

Without uttering a sound, he runs a single finger along my hairline and down the side of my cheek. Then he leans in and gently touches his lips to mine. It feels like my whole body has been set on fire. The sights and smells of the old diner fade away. The noises around me dissipate. And for a brief moment, it's just us. Standing ablaze in a hollow space.

When he pulls away, the grin has fully formed, lighting him up from the inside. "I hope that answers your question."

I nod, unable to speak as my feet find the floor again and my heart adjusts to its new, accelerated tempo.

Behind us, the entire booth erupts in applause. Even some of the surrounding tables join in on the ovation. My face turns all shades of red. I laugh and hide my face in Brian's shoulder.

"C'mon," he says, placing his hand on the small of my back and grabbing his jacket from the top of the booth. "Let's go outside."

We walk close together as we step out of the diner. Brian drapes his jacket over my shoulders and pulls it tightly around me.

"You look amazing, by the way," he says, admiring my outfit.

I take a step back and do a little twirl. "You like?"

He laughs and pulls me to him. Urgently. Ardently. I fall helpless into his arms and rest my head against his warm chest. "So," he says, amusement dancing along the edge of his tone. "It looks like Heimlich got the girl in the end. Who would have thought?"

It takes me a moment to realize what he's just said. And once I do, a gasp escapes my lips, echoing across the parking lot, and I leap backward. "WHAT?"

He shrugs, like it's just an everyday conversation. One we've had a million times. "I mean, I know Rhett Butler seemed like the front-runner for a while there, but I had high hopes for Heimlich. I knew it was only a matter of time before you came around."

I stare up at him, my mouth hanging open, my eyes as wide as the flapjacks they serve inside. "You knew?"

He shoves his hands in his pockets and flashes me that sheepish grin that I've come to love.

"For how long?" I demand.

"A while," he admits softly. "Around the time of the first posting."

"The *first* posting!" I echo in shock. My head is reeling as I think back to every blog post I ever wrote. Every poll I ever submitted. Every vote I ever counted. "But how did you find it?"

"Someone left it open on one of the library computers. I'm assuming it was you, although I didn't know that at the time. Anyway, it looked interesting, so I started reading it. And following it. By the second posting, I had a pretty good idea who wrote it. I mean, come on. *The Grapes of Wrath*? The field trip to the

Bodies exhibit? Rugby tryouts? I saw the bruise. You told me where you got it. But it wasn't until 'Heimlich' asked BB to join the debate team that I knew for sure."

My mind still can't seem to wrap itself around this new development. The whole time. He knew this *whole* time. And he didn't say anything!

"Although," he continues with a teasing smirk, "you weren't always entirely truthful, were you?"

"Huh?"

His eyes never stop sparkling. "We all voted for you to come to the diner with me that night."

"Oh, *that*." I laugh uneasily, remembering that fateful trip to the 7-Eleven and my little fib to cover it up. "Well, that was—" But another astonishing realization stops me mid-sentence. "Wait a minute. You *voted* too?!"

"Of course!" he exclaims. "That was the best part. I had to voice my opinion about whether or not you should go out with some other guy. Especially to a hot new downtown club. I have to tell you, it was a huge relief when I saw how many people agreed with me."

"But aren't you mad?" I ask. "I mean, that the only reason I said yes to you, that I even spent any time with you, was because a bunch of strangers told me I should."

He seems to find humor in this question as he adjusts his jacket tighter around my chest. "How could I be mad at something that brought you to me?"

The cold air mists my eyes. Or maybe the glisten of tears has nothing to do with the weather. I move toward Brian and sink back into him. But he grabs my shoulders and holds me at arm's length. His face suddenly very serious. Very still.

"Speaking of which. What about the blog?"

"Wh-what do you mean?" I stutter.

"Your last posting," he reminds me. "Heimlich vs. Rhett Butler. The ultimate showdown. I saw the results before I came here tonight. I saw that—"

But I don't let him finish. I already know everything I need to know. There's nothing else to say. So I kiss him. Long and hard and lustfully.

"I don't know what the results are," I tell him, our lips still millimeters apart. "I never looked."

It's evident he wasn't expecting this response. "Why not?"

"Because I don't care." I rise up to my tiptoes and rest my forehead against his. My eyes slowly close. "*I* choose you, Brian. Because I can. Because it's *my* choice. And because I know, without a shadow of a doubt, that it's the right one."

MY LIFE (NO LONGER) UNDECIDED

EPI-*BLOGUE*

Posted on: *Saturday, January 1st at 11:22 am by* BB4Life

Hi, everyone! Missed me? Sorry it's been so long since I've written. I figured there were probably some loose ends that I should tie up. I'm sure you're wondering what happened to me and Heimlich and Rhett Butler and even Her Royal Heinous. So I'll fill you in.

Rhett Butler is dating this new girl who just moved here from Kansas. They met on the night of the big winter formal. But don't worry, I'm not sad. Actually, I think it's great. They make a really cute couple. Her brother is going to be in some upcoming reality show so maybe they'll even come to our town to shoot something. Of course, I can't tell you what reality show it is, but if you just happen to be surfing channels one day and catch sight of a total hottie with a Southern accent, keep in mind that it just *might* actually be Rhett Butler.

And Her Royal Heinous? Well, let's just say she's not really "royalty" anymore. The "heinous" part is still true enough but it turns out all that money her dad has been making? Not really *his* money. He's been stealing it from his clients. Can you believe that? I certainly can. Like father, like daughter, right?

Apparently there was a huge bust right in the middle of her sweet-sixteen birthday party last month and her dad was taken away in handcuffs. Everything in their house was confiscated, including Her Royal Heinous's brand-new car (which was an early sixteenth birthday present) and her entire designer wardrobe. Tough break.

And me? Well, I've discovered that I actually *do* have a knack for community service. So I've decided to hang around at the nursing home even after my required court-ordered hours are up. We've added a new activity to the schedule. It's called *You Choose the Story* hour and I'm in charge of it. Basically it's like reading hour at the library . . . with an interactive twist.

Heimlich and I are doing great, too! We're preparing for the state qualifying debate tournament next month and I'm *really* nervous about it. I almost lost him to the wrestling team, but it turns out I'm not the only one who's learned to take responsibility for my life . . . and my choices.

So that's about it. You probably won't be hearing from me for a while . . . or *ever*, really. But I wanted to let you know how grateful I am that you decided to take this journey with me. Every day is a choice.

And I'm glad you chose me. Because without all of you, who knows where I'd be right now. So thanks for reading this. Thanks for caring. I promise I'll never forget you.

Your faithful friend,
BB

ACKNOWLEDGMENTS

Although writing can be a very "lonely business," as a writer, I never feel "alone." And that's probably because I'm surrounded by such an amazing, generous, loving, and supportive group of people. First of all, thank you to Michael and Laura Brody. I do believe that you choose your parents and I couldn't have made a wiser choice. Charlie, thanks for sticking around for yet another book (and consequently another tumultuous "act 2"). I'm getting better, right? *Right?* You're my rock and my sounding board and my plastic guitar hero. I love you. Thank you to Terra for letting me be such a bossy older sister and putting up with my *occasional* moodiness. And thank you to George, Vicki, Jennifer, and Addison for accepting me into your family with such open arms.

Janine O'Malley, my lovely, adorable, funny, talented, and (most important) *gentle* editor, thanks for guiding me through yet another book and reading it on your vacation! Our lunches are always the best part about coming to New York. To all the wonderful people at Farrar Straus Giroux Books for Young Readers and Macmillan Children's Publishing Group, my journey with you has been nothing but extraordinary.

I'd like to thank my awesome team of agents, Elizabeth Fisher and everyone at Levine Greenberg, for your undying support and enthusiasm for my novels, and Bill Contardi for introducing my characters to the world of film and television.

I also want to thank Deepak Chopra, Gotham Chopra, Carolyn Rangel, Felicia Rangel, and all the magnificent people at the Chopra Center for your support of my career and my novels. I have never met a more kindhearted family of generous souls.

Thanks to Christina Diaz, for keeping me sane and keeping my life afloat. Without you, I'd surely drown. And because I forgot to thank her two books ago, I need to thank Jen Marr—you know why! And of course, as always, thank you to Alyson Noël for inspiring me in ways you'll never know . . . I still say, I predicted everything!

To my fabulous group of friends who keep showing up at my book signings time and time again . . . without complaint. Ella, Leslie, Lauren, Jacey, Dan, Shalini, Kristin, Allison, Tina, Hilary, Stacey, Dom, Angie, Holly, Mike, Alicia, Brad, Katherine, Jerry, Jessen, and Lindsay. I am so blessed to have you guys in my life.

To the awesome people who work at the Champagne Bakery in West L.A., thanks for letting me stake out my office-away-from-office there and allowing me to stay for hours on end while I wrote this novel. And thanks to Mike Bachman, the master of titles, for summing it up so brilliantly in three words.

A huge thanks (and hug) to Lisa Nevolo, who has brought nothing but good things since she walked into my life! And to Danny Malakhov, Stephanie Friedman, Savannah Outen, Josh Golden, Cathy Golden, Nikki Boyer, and Jonathan George.

All the people who contributed to *The Karma Club* book trailer, I am forever indebted to you. Holly Karrol Clark, you are producer of the year! Your positive energy is infectious and good things always seem to happen when you're around. Jason Fitzpatrick, my wonderfully talented, creative, and *patient* cinematographer, editor, and co-director. Terra

Brody, fashion expert, style icon, and costume designer. Christine Schul, makeup genius and overall awesome human being. The hardworking crew, Steve Proctor and Adrian Ranieri, the rock-star music producers and songwriters, Tommy Fields, Matthew Clark, Mike Harold, and Ted Perlman, and the remarkable and beautiful cast: Madisen Hill, Megan Yelaney, Gina Cecutti, Leah Clark, Lyle Drucker, Nico Nevolo, Jaira Valenti, Savannah Polisar, and Deepak Chopra. Your talent is beyond measure.

Thanks to all the wonderful booksellers who continue to stock my books and welcome me into their stores, especially John Schatzel and Lori Christian.

And last but never ever, *ever* least, a warm and devoted thank-you to my readers—of all ages. It's because of you that I'm able to live my dream day in and day out and for that I am eternally grateful. You keep reading and I'll keep writing. Deal?

Deal.

A few fun facts about Jessica Brody's own life undecided:

- Jessica was born in Los Angeles, moved to Colorado when she was twelve, moved back to California after college, and now indecisively splits her time between both states.

- Jessica graduated from Smith College in Massachusetts with a degree in Economics and French because she was convinced she wanted to be an "important businesswoman." After a brief stint as a strategic analyst for MGM Studios, she abandoned her business background to become a full-time writer. Now she uses her mad spreadsheet skills to build complicated outlines for her books.

- Appropriately, when writing this book, Jessica couldn't decide on a title. So she polled fifty of her closest friends to finally come up with *My Life Undecided*.